STASI
77

East Yorkshire-born David Young began his East German-set crime series on a creative writing MA at London's City University when *Stasi Child* – his debut – won the course prize. The novel went on to win the 2016 CWA Historical Dagger, and both it and the 2017 follow-up, *Stasi Wolf*, were longlisted for the Theakston Old Peculier Crime Novel of the Year. His novels have been sold in eleven territories round the world. Before becoming a full-time author, David was a senior journalist with the BBC's international radio and TV newsrooms for more than 25 years. He writes in his Twickenham garden shed and in a caravan on the Isle of Wight.

Also by David Young

Stasi Child
Stasi Wolf
A Darker State

DAVID YOUNG
STASI
77

ZAFFRE

First published in Great Britain in 2019 by

ZAFFRE
80–81 Wimpole St, London W1G 9RE
www.zaffrebooks.co.uk

A CIP catalogue record for this book is
available from the British Library.

ISBN: 978-1-78576-714-2

Also available as an ebook

1 3 5 7 9 10 8 6 4 2

Typeset by IDSUK (Data Connection) Ltd
Printed and bound in Great Britain by Clays Ltd, Elcograf S.p.A.

MIX
Paper from
responsible sources
FSC® C018072

Zaffre is an imprint of Bonnier Books UK
www.bonnierzaffre.co.uk
www.bonnierbooks.co.uk

1

April 1977
Berlin

His heart started pounding, and his throat constricting, even before he reached the crossing point.

Checkpoint C.

C for Charlie.

A place where the glitz and decadence of West Berlin gave way to the colourless grey of the East. The contrast was always striking, no matter how often he crossed the border.

He'd done this journey countless times for work. Always driving – through France, Belgium, West Germany. And then the motorway corridor into West Berlin.

Each business trip was ostensibly about making money, making connections. Doing deals with the *Deutsche Demokratische Republik*, with its voracious appetite for foreign hard currency.

But his real reason for these trips was something quite different. It was to investigate.

To collect information.

To identify people.

And now he knew enough. Now he was ready to begin.

As the guard checked his papers, a deep wracking cough started, and he couldn't stop it. His body convulsed like a beached fish. The guard stared hard at him.

'*Aussteigen!*'

It was all going to go wrong now, he sensed it. He managed to control the cough – a permanent legacy of a day he wished he could forget, the day that this was all about – but beads of sweat formed on his brow, and his breathing was laboured and panicked. He climbed out of the Citroën, obeying the guard's gestures and shouts.

The guard circled the vehicle, opened its gently sloping hatched back, and pulled out the businessman's leather workbag.

'Open it, please.'

He flipped the catch. There was nothing in the bag that didn't match the stated purpose of his visit: all was as it should be, except for the one thing he wanted to be found. But the businessman still felt his face begin to colour up, to feel the guilt, even though he was guilty of nothing. The tension felt like it was intensifying in every sinew in his body, each second causing another twist to course through him.

The guard pulled out a plastic bottle of colourless liquid. He unscrewed the top, and immediately pulled his head back as he smelt the fumes, almost as though he'd been given a small electric shock.

'What's this?' he asked, grimacing.

The businessman didn't trust his voice to answer, and instead opened his papers, lightly running his finger over the entry which corresponded to the one litre of fire accelerant – approved for temporary import into the Republic as part of his business. The business of fire prevention. The Republic was developing fire resistant materials as an offshoot of its chemicals industry. His job was to test them so that they matched the standards of the West before sealing any import-export deal. In effect, he needed to be a fire-starter, in order to be an effective fire-preventer. It was a career he'd chosen for a reason. Part of that reason was this visit to East Germany via its capital, even though his destination lay hundreds of kilometres back towards the West. It was a circuitous route, designed to deflect attention. He didn't want some twitchy East German border guard ruining his plan.

The guard glanced over to his guardhouse, as though he was about to summon a superior. But then his attention turned back to the leather bag. He rummaged around again, and pulled out the multi pack of Gauloises cigarettes the businessman had deliberately left there – he knew it flouted customs regulations.

Waving the cigarette packets in one hand, and the bottle of liquid in the other, the guard shook his head, a theatrically severe look on his face. It was a young face, an inexperienced face – even though the businessman knew most of these officers in border guard uniforms were actually agents of the Ministry for State Security.

The Stasi.

'These don't mix well together,' said the guard. 'You might have permission for this . . .' He waved the bottle around again with one hand. Then the cigarettes with the other, as though he was making secret semaphore signals to his colleagues. 'But importing these . . .'

'I'm sorry. I must have forgotten to take them out,' said the businessman. He tried to give a calm, unflustered outward appearance. Inside he was churning up. He needed the guard to *want* to confiscate the cigarettes, and relish the thought of quietly smoking them, or sharing them with his fellow officers.

The guard's semaphore-like waving paused mid-air. This interaction had reached a critical point. The businessman held his breath – his heart tapping a steady drum beat. The guard placed both objects on top of the Citroën's roof, then glanced at his watch. He shrugged, picked up the bottle and placed it back in the bag, along with the man's passport and documents. Then he waved the businessman back into the driver's side, and picked up the cigarette multi pack.

If he knew the businessman had left them there deliberately – that it was an unofficial 'trade' – it didn't show in his deadpan face. 'We will be impounding these,' he said. 'Importing them is illegal. Do not do it again.'

He waved the Citroën past, while shouting through the open driver's window.

'Enjoy your stay in our Socialist Republic, Herr Verbier.'

2

Touchdown in the Hauptstadt – despite being bumpy – brought an overwhelming sense of relief to *Major* Karin Müller, the head of the *Volkspolizei* Serious Crimes Department. Her family holiday had been curtailed by the Telex delivered to her hotel on the Bulgarian Black Sea coast.

URGENT MESSAGE FOR COMRADE *MAJOR* KARIN MÜLLER, ROOM 411. RING COMRADE *OBERST* REINIGER AT THE PEOPLE'S POLICE HQ AT KEIBEL-STRASSE, AND PREPARE FOR IMMEDIATE RETURN TO THE HAUPTSTADT.

Her initial feeling had been one of anger at the premature ending of a long-planned family holiday, and that she'd had to leave her twin toddlers, Jannika and Johannes, in their great-grandmother Helga's care, fit and healthy though she was. But that anger had been swept aside as soon as she had reached Burgas airport, where it had been replaced by a fear, a terror, of flying.

Müller had gripped the armrests so tightly during the majority of the two-and-a-half hour flight that she had to flex her fingers now to try to free the tension in her upper body. It wasn't the irrational fear of something happening to the aeroplane that afflicted many others. Hers was well grounded, partly as a result of her fear of heights, but also the fact that she'd witnessed first hand the horrific aftermath of the 1972 Königs Wusterhausen air disaster. Plane crashes – even accidental ones – were the remit of the *K* – the *Kriminalpolizei*. One of her jobs as a young *Unterleutnant* had been informing the relatives of the more than 150 people who'd perished when the Ilyushin plane broke up in mid-air after an on-board fire. That had been an Ilyushin Il-62 taking holidaymakers to Burgas and was exactly the same model of plane on exactly the same route she'd just flown, albeit in the opposite direction. For much of this flight, she'd been unable to push the images out of her head of the blackened, broken wreckage of the plane in the middle of the woods just a few kilometres south of this airport. It had been Germany's worst-ever air disaster.

When she'd rung Reiniger, he'd been less than forthcoming about exactly why her holiday had had to be curtailed, other than to inform her that her deputy – *Hauptmann* Werner Tilsner – would be meeting her here at the airport, and then they'd both be travelling south to the scene of an apparent crime. The body of a middle-aged male had been found in a factory near Karl-Marx-Stadt in suspicious circumstances. That was pretty much all she knew. But for Reiniger to send the Serious Crimes

Department – effectively her, Tilsner, and their forensic scientist Jonas Schmidt – then there had to be something more behind it. Tilsner would be briefing her fully on the two-and-a-half-hour drive south.

She knew she was lucky, though. Her grandmother would face a forty-eight-hour train trip back to Berlin with two sixteen month olds. A nightmare. Müller had got off lightly.

'I see you've got the usual holidaymaker's souvenir.'

Müller furrowed her brow.

'The tomato face,' laughed Tilsner. Then he flicked his eyes towards the sky. 'You didn't need go away for that, though. It's been hot enough here. I wouldn't have thought you were too thrilled to be called back.'

'No. I hope this is all worth it. Reiniger wouldn't tell me very much over the phone.' She climbed into the Wartburg, as Tilsner held open the passenger door in a mock-chivalrous manner.

'Surely getting our teeth into any case must be better than what we've been doing for the past few months?' said Tilsner, getting into the driver's side. 'The job has become like a pair of dead trousers. Other than that Eisenhüttenstadt case, we've just been acting like administrative assistants, overseeing the cases of other murder squads without actually getting our hands dirty. As you know, I'd much rather be getting dirty hands than shuffling paper and pushing pens.' He turned the Wartburg's ignition key and the car fired up in its usual half-choked way. Because of the heat, Müller had rolled down her window as soon as she got in, and the fumes immediately hit the back of her throat.

'All I've been told,' she said, 'is that a middle-aged man was found dead overnight in a factory in suspicious circumstances, somewhere near Karl-Marx-Stadt. On the face of it, it's not exciting enough to pull me away from my holiday.' Her statement was almost a question, but no answer was immediately forthcoming from her deputy. She turned towards him, studying his chiselled jaw in profile. For an instant, she wondered who – if anyone – he was currently involved with. His wife, Koletta, had called time on their relationship months ago thanks to his constant philandering that had – on a couple of occasions – found Müller in his bed. A mistake she didn't want to make again, despite how attractive she found him, and how much she was missing male attention now that her spare time was spent with the twins. When the chiselled jaw still failed to move, she began to feel annoyed.

'Comrade *Hauptmann*, are you going to provide me with an answer?'

'I wasn't aware you'd asked a question, Comrade *Major*,' said Tilsner, manoeuvring the car into the lane for the autobahn towards Dresden and Cottbus.

Müller gave a long sigh. 'Quit the games, Werner. And tell me everything you know. Now.'

On the banks of the Zschopau river, the site itself was grey, high-walled and slightly forbidding – a fabric-spinning factory next to Sachsenburg castle, near the town of Frankenburg, to the north-east of Karl-Marx-Stadt. Müller felt a frisson of excitement, tempered by wariness. There was an incongruous contrast between the decaying, decrepit-looking factory and its pictur-esque surroundings. The river itself cascaded in a man-made waterfall over a weir, alongside timber-framed buildings, over-looked by the majestic white-walled castle, high on a wooded promontory. The view was almost like the scene from a fairy tale picture book. If Müller ever got the chance to catch up on her curtailed holiday with Helga and the twins, they could do a lot worse than spend it around here.

Outside the factory, a couple of uniformed officers on guard pointed to the meeting room where the body had been found.

Müller was surprised to see a female police officer in plain clothes apparently directing proceedings outside the room. Female detectives weren't that uncommon, though when Müller had been promoted to lead a murder squad she had been the only woman in charge of one, as far as she knew, in the whole Republic. The surprise was that both Tilsner and she knew the young woman. It was Elke Drescher, who they'd last encoun-tered as a student detective in the Hauptstadt, helping them in the office on the graveyard girl case more than two years earlier. A coincidence, perhaps, but the Republic was a small country. In Müller's experience, coincidences were all too common.

Drescher herself showed no surprise at the appearance of her old boss. 'Comrade *Major*. It's good to see you again. I just wish it was in happier circumstances. And Comrade *Hauptmann* Tilsner too, I see.'

'Have they made you head of a murder squad already, Elke?' said Tilsner. 'If so, I hope you're better at that than you were at making coffee in the old Marx-Engels-Platz office.'

'Ha! I don't think even I could ruin a cup of the new *Kaffee Mix*.'

'You're not wrong there,' laughed Müller's deputy. 'It tastes shit even when it's made properly.'

Müller couldn't disagree with Tilsner's assertion. The new ersatz coffee was the government's solution to the coffee price crisis. The problem was it tasted vile, with only fifty per cent of its weight made up of real coffee and the rest consisting of substitutes such as chicory. The Republic's citizens hadn't been slow in letting their feelings be known.

'Exactly, Comrade *Hauptmann*. You've got it in one. Anyway, I'm sure you and Comrade Müller haven't come all this way to discuss my coffee-making skills. And no, I'm not the head of the murder squad. I'm his deputy. But he's been off ill for a couple of weeks, and it doesn't look like he's coming back to work soon. So I'm in charge technically, but I'm still an *Unterleutnant*. That may be why they've brought in back-up from Berlin.'

Maybe, thought Müller. But equally, if *Unterleutnant* Elke Drescher was trusted enough to take charge – even on a temporary basis – then she must have been considered capable. There had to be some other reason Reiniger had despatched them here. And it certainly wasn't to discuss the coffee crisis. 'So, Elke. We need you to bring us up to speed,' said Müller.

'Of course. You'd better put these on first.' Drescher handed each of the Berlin detectives a pair of protective gloves.

When they entered the building, Müller's nostrils were immediately hit by a strong residual smell of burning. Drescher noticed her sniffing the stifling atmosphere. 'We won't know till the autopsy,' she said, 'but it looks like the victim was overcome by smoke inhalation.'

'And just explain to me who exactly the victim is, or was,' asked Müller. Already, her internal antennae were sensing that there was something different about this case.

'He was a leading local Party official, from Karl-Marx-Stadt.'

A leading local Party official? Why hadn't this been handed straight to the Ministry for State Security, thought Müller. Why were they allowing her team to become involved? She kept her thoughts silent.

Tilsner frowned, posing the same question out loud, but for a different reason. He let out an elongated sigh. 'If his death was simply caused by a fire, why have we been brought here?'

'I can't tell you,' replied Drescher. 'But for someone to die in a fire, in an enclosed space like this, you'd expect the victim to have burns. The only place he has burns are on his wrists.'

'His *wrists*?' echoed Müller. Already the apparently complicated, political nature of this case had taken a new twist.

'Yes. It's odd, isn't it?'

Müller nodded. Why would the victim only have burn marks around his wrists? Had he been tortured? If so, by whom? And why? For the moment, although these questions raced around her head, she was content to allow Drescher to continue her account.

'The seat of the fire was in the centre of the room.' She gestured with her arm. Müller's eyeline followed, scanning the space; a scorched, blackened area, about two metres in diameter. Some of the wooden beams above were slightly charred – but it wasn't a huge conflagration. 'Your forensic scientist has already bagged up the remains of the combustible material and is testing it in the lab as we speak,' said Drescher.

Kriminaltechniker Jonas Schmidt. In that initial phone call from the hotel in Bulgaria – after she'd responded to the Telex message – Reiniger had already told Müller that Schmidt had travelled on ahead to Karl-Marx-Stadt by train, before Müller and Tilsner had even set off from Schönefeld.

'And then the body was found here.' Drescher strode across the room, with Tilsner's eyes watching her carefully with the same animalistic hunger Müller had seen when she'd been a student detective in the Hauptstadt. Maybe, Müller admitted, she was jealous that he never seemed to look at her in that way these days, now her thirtieth birthday was consigned to history. Still, men like Tilsner would never be able to jump over their own shadows – it just wasn't in their nature.

Drescher stopped when she reached a doorway. The light coming around the frame suggested that the door led outside. The body itself had been removed, but an approximate chalk outline of its position had been marked on the floor, one arm apparently stretched out, reaching in desperation for the fresh air outside. Reaching in vain.

'What a way to go,' sighed Müller. She turned to Tilsner, who'd hung back slightly. His face was creased in a severe frown. 'Any thoughts, Werner?'

Tilsner looked momentarily startled. 'What?'

'Thoughts, theories, hunches? You know. It's what we do. We are supposed to be *detectives* after all.'

'Sorry. It's just shaken me a bit. It must have been a desperate situation for him.'

It wasn't unusual for detectives at murder scenes to react like this. Müller had been guilty of it plenty of times herself. But it was unlike Tilsner. Normally he was laidback, unflustered – and if anything, it was his insouciance which riled her.

'What is this place exactly, anyway, Elke?' asked Müller.

'Nowadays?'

'Yes.'

'It's Sachsenburg-Werke. A state-owned cotton-spinning mill. In fact there's been a cotton mill here since the mid-1800s, and before that there was a flour mill. It was ideally positioned to get power from the fast-flowing river.'

'I wonder if our Party official had somehow crossed swords with someone at the mill?' mused Müller.

'Maybe. I can check that out,' replied Drescher. 'As far as I know, he had no particular link. But, as I said earlier, he was a high-up. Number Two in the Party in Karl-Marx-Stadt. I'll give you all we've got on him. Of course, the Ministry for State Security may know more.'

'Have they been in touch with you yet?'

'No. Well . . . not as far as I know. Not through official channels.'

Tilsner had been deep in silent contemplation, but now he spoke. 'And this place. You say it's always been a mill . . . at least in recent history?'

'Yes . . . well, except in the 1930s. There were a few problems in the twenties: a fire destroyed the spinning mill, and then the Depression hit. One firm went into bankruptcy and another issued new shares, but then the new company faced liquidation in 1930, and by 1933 the building was empty.'

'But operations started again?' asked Müller. She was impressed by the thoroughness of Drescher's research. The young woman could go far. Müller's position wasn't *that* senior, but as the most senior female in the *Kriminalpolizei*, it could be under threat. It didn't worry her. The prestige and responsibility of a leading role wasn't something she coveted. Major was about as high as she would go and probably higher than she'd wanted to go.

'Yes. In 1938.'

'And the war didn't shut things down?' asked Müller.

'No. There was some bomb damage. But production continued.'

'In private ownership?' asked Tilsner.

'Yes. Until 1952. And then it was taken over by the state.'

State nationalisation. She'd come across that before. Of course, it was for the greater good of the Republic and its workers. But for those whose property was confiscated, it still created resentment, to put it mildly. Even though he'd become a leading Party official, could the dead man have borne some grudge against the factory and its nationalisation, and started the fire himself? Perhaps his wrists had been burnt as he set the fire. But in such a regular pattern? That didn't make sense. Perhaps, if this *was* a murder, the victim had been in some way responsible for the appropriation of the once private company? Was this a revenge killing by someone whose capitalist enterprise had been taken over for the good of the people of the Republic?

'What else do we know about the victim?' asked Müller.

'His name was Comrade Martin Ronnebach. He was married, with no children.'

'Did he live here in Sachsenburg?'

'No. Karl-Marx-Stadt. In an apartment with his wife on a relatively new estate. But the apartment is no different to that of many other workers' apartments. He didn't receive any special privileges in terms of housing.'

'We wouldn't expect him to,' said Tilsner, eyeballing Müller as he did. They both knew she *had* received special privileges – a larger than usual apartment, just off Karl-Marx-Allee in Berlin, the trade-off for accepting her promotion to head up their new Serious Crimes Unit.

Müller ignored his pointed look.

Then Tilsner turned back to Drescher, and frowned. 'Let's go back to your history of the mill. It still leaves some missing years, doesn't it? In the 1930s.'

'Ah yes, of course. I assumed you knew about that,' said Drescher.

'Knew about what?' said Tilsner.

'The camp. From 1933 to 1938 this was Schutzhaftlager Sachsenburg. A Nazi concentration camp.'

Müller glanced at her deputy. She'd already realised this was going to prove another 'difficult' case. From the look on Tilsner's face, that had just registered with him too. The question was how difficult. And how much interference were they likely to face from other agencies.

Especially the Ministry for State Security.

The Stasi.

3

October 1943
Kohnstein mountain, near Nordhausen

I'm not a religious man. But if I was – and if I'd done some of the things that have been done to me and my compatriots and fellow prisoners – then I might imagine, one day, entering Hell.

Today, I no longer need to imagine.

For I have arrived.

The giant wooden door shuts behind us, and we're engulfed in darkness. But we're shoved on and on, even though most of us are too exhausted to lift one foot in front of the other. Marcellin and I try to look out for Grégoire; we know he's weaker than we are. On the tunnel floor, we have to watch out for cables, beams, lumps of rock in pools of stagnant water. Our wooden soles slip and slide on the muddy damp slime. Occasionally, an acetylene lamp gives out a weak light, and I can see the silhouettes of fellow prisoners up ahead. They are hunched, broken, desperate.

We are three brothers. Myself, Marcellin and Grégoire. But we don't talk to each other. No one talks. No one dares to. No one except the *Kapos* or their SS overseers, barking out orders. It's the

Kapos who are the most dangerous. *Kameradschaftpolizei.* That's supposed to be their full name. With the first syllable and third-to-last of the full German name forming the abbreviation. I don't know why I'm thinking about this. I'd rather remember living in Loix, sipping a pastis in the village square, or cycling along the sea wall. The smell of the salt marshes, and the rotting seaweed. I try to keep those memories alive, but each day it's harder. The pictures fade. The pictures that I want to draw, to paint. I know that if I manage to prevent my meagre supplies of pencils and paper from being confiscated, that I will be drawing this instead.

This Hell. Staffed by collaborationist *Kapos.*

The *comrade police force.* Ha! They are pigs. Criminal pigs. I'd had my fill of them at Buchenwald. But they are here too.

The tunnel we're stumbling through suddenly opens out into a bigger cavernous space. It's another tunnel, perhaps three or four times as high and wide. And then at right angles, there are a series of smaller passages or halls hewn from the rock.

We're pushed towards one of these. Dirty, half-stuffed mattresses lay in piles on one side. Amid blows and shouts, we scrabble to claim the best of them. And then we lay them out, over the sharp stones, the stagnant puddles, the muddy floor, and try to sleep.

Exhausted after our transit from Buchenwald, I try to lose myself in dreams. Of Loix, pastis, the salt marshes, puncturing my bicycle, eating oysters raw from their shells, freshly stolen from the oyster farm. I try to remember warm, sunny days, when a soft breeze would blow from the direction of Ars-en-Ré, and how, at its most ferocious, the sea could swallow our little island whole, but at its calmest, the waves would gently lap at the harbour wall like a cat carefully licking the last drops of milk from its bowl. Marie-Ange and I would sit on the wall, our feet dangling over the drop. I would try to summon up the courage to tell her that I loved her, that I wanted to be with her always. But I never did. I was frightened that simply doing so would dissolve my devil-may-care, piratical image. And I was worried that in telling her this, I would lose whatever it was that attracted such a beautiful creature to me in the first place.

I dream of the warmth of her body hugging me, and try to draw some comfort from that memory. Because down here it's so very, very cold. A damp, dripping cold. A cold to rot your bones.

4

Müller drank in her surroundings as they followed the local police in a convoy through the newly built streets of the city. She felt a sense of pride in its functional modernity. The regular-planned blocks were unusually built with a slight curve in the centre. Window after window reflected the strong July sun like a glittering array of precious gems. All these buildings had been rebuilt by the Republic after the terrible destruction wrought on it by the Anglo-American bombing in the war. This bombing had been an attempt to undermine the production base of the future Soviet zone. Dresden had paid a higher price, but the factories of this city had been regular targets too. It spoke volumes of the workers of this small republic that they had revitalised it to such an extent. In the distance, chimneys belched out smoke like giant perpendicular cigarettes – helping the factories to meet targets, factories that were another beating heart of the Republic's industrial might. This one, she knew, contributed around a fifth of the country's industrial production.

The giant sculpture of the man who lent his name to the city came in to view. She'd seen the Karl Marx monument often enough in photographs and magazines. But here it seemed to take on new meaning – the huge granite head surveying the socialist republic his ideas had helped to inspire, a severe expression on his face. Would he have approved of this tiny, imperfect country, built on ideals? Müller hoped so. Even if her many brushes with the feared Ministry for State Security often made her question whether this really was a model society. But she worked for the state too. She was part of the same machine.

After they passed the monument, she turned and looked back. It was an almost Pavlovian reaction rather than a desire to take a second look. She still expected to see Stasi agents, it was now almost ingrained in her psyche. She glanced over her shoulder to check that no one was tailing the Wartburg. There was nothing obvious to see, but she felt the electric tingle of a shiver down her spine. As she glanced at her tanned forearms jutting from her summer blouse, she saw what she felt: the tiny hair muscles had contracted into bumps – the hairs themselves standing on end.

'Don't worry,' said Tilsner, breaking the silence with a thin smile. 'There's no one following us. I've been keeping a lookout too.'

The *Volkspolizei* headquarters seemed to be one of the few structures here to have survived the bombs and bulldozers – it looked to Müller like it dated from the Nazi period, or possibly Weimar Germany before that, with its neo-Baroque architectural details. It had a forbidding feel that did nothing to dispel Müller's unease – an unease which she hoped was irrational. But it was the more obvious unease of Tilsner that concerned her.

'You seem about as keen on being involved in this inquiry as I was at being summoned back from holiday. There's nothing wrong, is there? Nothing I need to know about?'

He found a parking space and turned off the ignition. Then he held her gaze with another smile. 'It's nothing to do with the inquiry, and don't worry, I'm fine. Just a bit of new girlfriend trouble back in Berlin. I thought things would be simpler once Koletta and I had finally parted ways.' He gave a rueful laugh, and slapped the steering wheel. 'Let's just say the cherries in the neighbour's garden don't always taste sweeter. If I'm called away with messages from Berlin, you know what it's about.'

Behind the smile and the laugh and the ice-blue eyes that Müller had once found so attractive, there was a vacant, far-away look. Maybe he was regretting finally ending it with the mother of his teenage children.

Drescher had arranged a meeting with various *Kriminalpolizei* and uniform officers to bring Müller and Tilsner up to speed. Müller smiled at Jonas Schmidt – who'd torn himself away from the local police's forensics lab to attend. She received a warm smile back: it was heart-warming to see the *Kriminaltechniker* putting the previous year's troubles behind him. He had struggled to come to terms with his son's sexuality and temporary disappearance. The three of them had arranged themselves in a semi circle facing Drescher, who in turn was standing in front of a notice board that was liberally covered in police photos from the scene. Müller found herself having to look away from some of them. Tilsner seemed to be doing the same.

'Thanks for coming here, Comrades,' said Drescher. 'I'm delighted to be able to introduce you to Comrade *Major* Karin Müller and Comrade *Hauptmann* Werner Tilsner of the Serious Crimes Department in Berlin. They've been asked to oversee this case. I'm sure we welcome any help we can get, and you've already met their team's forensic scientist, *Kriminaltechniker* Jonas Schmidt.' She glanced across and nodded at Schmidt. 'I'm going to give a short summary of the case for the benefit of our comrades from the Hauptstadt, and then if anyone has any questions for *Major* Müller about her team's role I'm sure she'll be happy to answer them.'

Müller had a fleeting thought that perhaps she should be the one leading this meeting. But Drescher appeared to be taking things in her stride. She cut a very different figure to the trainee detective from more than two years ago. She was now a confident professional.

Drescher turned towards the police photograph of the victim, discovered at the scene. This time, Müller had no choice but to look at the photo, shocking though it was.

'As most of you know, this is Comrade Martin Ronnebach, deputy chairman of the Socialist Unity Party here in Karl-Marx-Stadt. We won't know the exact cause of death until the results of this afternoon's autopsy, but some things are clear from the position of the body and the crime scene. Comrade Ronnebach appears to have died from smoke inhalation – that was the pathologist's view from the initial examination of the scene. But this was no accidental death.'

'How can you be so certain?' asked Müller, aware of the scrutiny of the other officers as she posed the question. Despite asking this, she knew that had it been thought an accident, there was no way she, Tilsner and Schmidt would have been despatched from Berlin.

'Sorry, perhaps I should have phrased that differently,' said Drescher. 'Our *initial conclusions* are that this was no accident.' She pointed to each of the victim's wrists in the photographs. 'See the discolouration? The pathologist's view at the scene was that these are burn marks.'

'I think we'd expect to see burns,' interrupted Müller, 'even if the fire started accidentally. But I agree it's very odd that the *only* burns are around the wrist, and in such a defined pattern. I was thinking about that on the way here. To me, the only logical conclusion is that he must have been restrained, using material that caught fire more easily than his clothing. Synthetic rope, something like that.' Müller could sense Drescher was frustrated by her interruption. 'Sorry, Comrade Drescher. You were probably going to say exactly that!'

Drescher shrugged. 'Well, the pathologist's view was that the victim had deliberately burned his own wrists. But perhaps that fits in with your theory too. If he was restrained in some way, maybe he deliberately tried to burn through the restraints in his desperation. Anyway, it seems that the fire itself was relatively small – constructed to give out the maximum amount of smoke, but not intended to ignite into a large conflagration. It was almost like the sort of fire beekeepers might set to smoke their bees. Although there, the effect is to calm the bees. Here, it was the opposite. We believe this fire was set to terrify Herr Ronnebach, and not necessarily to kill him. Jonas, you said you had some information to corroborate this?'

'Yes, Comrade *Unterleutnant* Drescher. At least to lend weight to the theory that the fire was set deliberately. The material we recovered also indicates that this was a smouldering fire, designed to maximise the amount of smoke, while producing minimal flames. The pattern of burning, and the presence of hydrocarbon residues – indicated both by laboratory investigations, and sniffer dogs used at the initial scene – tell their own story. This fire was set deliberately.'

Tilsner had been maintaining his quasi-monastic silence. But now he raised his hand to speak.

'Comrade *Hauptmann*?' said Drescher.

'You say the fire was set deliberately, Jonas,' said Tilsner. 'That may be so, but how do we know Comrade Ronnebach was the intended victim? How do we know there was an intended victim? Could it have been an elaborate suicide?'

'Surely the burn marks on his body answer that?' said Drescher. She tapped the crime scene photograph of the victim, pointing to each wrist in turn. 'The pathologist's findings support what *Major* Müller is suggesting – that material had been lashed round the victim's wrists. This is something that would be hard to do yourself. It looks as though he tried to burn the material off in desperation to free himself. He managed to locate the door to the outside through all the smoke.

But it was locked. All the doors to the room had been locked from the outside.'

'And there was something else we found,' said Schmidt. 'Fingernail marks on the inside of the door. From Comrade Ronnebach's vain attempts to scrabble his way out as his life ebbed away.'

5

October 1943
Kohnstein mountain, near Nordhausen

Myself, Marcellin and Grégoire – the band of brothers. We were fearless. Strong. Invincible. Or so we thought. But there is a thin line between human strength and total weakness and vulnerability. And we had crossed that line.

We never believed it was possible, of course. In the family fishing boat out of Loix, we always knew that the *Celestine* would right itself, no matter how big the wave that hit. We could fish for days without any significant catch, but then we knew we would find a shoal. When the Germans came and they turned our island into an Atlantic fortress, we three – who had been too young for war – joined up with the Resistance. We were involved in low level interference, sabotage, making sure the well-oiled Boche machine wasn't quite so well-oiled. Such was our confidence, we never thought we'd be caught.

But one night we were.

And then we were sent to Compiègne.

There we had the *Milice* to guard over us. Here – and in Buchenwald – it's the *Kapos*. They are cut from the same cloth;

traitors, criminals, scum without any backbone, without an ounce of moral fibre in their bodies. Looking after themselves and only themselves.

We've been lucky to be kept together, and we've had to fight for it. But Grégoire looks like he's fading day by day. He's more fragile now than the girl he was sweet on back on Ré. What was her name? *Gisele*. That was it. She was a tiny thing, who looked as though she could be knocked over by the gentlest Atlantic breeze. She wasn't really cut out for the life of a fisherman's wife.

Marcellin doesn't agree about Grégoire. He says he'll be fine.

The price of being together, though, is being assigned to a mining Kommando – where you are put to work lengthening one of the two main tunnels.

The dust gets everywhere. You want to scratch yourself every minute, but you're not sure if it's the dust or lice, which wriggle over you every night in the few hours' sleep we get, like a thousand simultaneous caresses from a thousand women.

Each day is twelve hours of dust, explosions, and drilling. It will send us mad. We cannot talk to each other for fear of a beating from a *Kapo*. The best we can do to communicate is the occasional look full of meaning. And hope. The hope that one day, rescuers will come and this Hell will be over. There are countless things that can kill you down here: a sadistic SS guard you look at the wrong way, a *Kapo* who hits you just a little too hard, and the hope.

The civilian *Meister* shows us where to put the charges. He blasts the horn. Then there's a crack and thud as the charge explodes and the rock fractures and falls. There are hacking coughs all round. All of us are desperate for water, but most of the water in pipes down here is undrinkable – it's for mixing concrete and cement.

Grégoire has fallen backwards from the blast. He's too weak to stand. I go to try to help him.

'Stand back,' shouts a *Kapo*, clubbing me over the shoulder. He hauls me away. 'Get back to work, you French piece of shit.'

I try to look back, to see how my younger brother is. When the *Kapo*'s attention is diverted by something else, Marcellin gently lifts Grégoire to his feet. We don't want him to go to the sanatorium. People don't come back from there.

Marcellin and I struggle to lift the rocks, one by one, into the carriage. It's back-breaking work, but if we are slow, if we shirk, we'll get another clubbing from the *Kapos*. But even once we load them up, it's not finished. Because the trucks themselves, and the rails they're on, are twisted, deformed and not fit for purpose.

We push and shove, and finally get it moving with what little strength we have left.

But then it derails.

Of course, we want this project to fail. We would do anything we could to wreck it. But not like this. This just means more pain. The whole mining gang has to use their shoulders to try to lift it back onto the tracks.

We manage it, eventually. No thanks to Grégoire, who is now next to me again. He has no strength left. He's just going through the motions.

I fear for him. That he will never see his little Gisele again.

6

Müller and Tilsner made a brief visit to the formal autopsy, but the pathologist didn't deviate from the story Elke Drescher had given in her briefing. Tilsner seemed to be hanging back at the rear of the room, as though he couldn't face looking at the body on the mortuary slab.

When it became clear they weren't going to get any further information from the pathologist – and that any detail would be in his report – Müller turned her attention to what was known about Martin Ronnebach. She sent Tilsner to interview Party colleagues, while she sought his private address from Drescher. Immediately, though, she encountered a problem.

'We don't actually have his address listed,' explained Drescher, apologetically. 'We asked the Party offices who referred us to the Ministry for State Security.'

Müller frowned. 'I thought you said the Stasi weren't involved?'

Drescher blushed. 'Well, not involved in the investigation. As far as I know. But they said they would handle any questioning of Comrade Ronnebach's colleagues, friends or relatives.'

'That's a very peculiar definition of not being involved.'

The younger officer shrugged.

'I've just sent Tilsner off to the Party offices to ask questions there,' said Müller.

'Sorry. He won't get very far without the Stasi's permission. I can give you the phone number of the police liaison officer at their headquarters. I doubt you'll have much luck, but it's worth a try.'

With Tilsner taking the Wartburg to the Party offices, Müller was left to get the tram. She'd expected a leading Party official to have a large apartment in the centre of the city, or perhaps a house on the outskirts, but Ronnebach seemed to have eschewed that. Instead, he and his wife lived in one of the new residential areas. It looked like a city within a city, with rows of slab apartments, much like Müller had encountered in Halle-Neustadt or Eisenhüttenstadt, or where her ex-boyfriend, Emil, had been planning for her little family to move to, had they stayed together, in the Marzahn area of the Hauptstadt. The Ronnebachs had been handed the keys a couple of years earlier to one of the first new homes in the Kappel area, the first building zone to be completed.

Müller had got permission to interview Comrade Ronnebach's widow on one condition: she was to be accompanied by a Stasi officer. A *Hauptmann* Ole Strobl of the *MfS* would be meeting her outside the apartment block, and would be sitting in on the interview.

To Müller's eyes at least, Frau Maja Ronnebach didn't seem to be over-troubled by her husband's death. The tiny, almost child-sized woman sat erect and composed on the couple's lounge sofa, apparently eager to help the *Kriminalpolizei*.

'I realise you're just doing your job, *Major* Müller. I'm happy to answer your questions where possible.'

When she said this, though, she gave a slight nod towards the leather-jacketed *Hauptmann* Strobl, and put undue emphasis on the words 'where possible'. Müller started to get an inkling about where this might be going, although Strobl, himself as tall as Frau Ronnebach was short and equally as thin, didn't acknowledge the woman's glance. He sat impassively, pen in hand, looking down at an open notebook, not writing anything. It was almost as though the pen and paper were there as props.

'Thank you, Frau Ronnebach. I'll keep this as brief as I can.'

The woman gave a slight nod.

Müller decided to steer a path to the heart of the matter right from the start. 'We understand, from our initial inquiries, that your husband was involved in the decision to nationalise the mill where his body was found.'

'That's correct,' said the woman. Out of the corner of her eye, Müller saw Strobl make a stabbing motion with his pen on the notebook, but he didn't interrupt.

'Had he ever received any criticism for that? Did anyone hold a grudge against him for it?'

Frau Ronnebach's gaze was unwavering. She gave a slight shake of the head. 'Not as far as I know, although I wouldn't know the details of Party business. Martin certainly didn't mention anything like that. He was simply carrying out the wishes of the Party and the people. Why should a few capitalists reap the benefit of a whole enterprise? He was a firm believer in socialism. As we all are.'

There was another stab of Strobl's pen at the end of the woman's sentence. 'Of course,' said Müller. 'And did he often visit the mill?'

'Not that I'm aware of. But he may have . . . for Party reasons.' Another pen stab.

'And can you think of any other enemies he may have made? Has anyone threatened him at all? Had you noticed him acting oddly?'

The woman shook her head. Again, her expression was neutral. There was no sadness, no red-rimmed eyes, no signs of grief whatsoever. 'Although on the day he . . . died . . . he'd said he might be late. He said he had to go out to somewhere near Frankenburg in the evening.' This time there were two stabs of the pen from Strobl. Müller found the man's silent vigil more annoying than if he'd actually been intervening.

'But he didn't mention Sachsenburg?'

'No.' This time Strobl's pen movement was just a gentle tap.

'So you can't think of anyone from your life here in Karl-Marx-Stadt, or from your husband's work, who would wish him harm?'

'No.' This time Strobl's pen failed to move at first. Then came a light tap after a couple of seconds. The woman turned down the sides of her mouth. 'Sorry. I don't feel I'm being awfully helpful.'

'Don't worry, Frau Ronnebach. As long as you answer truthfully, that's all you can do.'

'Of course.' There was the tiniest flick of the pen from the Stasi officer.

'And how long have you both lived here, in this apartment?' Müller knew the answer, but just wanted to keep things ticking over while she thought of a more probing question.

'We moved in a couple of years ago. I can check the exact date on the rental agreement if you like.' This time, there was no pen stab or movement at all, as though Strobl had almost stopped listening, as the answers were so mundane – and, if she admitted it to herself, the questions too.

'And before that?'

'We lived in Altendorf – to the west of the city centre.' Strobl had by now rested his pen, and was leaning back in his chair, with his hands clasped behind his partially bald head, a thoroughly bored expression on his face.

'And have you always lived in Karl-Marx-Stadt, or Chemnitz as it was known before?'

All of a sudden Strobl leant forward, and jabbed the pen again, harder than ever into the notepad. 'Frau Ronnebach is not permitted to answer that question.'

Müller pulled her head back. *Had she heard correctly?* It was an innocuous question. She'd only really asked it to keep the interview ticking over.

'Well . . . I'm happy . . .' started the woman.

'You're not permitted to answer that question,' repeated Strobl, firmly but without anger. His voice sounded almost robotic.

'Very well,' sighed Müller. 'What about your own relationship with your husband? Were you happy together?'

'Perfectly happy, perfectly content.' The woman looked down, and picked at the cuff of her long-sleeved blouse. 'Well, as much as you can be after so many years of marriage.'

'And as far as you know, your husband had never been unfaithful?'

'No . . .' Frau Ronnebach frowned. 'Is there a particular reason for this line of questioning? Have you found something out? I wouldn't necessarily know everything about my husband. We weren't in each other's pockets twenty-four hours a day. He has . . .' She paused a moment, as if grief was catching up with her for the first time. Then she gave her head a small shake, as though to gather her thoughts. 'He *had* his interests, and I have mine. But I think I would know if he was having an affair. There would be little signs.'

Strobl had picked up his pen again, and seemed to be noting something on his pad, although from her angle Müller couldn't see exactly what.

'You talk about his interests. What were these, aside from Party business? Was there anything which was particularly time-consuming, which might give him the opportunity to be . . . doing something other than what he said he was doing?'

The woman skewed her face in confusion. 'That's an odd question. But . . . yes, his main passion away from Party business was hunting. He was a member of a hunting club in Hermsdorf, near the Czech border, just over an hour from here. We've a little weekend cottage there. I don't particularly like it. It's dark and a bit cold. But Martin would sometimes go for weekends there with his hunting friends. I suppose . . .' The woman's voice trailed off, as though she was thinking about the rest of the sentence in her head.

'What do you suppose?' said Müller.

'I suppose that if . . . if he *had* been having an affair . . . not that I think he was . . . that might have given him an opportunity.'

'Do you have the name of the hunting club? I'll also need the address of this cottage.'

The woman rose from her chair, and walked over to a writing bureau. She wrote something down on a pad, and then picked up a business card from the side of the desk. She handed the piece of paper and card to Müller.

'I've written down the address for you. And the details for the hunting club are on this card.'

Strobl had by now reverted back to his pose of 'hands on head, leaning back in chair with bored expression on face'. Having been allowed a few questions without intervention, Müller decided to test the water again.

'Was your husband always a member of the P—?'

Müller didn't even manage to get the question fully out of her mouth this time, as Strobl leant forward.

'Frau Ronnebach is not permitted to answer that.'

The woman shrugged, as though helpless.

'Questions such as these will not be permitted.'

This was becoming pointless. Müller put her notepad and pen back in her handbag, and started to rise to leave.

'Sorry I couldn't be more helpful,' ventured the woman. She glanced over at the Stasi officer, as though he was annoying her just as much as Müller. 'If I think of anything else, I'll get in touch.'

Müller handed the widow her card.

Strobl gathered up his own notepad. 'If you do want to talk to each other again, please make sure I'm in attendance.'

Müller gave a slight nod. Strobl held his notepad so that the page he'd been writing on was facing outwards. Müller realised it was just a series of dots joined together with lines – nothing more than an elaborate doodle. A waste of time. Exactly what this interview had been.

7

As she left the apartment block, Müller checked her watch. Would there be enough daylight left once she got back to the People's Police office to make a visit to the Ronnebachs' weekend cottage? His wife had said it was near the Czech border – Müller didn't have a map with her, but knew it would be at least an hour's drive away. She looked up at the sky. It was a bright summer's late afternoon. If Tilsner had returned with the Wartburg by now they would be able to make it – if not, it would have to wait till the next day. She got out the piece of paper the address was written on, and realised that Frau Ronnebach had added a short note – possibly something she didn't want to say in front of the Stasi officer.

The key is kept under the barrel at the side of the porch. By all means let yourself in, though I doubt you'll find anything.

Her deputy had indeed returned, but was dubious about her plan.

'Where is it you want to go?' he asked, frowning as he pulled the red plastic-covered road atlas from the shelf under the Wartburg's dashboard.

'Near Hermsdorf. The Ronnebachs have a country cottage there, and the victim was a member of the local hunting club.'

Tilsner exhaled slowly. 'There are seven Hermsdorfs listed here. Which one?'

'South of Dresden. Near the Czech border.'

'That's in the Ore Mountains, nearly seventy kilometres each way. It's going to be a three-hour round trip. Wouldn't we be better waiting until tomorrow?'

'No,' said Müller. 'By all accounts, Martin Ronnebach was there regularly – without his wife. That's something worth investigating. So let's do it before the trail goes cold. And on the way you can brief me about what you found out at the Party offices.'

'That's not going to take very long, I can assure you.'

They headed east to begin with, along the main non-motorway route towards Dresden.

Tilsner's hands appeared to be gripping the steering wheel hard, and his knuckles were turning white. Müller knew what he'd be thinking: that she was taking him on another wild goose chase. Or perhaps it was the 'girfriend trouble' he'd mentioned that was making him such bad company.

As they passed a sign for the village of Oberschöna, she fixed him with a stare and raised her voice above the roar of the Wartburg's two-stroke engine.

'What did you find out at the Party offices, Werner?'

'Not a lot. Everyone just repeated in parrot fashion that I would need to get the permission of the Stasi before I spoke to them.'

'And did you?'

'Did I what?'

'Did you ask the Ministry for State Security?'

'There doesn't seem a lot of point, does there? There's clearly something they don't want us to know. What about your interview with Ronnebach's widow?'

Müller tried to bite back her annoyance – both at her deputy's lack of persistence, and his convenient change of subject. 'The most useful thing I uncovered seemed to be this weekend cottage and the nearby hunting club. But I had an *MfS* agent sitting in on the interview.'

The mention of a Stasi agent had Tilsner glancing into the rear-view mirror. Müller turned her head. 'Do you think we're being followed?'

'Hold on!' bellowed her deputy, yanking the steering wheel. Müller braced herself as she was thrown against the passenger door. Tilsner had made a savage U-turn. Müller swallowed back bile as her stomach lurched.

They were heading back to Karl-Marx-Stadt.

Then there was another spin of the steering wheel and they darted across the other carriageway and down a minor road.

Tilsner reached up to the rear-view mirror and adjusted it. He snorted and then turned and smiled at her. 'I'm not sure it *was* someone following us.' He glanced into the mirror again. 'But whatever they were doing, they're not there now.' Holding the steering wheel with one hand, he used his other to pick up the road atlas and flick through it to the correct page. 'This road is fine. It'll take us round the south of Freiberg and then we can pick up the route to this Hermsdorf place.'

Müller half-expected that the Ronnebachs' weekend cottage would have been sealed off by the Stasi, with a guard placed outside. But nothing looked out of the ordinary. The neat house sat proudly in the sun, its grey-rendered lower portion looking new, or newly cleaned. On the second floor there was treated brown timber, and even a dash of colour – brilliant red – highlighting the window frames. The Ronnebachs might call it a cottage, but to Müller this was a house. It was not unlike her adopted parents' guesthouse in Thuringia. This part of Hermsdorf – a hamlet called Seyde – had much in common with Müller's childhood hometown of Oberhof too. Low, rolling mountains that in the winter would be blanketed with sparkling white snow. Now, in the height of summer, the colours were the verdant greens of the meadows, interspersed with the rich browns of the timbered houses. As she climbed out of the Wartburg, and Tilsner killed the motor, she let the tang of newly mown grass fill her lungs, replacing the petrol fumes of the car.

An old beer keg stood to the side of the front door like a sentry, its wood stained dark brown to match the timbered upper storey of the house. Müller strained to tip it sideways slightly, surprised by its weight. It must have been filled with earth or sand. As promised by Frau Ronnebach, the key ring was underneath, surrounded by wood lice and beetles. Either the Stasi hadn't visited themselves yet, which Müller found hard to believe, or they had already been. In which case, they would have removed anything they didn't want the *Kriminalpolizei* to find.

'What precisely are we looking for?' asked Tilsner, his face still sour-looking, as though he'd rather be anywhere else.

'You shouldn't need to ask that, Werner. You're a detective. Anything that helps to shed light on the case. Anything at all. Are there any official papers to do with the mill nationalisation? Had he received any threatening letters? Was he really coming here to go hunting, or did he have another woman he was seeing here? Can you start with the downstairs? I'll do the first floor.'

The cottage was neat, tidy, clean. But there was something slightly odd that Müller couldn't quite put her finger on as she climbed the stairs. Then it came to her. Behind the usual aroma of stale cigarette smoke, there was a slight musty smell. Not of damp, but of men – there was a maleness about the place, as though women weren't welcome. It was reflected in the décor too. There was nothing feminine here. The pictures on the wall were of hunting scenes. Horns of various small mammals lined the stairwell.

At the top of the stairs, Müller took a quick glance in the rooms. Two were bedrooms, a third appeared to be used as a study. And then there was a private bathroom with a toilet, which wasn't always a given in the Republic, even now in the mid-to-late 1970s. The bedrooms seemed very much 'his' and 'hers'. In fact, the smaller of the two was the only place in the house so far with any sign of a feminine touch: a flowery bedspread, lighter patterned wallpaper, and perfumes and cosmetics on the dressing table. There were photos on the wall of a younger Frau Ronnebach – at least Müller assumed it was her – singing in some sort of choir.

With her hands covered in protective gloves, Müller quickly rifled through the drawers and cupboards in this room, finding little, and still wondering if the Stasi had already been here. Then she moved to what she assumed was the dead man's bedroom. Again she worked quickly, finding little at first. Then, in the drawer of the bedside table, she made a discovery. She recoiled slightly from the smell as she opened it. There was the aroma of rubber, and behind that something else, something unpleasant. It was fishy, like a mussel or oyster that had been left to rot.

Although she was wearing gloves, she still picked it up gingerly – as though it could suddenly burst and shower her with its foul contents. It was a used condom, tied and sealed, yet still out of keeping with the rest of the neatness in the house. She pulled an evidence bag from her pocket and put the condom in it. Then she noticed some black material stuffed at the back of the drawer. Again, she removed it carefully, almost reverentially. Women's knickers. A small size, lace-trimmed. She looked at the marque and didn't recognise it. But the New York-Paris-London city geography under the manufacturer's name told her what she needed to know. Western underwear. Expensive capitalist underwear. She tried to picture Frau Ronnebach wearing them – without success. Was this their evidence of an illicit affair? If so, was Comrade Ronnebach's widow aware of his infidelity after all? Was it a motive for murder – with the widow as a suspect?

Müller again bagged the article, then moved to the room used as a study.

Here there was more – almost too much. Reams of official papers sat on top of the desk and in the drawers. It was untidy too, and almost as though someone might have done this before her, given the neatness of the rest of the house – save for what she'd found in the bedside cabinet.

She riffled through the pages; minutes of no doubt irrelevant, boring committee meetings. Was there anything about the mill here? Possibly – but they would just have to bag it all up, and then get one of Drescher's team to read through it all, looking for any evidence. Müller began to collect the sheafs together, banging each end on the desk in turn to align them. It was when she did this to a collection of papers at the back of the desk that she saw it. A blue envelope. Not an official-looking envelope – it was more like something from a special writing set. Something a lover might use. She felt a lightness in her chest as she picked the envelope up in her gloved hands, but that feeling immediately evaporated. The envelope was empty.

It *was* luxurious, though. And she was sure it wasn't from any modern writing set in the Republic. She flipped it over. There was no writing on it. She held it up to the fading light to see if there had been an imprint of anything written on top of it. Nothing.

Then her heart start pounding again.

A very faint watermark.

This could indeed be something. The name of a company. *G Lalo*.

More importantly, there was a place name, just as there had been on the lingerie label.

But this narrowed things down to just one city.

The French capital, Paris.

8

Unterleutnant Elke Drescher managed to arrange a room at the People's Police headquarters for Müller to lead a summit on the case so far. Jonas Schmidt joined them, polishing his thick spectacles on his white lab coat. Each officer took one side of a square table in the centre of the room. Drescher had moved some of the photos of the crime scene and pinned them to a notice board on one of the walls.

Müller held the gaze of each officer in turn before she began to speak – or at least she tried to. Tilsner was staring down at his shoes – his mind probably on his new girlfriend back in Berlin and whatever grief she was giving him. She cleared her throat to try to attract his attention.

'We need to discuss a few of the possible theories, so that we can channel our resources in the right direction,' she said. 'I think the nature of the killing is the key here. It's annoying that we can't get more information from the Party. I wonder if Herr Ronnebach has approved some measure in the past which influenced fire safety in a negative way. Maybe someone holds him responsible for the death of a loved one as a result?'

'That's not a bad theory,' said Drescher. 'We can check that in the newspapers.'

Müller nodded. But she knew that everyone in the room was aware that if something had gone wrong with a Party decision, nothing critical would ever have been published in any newspaper anywhere in the Republic. Müller was treading on thin ice even by raising the possibility.

'What about motives?' she asked, looking round the room again. 'Werner, any theories?'

Tilsner shrugged then started rubbing his chin. 'Potentially, the usual ones. Money – if it was the former mill owner or an employee who felt they'd lost out when the state took it over. Love or lust – if Herr Ronnebach was seeing someone on the side, and his bit's husband or boyfriend killed him in a jealous fit. Or if he was having an affair and his wife found out.'

Müller nodded slowly. 'Werner and I spent the afternoon and early evening at his weekend cottage. There are perhaps some indications that his wife didn't know everything that was going on there.'

'So you're saying Frau Ronnebach could be our murderer?' asked Drescher.

'She's got to be considered a suspect,' replied Tilsner.

Müller sighed. 'Frau Ronnebach *does* seem remarkably untouched by grief. But in my interview with her it also became clear that the Stasi don't want us to dig into their past. Why is that? And how are we going to circumvent it?'

'I can get any spare members of my team to look into anything about them both that is public knowledge,' offered Drescher. 'They don't have children – so there won't be birth records for kids. But there might be for the Ronnebachs themselves, and there could be details of their marriage. We can also take a look through newspaper records for mentions of Herr Ronnebach. As a high-up Party official he'll probably be seen glad-handing in a few photos.'

'Good,' said Müller. 'Werner and I didn't have a chance to actually visit the hunting club, or indeed knock on doors in the village where the cottage is. That's also something I'd like your team to look after, please, Elke.'

Müller moved over and studied the photos of Ronnebach's body, and the chalk outline showing how he'd desperately tried to escape before finally being overcome by the smoke. She tried to imagine the terror in his head, knowing his life was about to end. 'We also need to get to the bottom of the potential motive – the potential grudge – to do with the nationalisation of the mill. It's going to need some foot soldiering. Does anyone have a particular grudge to bear? Was anyone thrown on hard times as a result? Had the victim been seen in the area of the mill in recent weeks? That sort of thing.'

She tapped her pen on the table, then looked up at Schmidt. 'What about you, Jonas? Anything more you can tell us from the forensic side?'

'Well, I was a bit naughty. We – that is myself and *Unterleutnant* Drescher's forensic scientist – were waiting outside the flat when you were interviewing Frau Ronnebach, in a car on the other side of the road. When you left, we explained to her that there were a few forensic tests the officers wanted us to perform.'

'The *officers*?'

'Well, I meant you and *Unterleutnant* Drescher. But I was hoping Frau Ronnebach might assume I meant the Stasi officer who was shadowing you. And I think she did because she let us in without question. So we've been able to fingerprint the entire flat without any suspicions, and without the widow contacting the Stasi.'

'Good work,' said Müller. 'Let me know as soon as you have any results from that. Maybe we need to pull a similar sort of trick to get in Herr Ronnebach's Party office.' She steepled her fingers together on the table. 'We need to try to piece together the Ronnebachs' past history too. That's something I'm going to look at. Each time I tried to ask something – even innocent-sounding questions about whether they'd always lived in Karl-Marx-Stadt – the Stasi officer stepped in and prevented Frau Ronnebach from answering.'

'Couldn't we try to get her on her own?' said Drescher.

'Perhaps,' agreed Müller, 'one of us could bump into her – maybe even literally – in the Kaufhalle, for example. Get her talking that way. I got the impression she was prepared to say more.'

Drescher and Schmidt nodded. Tilsner sat in silence.

Then Schmidt's face lit up. 'I just had an idea about their history and background, Comrade *Major*.' Müller raised her brow, inviting him to continue. 'Did you notice anything regional in Frau Ronnebach's accent?'

Müller shook her head. 'I'm afraid not, Jonas. I should have had Werner with me – he's good at putting on accents, so presumably he's good at recognising them.'

Tilsner gave a sarcastic grin.

'Well, what I could do,' continued Schmidt, 'together with *Unterleutnant* Drescher's forensic team – if she's happy with that idea – is analyse voice recordings of Herr and Frau Ronnebach. It may tell us whether they're from this area, or whether they're originally from elsewhere, and therefore whether it's worth making inquiries elsewhere.'

'Where would we get those voice recordings?' asked Müller.

'It's easy with the widow,' replied Schmidt. 'We secretly make sure we record our next interview with her. The victim was number two in the Party here. He'll have made speeches – recordings will exist. He's probably even appeared on television or the radio talking about such and such. I can't imagine it will be a problem.'

'That seems worth a try, Jonas. Good. You and Elke have important things you can be getting on with. I think Werner and I need to go through the records and see if there have been any reports of similar murders. It's an odd one. Almost ritualistic. That's why I think it holds the key to cracking this case.'

The others left the room to get on with the various tasks Müller had delegated to them. Tilsner, too, asked for a few moments to try to address his domestic issues back in Berlin. Müller took advantage of their absence by putting a call through to Bulgaria. She was aware she'd left Helga in the lurch, as a woman well into her sixties having to look after two lively toddlers on her own. It wasn't the deal her grandmother had signed up for. She checked her watch, 7 p.m. With a bit of luck, Helga would at this very moment be starting to put the twins down to sleep, before going to dinner herself. A babysitting service would visit the hotel room in her grandmother's absence. Müller just hoped she could catch her before she went down to the restaurant.

The operator put her through to Helga's room, and the phone rang. Müller was on the point of replacing the handset, worrying that she might be waking Jannika and Johannes, when Helga answered sleepily.

'Are you OK?' asked Müller.

'Yes, I'm fine, darling. I've got the twins down, and I'm just having a little rest myself before dinner.'

'I hope they haven't been causing too much trouble.' Müller found herself half-shouting, the line was so bad.

'Well . . .' Müller's heart sank at the pause. She knew it was selfish, but she was hoping, somehow, Helga could cope. 'I won't lie: it has been difficult on my own. I went to the station to ask about the possibility of coming back a few days early. They didn't seem very willing to change my ticket. It's fine in the mornings, when they're at the club, and it's fine now when they've tired themselves out. But I tried taking them to the beach and that was a disaster.'

Müller wracked her brain, wondering what she could do to help. 'Do you really *want* to come back by train? Two days on a train even *without* young children is a nightmare. Two days with children for a couple would be a nightmare too. But on your own . . .'

'I know. I'm not looking forward to it, but we'll manage. We'll have to.'

'If I could sort out plane tickets, would you prefer that?'

'That would be a godsend. At least then the air hostesses could help with the little ones. And it's so much quicker. But can you afford it? It will be so much more expensive.'

'Don't worry about that. I'll make some calls and try to arrange it. It was the People's Police who called me back and want me here – it's up to them to sort it out.'

9

December 1943
Kohnstein mountain, near Nordhausen

Grégoire has gone.

I should be grieving. I should be fighting on his behalf, to have his body repatriated, to ensure a proper burial.

But I'm not. And Marcellin isn't either. We feel numbed by death. And sickness. It is everywhere around us. Sickness and death.

It wasn't a surprise. He had been fading day by day. Worked to death by twelve-hour shift followed by twelve-hour shift on the mining Kommando. And then trying to sleep in the underground halls, amid the damp, the cold, the stink of shit.

He was always a sickly child. A mummy's boy. And perhaps without a mother to protect him then we, his older brothers, should have done more. But really, we were as powerless as he was.

I learnt about it in the most awful way possible.

He'd been taken to the sanatorium. Marcellin and I knew then that he was unlikely to come back.

'He is too weak, Philippe,' my brother whispered, the first night without him. 'Prepare yourself for the worst.'

They never gave us the news. We discovered it ourselves.

During the roll call, we saw piles of what we thought were sacks outside the sanatorium, or *Revier* as it was called by the Nazis and *Kapos*. From a distance, they looked like what could be medical supplies. Somehow Marcellin and I managed to get nearer by shuffling back through the lines of prisoners. Our aim was unspoken. I think we wanted to somehow enter the *Revier* to see if we could find Grégoire. To see how he was.

We saw the sacks.

They weren't sacks. but piled up bodies.

And then we saw his face.

It was staring at us. Hollowed eyes, hollowed cheeks: a skeleton covered by parchment-like skin. Almost unrecognisable as a human form.

Yet we knew straightaway that it was him.

I saw a movement. A clawing hand, making slow grasping motions.

Not from Grégoire, but from the body above.

The man was still alive. He had been dumped there to die.

As we watched, the clawing stopped. He had breathed his last breath.

Grief is a strange thing. You need space for it. You need time. You need energy to grieve. We didn't have that space or time. We certainly didn't have the energy.

I thought back to our days as young boys, playing our own version of *petanque* amongst the oyster beds.

Eating the contents of the oysters, raw and whole. Savouring the taste of the ocean, the texture like the white of a fried egg, and the slightly metallic tang. And then using one of the smaller empty shells as the piglet ball, and the larger ones as our *boules*. Of course, we should have let our little brother win occasionally. We never did. Brothers can be cruel like that, and Grégoire would often end up in tears.

Remembering his tears finally start mine, later, when we are back in the tunnel. But I do not have time to cry or stop work. There is a crash of the *Kapo*'s baton on my back, and a shout of 'Work, you French piece of shit!' I know Marcellin would defend me if he dared. But if he did, the punishment for him would be even harsher.

For both of us, Grégoire's death was a turning point. The hope has gone. It's been extinguished. Whatever happened, we would never be that team of three brothers again. So we no longer care. And because we no longer care, we are dangerous. We are dangerous and can start to fight back. What more can they do to us?

We manage to stick together in the same work Kommando. After the tunnels were finished, we somehow get one of the easier jobs as welders through our knowledge of mending fishing nets, and generally repairing things. For some reason, we French are trusted more than the Russians, who tend to be kept on the manual, unskilled tasks.

And as welders, we begin to take risks.

Nothing is spoken, there is no organisation down here in the work tunnels, no system for undermining the Reich. But that is still our aim.

I notice Marcellin doing it first. The quality of the welded seams of the rockets is often poor. Perhaps deliberately so, as a result of sabotage further down the line. Our job is to strengthen these seams with rivets or spot welding.

But it is easy enough to hide a missing spot weld with the slag from the electrodes.

That's what we do. Again, again and again. Hoping that by our little actions these weapons of mass destruction will fail on launch, or fail in mid-air, before they can complete their murderous intent.

This is how we will avenge Grégoire.

It isn't much. But it is the best we can do.

10

Müller sorted her family problems via a call to *Oberst* Reiniger, her People's Police boss back in the Hauptstadt. He agreed to get his secretary to sort the necessary plane seats and travel warrants for Helga and Müller's children. It meant Müller felt less guilty, and that she could concentrate all her mental resources on the current case. And the current case had just widened, thanks to a Telex delivered to her by Elke Drescher.

'Your national appeal to other police districts about similar murders seems to have come up trumps already,' she said.

Müller eagerly snatched the note from Drescher's hands.

'Leinefelde?'

Drescher nodded.

'But that must be more than two hundred kilometres away?'

'More like two hundred and fifty. Around two and half hours by car. Not far from the state border.'

Müller sat back in her chair, her hands clasped together on her lap. 'At the back of my mind, there's something clicking about Leinefelde.'

'The answer's in the name,' said Drescher. 'It literally means *linen fields.*'

'Of course!' Müller clicked her fingers, then ran them over her cotton blouse. 'It's another new town, isn't it? Another socialist city.'

'Exactly,' said Drescher. 'Built around a cotton-spinning mill.'

Drescher stayed behind to lead the investigation at the Karl-Marx-Stadt end. Jonas Schmidt had unfinished business with the forensics there too.

So it was left to Müller and Tilsner to set off for Leinefelde. Their route took them on the motorway north of Leipzig, then through the centre of Halle. Müller realised Tilsner was taking her right through Halle-Neustadt – along the raised roadway with its giant street lamps that looked like something from a spaceport, and then over the Saale river, and straight along the Magistrale – the main road that bisected this new city. It was a city where Müller's life had changed for ever. Awful things had happened here, and she had been at the centre of them. But the end result had been two little miracles in the shape of Jannika and Johannes – the children that doctor after doctor had said she'd never be able to have after what had happened to her at the police college all those years ago. Some things she didn't want to remember, but her twins had changed her life. Thanks to Reiniger, they would soon be on a plane high above Bulgaria, or one of the other friendly socialist countries, on an Interflug flight to Schönefeld. She just hoped they – and her grandmother – would arrive back in the Hauptstadt safe and sound.

As they approached Leinefelde, Tilsner seemed to snap out of whatever troubles were weighing him down.

'Are you aware of the history of this area?'

Müller stared at him blankly. 'What do you mean?'

Her deputy took one hand off the Wartburg's steering wheel and made a sweeping gesture. 'All this was once countryside. The Eichsfeld. A very poor region, cut off from the larger cities on the other side of the state border. Our leaders were worried it might be a centre of revolt and insurrection.'

'Why?'

'Because the glue that brought the area together was religion. Catholicism held sway rather than socialism. The idea of building the cotton mill here – of developing Leinefelde into an industrial centre – was to break the grip of the Catholic church.'

Müller gave a doubtful look. 'Why's that relevant to our inquiry?'

Tilsner shrugged as he drove. 'It might not be relevant at all. But you said the Stasi didn't want you asking about Herr Ronnebach's past. If he was linked to the cotton mill at Sachsenburg, maybe he also had some link here. Here you would have a motive: church leaders who didn't want their grip on power broken.'

The theory sounded a big and fanciful leap to Müller. But she nodded thoughtfully, more for show than anything else. At least Tilsner seemed to be engaging in their work again. What she needed was a fully functioning deputy, not someone in a perpetual sulk over his girlfriend troubles.

Leinefelde was like Halle-Neustadt in miniature. Block after block of concrete slab apartments, and on one side of the new town, the cotton mill. Their destination, though, was just beyond the main Kaufhalle and shopping centre: Leinefelde People's Police office.

Tilsner had radioed ahead from the car, and an officer was waiting to show them an allocated car parking space. Once they'd parked, he ushered them into the building.

'I'll take you straight to *Hauptmann* Ingersleben. He's expecting you.'

The officer led them to the first floor of the four-storey block, and then knocked on a door.

'Enter,' barked a voice from inside.

'Comrades Müller and Tilsner from the Serious Crimes Department in the Hauptstadt are here, Comrade Ingersleben,' said the officer.

'Aha. Good.' A sharply dressed man with a wide blue tie, white shirt, and neatly pressed blue-grey suit rose from behind his desk to greet them, extending his hand to Müller. 'Dolphus Ingersleben. I'm head of the murder commission here.'

'*Major* Karin Müller, and this is my deputy, Werner Tilsner.'

'Please. Sit down,' said Ingersleben, gesturing to two seats opposite his, with his desk in between. 'Did you have a good journey from the Hauptstadt?'

'It's actually Karl-Marx-Stadt that we've come from,' said Müller. 'But yes, a clear run. Lovely weather and little traffic.'

Ingersleben smiled. 'Of course. The murder at Sachsenburg that you wanted to compare to any other similar murders. I think ours fits the bill. To be honest, we had it down as an accidental death to start with. In fact it was the Stasi who'd investigated it. We got involved somewhat fortuitously – otherwise it might always have remained an accident.' He opened a file on his desk, and drew out a photo, then rotated it for Müller and Tilsner's benefit. Tilsner picked it up for a closer look, then placed it down quickly.

Ingersleben seemed to stare hard at her deputy for a moment, before continuing. 'Herr Ingo Höfler. He is – or rather was – the managing director of the VEB Baumwollspinnerei Leinefelde – the cotton-spinning mill you may have seen on your way here. It's the biggest employer around here, with several thousand workers.' Ingersleben slid across another photograph from the file, and again turned it towards the two Berlin detectives. 'And this is how he was found, slumped on the factory floor, overcome by smoke.'

This time Müller picked up the photograph, then immediately recoiled. At first glance, the similarity with Ronnebach's death in the Sachsenburg mill was uncanny.

Höfler's body – like Ronnebach's – had been found by a closed exit doorway. His arms were clawing out, as though he was desperately scrabbling to escape.

She offered the photo to Tilsner. He glanced at it for a moment, shook his head, and replaced it on the table.

'So, Comrade Ingersleben, why are you now certain this was a murder?' asked Müller.

Ingersleben stroked his chin. 'Well, it was soon obvious that arson was involved – that the fire was set deliberately. We're very near the state border here as you know. It's a sensitive area. Before the factory and all the apartments for workers were built, there were fears that this area could be a centre of revolt against the state, fomented by the church. This was the Ministry for State Security's reasoning for why they should take control of the case. We initially didn't get a look in.'

Tilsner gave Müller a knowing look, no doubt pleased that the theory he'd espoused on the journey was being echoed back to them.

'What changed?' asked Müller.

'Well, I don't think the Stasi could find any real evidence of a plot. So they lost interest.' Ingersleben paused, and leant back in his chair, his hands clasped behind his head. 'Also it's mainly a rural area, apart from pockets of industry like here in Leinefelde, so pathologists are rather thin on the ground. We have to share one with the Ministry for State Security. And our friendly pathologist didn't particularly like the way this arson attack was being portrayed as simply a grudge by so-called counter-revolutionaries. You see, to the pathologist, it was clear that Herr Höfler was the target.'

'Why?' asked Müller, though she suspected she knew the answer.

'His hands and feet had been lashed together. All the doors to the factory unit where he was found were locked from the outside. He wasn't meant to escape . . . and he didn't. I gather that is a very similar modus operandi to your murder in Sachsenburg.'

'It's uncannily similar,' said Müller. 'The hallmarks of some sort of ritualistic killing.'

Tilsner leant forward in his chair, his hands on his knees. 'Could someone have borne a grudge against Herr Höfler to do with the factory? Perhaps someone who'd lost their job?'

'We've looked into that,' said Ingersleben. 'And drawn a blank amongst the employees. You have to do something pretty awful to lose your job in the Republic, as you're no doubt well aware.'

'But you say this area was mostly countryside before the factory and town were built?' continued Tilsner.

'That's right. Leinefelde existed – but it was little more than a village.'

'And the land the mill was built on?' asked Tilsner.

'Farmland, I would think,' said Ingersleben.

'At one time, no doubt owned by a farmer who then lost his land.' Tilsner slapped his hand on the desk. 'There's your possible motive. And it fits in with the Sachsenburg murder too. The victim there was involved in the decision to nationalise that mill.'

Ingersleben looked doubtful. Müller was too. Tilsner was just a little too eager to push them down one line of inquiry when they should – at this stage – be keeping an open mind.

11

When she went to question Herr Höfler's widow, Müller toyed with the idea of leaving Tilsner behind. The fact that the Ministry for State Security here in Leinefelde hadn't yet twigged what she was up to gave her a slight window of opportunity to find out information without the presence of a Stasi agent obstructing any of her questions. In the end, though, she decided to take her deputy. Tilsner had never let her down before, not when it really mattered. She wanted him concentrating on the task, not sulking about whatever it was that was getting him down.

The Höfler residence was a half-timbered, mediaeval-looking house, that appeared to have once been a private farm, just off the main road towards Worbis, to the north of Leinefelde itself.

As they parked, Tilsner echoed what Müller had been thinking. 'A farmhouse, a former farm, built on farmland and now occupied by the head of a state cotton mill. Plenty of potential motives there.'

'Perhaps, Werner. But let's not prejudge things,' replied Müller.

After the introductions, Frau Höfler led them into a spacious, rustic kitchen, and offered them coffee. The middle-aged woman's hands shook as she poured into three mug-like cups, and offered two of them to the detectives. She gestured to the wooden kitchen table.

'We can talk here, if that's all right. I've been struggling a bit since Ingo passed away. But I want to help if I can.'

'You understand why we're taking an interest?' asked Müller.

'Well . . . I was told by the police here that things might not have been how they first appeared with Ingo's death, yes?'

Müller took a sip of the coffee. It was the real thing – clearly the Höflers didn't have to rely on *Kaffee Mix*. Then she stared hard at the woman. 'We want to know as much as possible about your husband to enable us to get to the bottom of all this.'

The woman frowned in confusion, her faced framed by a mass of dyed blonde hair, permed into tight curls. 'Well, I said everything I could to the Ministry for State Security and then later the police in Leinefelde.'

Tilsner sighed. 'We'll need to go over it all again. Can you think of anyone who may have wished your husband harm?'

The woman shrugged. 'I wouldn't know all his business. We tried to keep our work and private lives separate. It was a bit of a rule.'

As Tilsner continued to question the woman, Müller found herself losing concentration and scanning the room. She wasn't sure what she was looking for, but her eyes were drawn to a dresser, and the centre shelf which held a framed photo of a young-looking couple.

'I must say,' said Tilsner, 'this house of yours is lovely. It's more like something you'd expect in the West.' Müller could hear the accusatory note in his voice, as she got up to study the photograph more closely. 'How did you come to acquire it?'

The question hung in the air without answer, as Müller picked up the framed photograph and studied it more closely. It showed a young couple outside an ivy-clad historic town hall, with a steep red-tiled roof punctuated by low dormer windows, above a grand-looking first floor which in turn straddled the arches of a colonnade at ground level.

'Who's this?' asked Müller. From what she could tell, the photo was taken in the 1930s.

'That's myself and Ingo, of course, just before we were married.'

Tilsner got up to study the photo too.

Müller looked for clues about the location. 'Where was it tak—'

There was a sudden roar of car engines and then furious braking coming from outside. The three of them peered out of the kitchen window as there was a hammering on the kitchen door.

Frau Höfler went to open it, and Müller tried to repeat the question. 'Where, Frau Höfler? I need to know. Now!' While the woman's back was turned, she quickly removed the photo from the frame, and slipped it under her jacket.

'Hang on,' said the woman. She opened the door.

Müller almost didn't believe who was standing there. *Why is he here again? Always interfering. Always controlling everything I try to do.*

Her sometime nemesis.

Her sometime saviour.

Oberst Klaus Jäger of the Ministry for State Security.

The sudden intrusion by the Stasi seemed to reawaken Frau Höfler's grief. Jäger instructed a female agent to sit with her at the kitchen table, while barking orders to other officers – apparently sealing off the farmhouse. Then he ushered Müller and Tilsner into the lounge.

He was dressed neatly, with collar-length sandy hair. Immediately, he slipped into the suave patter that always reminded Müller of the smooth-voiced news presenters of West German TV – something that, as a major with the People's Police, she wasn't even supposed to watch.

'Sorry about all this, Karin and Werner. We've received new information about both the Höfler killing here, and the one of Ronnebach near Karl-Marx-Stadt, which means we're having to take over both cases.' The Stasi colonel looked apologetic. Müller knew he wasn't.

'I'll need to check what you have said with Keibelstrasse, Comrade *Oberst*.' It was futile to put up any resistance, but she had to at least go through the motions. '*Oberst* Reiniger may not agree with this.'

'He will. He has his orders, just like I have mine. And now you have yours too, but by all means ring or radio in to check if you wish.' Jäger's face wore a thin, supercilious smile.

Müller gave a long sigh. She turned briefly to Tilsner alongside her. He seemed relieved. *He can get back to his new girlfriend now.*

She clenched her teeth, and returned her gaze to Jäger. 'What exactly is this new information?'

'I'm not permitted to tell you everything. But what I can say is it is connected to that so-called Committee for the Dispossessed.'

'The group agitating against the nationalisations?'

Jäger nodded. 'The one your childhood friend was involved with.'

'But in Halle-Neustadt you said the group had disbanded, that all the active members had been arrested?' Müller knew something wasn't right with this convenient excuse for getting her off the case. She just didn't know precisely what.

Jäger gave a small shrug. 'Clearly I was wrong. Anyway, as a result of that, I'm sure you can understand that further inquiries into these murders have to be conducted by the Ministry for State Security. You're free to go back to Berlin and Keibelstrasse.'

'That's a stroke of luck,' said Tilsner, once they were back in the Wartburg. The transformation in his mood was near miraculous. 'I could tell both of those cases were a can of worms from the start.'

Müller didn't bother to answer. She felt frustrated and powerless. She tried to picture the photograph of the young Höflers in her head. The location was significant, she was sure.

'It'll be good for you too,' continued Tilsner. 'Will you go back out to Bulgaria for the rest of your holiday?'

The futility of cutting short her family's Black Sea break was the least of Müller's worries at the moment. Again, she didn't answer her deputy, as he indicated to join the main road back towards Nordhausen and Berlin. She turned to him and studied his face. He looked as though all the cares of the world had been lifted from his shoulders.

'Have you noticed how Jäger always seems to arrive at key moments?' she asked.

Tilsner shrugged. 'So? The Stasi have eyes and ears everywhere.'

Müller looked down at his watch. The glittering western watch. The one that no one on a police captain or lieutenant's salary would be able to afford. The one that, to her, was almost like a badge that betrayed Tilsner's Stasi sympathies.

'On the Brocken, Jäger appeared with his cronies soon after you'd used the police radio in the car. That was convenient.'

Tilsner said nothing.

'In Guben, the same thing happened. You use the radio. You refuse to tell me who you're talking to. Not long after, as if by magic, Jäger is there on the scene.'

'I'm not sure what you're driving at, Karin.'

'Oh, I think you know very well what I'm talking about, Werner. But this time, I'm determined to get to the bottom of things – with or without you.'

The sides of Tilsner's mouth turned down. 'Jäger has said we're off the case. That's an end to it as far as I'm concerned.'

'Well, we'll just have to see about that, won't we, Werner? The Frankfurt Stasi tried to pull the same trick last time. Reiniger managed to let us circumvent it. I wouldn't bet against him doing the same thing again.'

12

It was evening when they arrived back in Berlin. Tilsner invited Müller for a drink. It was presumably his attempt at a peace offering. She wasn't interested – and in reality, probably neither was he, no doubt eager to get back to his new woman. Instead she checked whether Reiniger was still in his office. He was, despite the relative lateness of the hour.

'Ah, Karin, come in,' he said, after answering her knock on the door himself, as his secretary had long departed at the end of the working day. 'Please sit down.' He gestured to one of the armchairs by a low coffee table. He arranged himself in one of the others, hitching up the legs of his uniform trousers. 'I'm sorry I can't offer you coffee. Truda's already left. I was just trying to get on top of my in-tray before calling it a night. What can I do for you?'

'You've heard about the Karl-Marx-Stadt and Leinefelde cases, Comrade *Oberst*?' asked Müller.

'Yes, very unfortunate. And particularly annoying for you as you and your family cut short your holiday because of the cases. Take the rest of your leave, of course. If you like, I can obtain travel warrants for a new trip?'

Müller shook her head. 'That's not what I want. What I need is your permission to continue investigating these two killings. Something just isn't sitting right with them for me.'

Reiniger frowned, clasping his hands across his stomach. Then he opened his hands towards her and shrugged. 'Why do you think I have any more control over this than you do? The decision has been made. The apparent involvement of this counter-revolutionary group means it has to be a matter for the *MfS*.'

Müller placed both her elbows on the chair arms, and steepled her fingers. 'Can you at least tell me what this new information is? Why they are convinced that this Committee for the Dispossessed is involved?'

'I believe it was an anonymous tip-off.'

'An *anonymous* tip-off? How convenient.' She thought of Tilsner and his uncanny ability to mimic regional accents. He'd pulled a similar trick before, and she wouldn't put it past him to have done the same again.

'Don't be like that, Karin. I can appreciate you're annoyed and frustrated. But as I told you when we set up this new unit, we need to work with the Stasi, not against them. We're all on the same side.'

The consolation for Müller was that she could now drive to Schönefeld the next day to welcome Helga and the twins as they arrived back from Bulgaria.

She managed to get hold of Helga in a late evening phone call to tell her the news.

'That will be much more convenient than getting the S-bahn. And the twins will be delighted to see you.'

'How are they?'

'Well, Jannika's been as good as gold.'

'And Johannes?'

'Hmm. I suppose you could say he's been rather spirited. You know how he is.'

Müller vowed to herself to give more help to her grandmother now that she was between cases again. But at this stage, she didn't tell the older woman about being taken off the case so quickly. She didn't want Helga realising yet that their holiday had been cut short in vain.

The next day, Müller felt such a rush of joy – such breathlessness – as she saw Helga wheeling Jannika and Johannes in the pushchair, that she had to fight back the tears.

She gave Helga a hug, kissed Jannika, and then gave in to Johannes's back-arching and screaming and scooped him into her arms. She covered him in kisses as he yanked at her hair. Then she handed him to Helga, as she picked up Jannika. 'Mutti, Mutti,' shouted her daughter, clapping her hands and smiling broadly.

'We should celebrate,' said Müller. 'I've got a few days off now.'

Helga's face creased into a frown. 'I thought you'd been called back because of a new important case.'

Müller shrugged. 'I was. But there's been a bit of . . . a bit of a misunderstanding. It looks as though we came back from Bulgaria for no reason.'

'How odd. And annoying,' said Helga, her frown deepening.

'I'm sorry. There was nothing I could do about it, and I've only just found out. But I've still got a few days off. We can go to the park, the lakes, maybe even the Kulturpark Plänterwald.'

Helga smiled. 'That would be fun. They're a bit young for the rides, though.'

'We can go on gentle things like the Swan Boats. Even Johannes couldn't get up to much mischief on those.' She tweaked her son's nose, eliciting a giggle. It was so good to have them back.

The following day was a beautiful summer day in Berlin with blue skies and a light breeze to take the edge off the warm temperatures.

Rather than go to the Kulturpark, Helga's preference was for more sunbathing and paddling – to try to extend the holiday feeling they'd just had snatched away from them. They took the tram out towards Hohenschönhausen – the site of the Stasi prison where Müller's ex-husband Gottfried had been held. But Müller had no intention of visiting there again, not if she could help it. Instead their destination was *Strandbad Orankesee*.

Müller looked after most of the childcare to give Helga a rest, but at one point her grandmother took the twins off in the pushchair to get an ice cream, leaving Müller a few moments to sunbathe in her bikini, and think over the events of the past few days. At the forefront of her mind was a feeling that somehow she'd been cheated. She tried to relax as she lay back, picking up fistfuls of sand with each hand, then letting the grains slowly run out between her fingers. As she closed her eyes, the image that seemed to be projected onto her eyelids was the one of Herr and Frau Höfler as a teenage couple, in front of that town hall. It would be a long task, but surely if she looked through books on German architecture or history, or significant buildings, she could find out where it was?

When they got back to the apartment block in Strausberger Platz, Johannes started playing up again, as though he didn't want his day out to end. While Helga tried to calm the children before they got in the lift, Müller had a quick check of the apartment's mailbox in the lobby. There seemed to be nothing of much significance, except for one handwritten letter, addressed to her at Keibelstrasse, and obviously forwarded by the office there. Presumably her colleagues had assumed it was personal mail, and had sent it on thinking Müller wouldn't want to wait till after her leave to open it.

She looked at the handwriting. She felt a knot tighten in her belly.

It looked suspiciously like Gottfried's. She dismissed the thought. It wasn't possible – Jäger had said he was dead. He'd even taken her to the execution site in the forest.

She looked at the stamp and postmark. A DDR stamp, so from within the Republic. The postmark: Gardelegen. At the back of her mind she'd heard of the place, but she wasn't sure why or exactly where it was. She tore the envelope open, and immediately realised it wasn't from her ex-husband.

But she didn't know who it was from, because it was unsigned. She read the note:

I understand you are looking into the killing of 'Herr Ronnebach'.

I can give you some information.

Meet me in a week's time (Saturday 29 July) at 1 p.m. at the following grid coordinates: 52°34'26.3"N 11°20'55.3"E

I will wait there for thirty minutes.

13

March 1945
Kohnstein mountain, near Nordhausen

We know it's nearly over for the Germans – that they're facing defeat. I can't believe Marcellin and I have survived eighteen months down here. Conditions got a little better when the camp itself was completed. We no longer had to sleep in the tunnels, amid the stink of shit and the dust.

There are various signs of imminent defeat for the Nazis. We have to cling on and survive until then. I try not to dream of going back to the island, to the village. I don't want to kill myself through hope. But sometimes my mouth salivates at the thought of gulping a raw oyster down whole. The most tangible sign is the number of air raid alarms, the number of alerts about enemy plane movements. If it looks like the complex itself will be bombed, one of the *Kapos* bangs an iron bar against a suspended piece of scrap iron. We always feel a frisson of fear then, but also the buzz of excitement – willing the Allies to strike home. Sometimes when we're above ground we'll even see a plane dive-bombing in the distance, attacking a German target.

Parts become scarce. There is less work because of that. And the lights have been dimmed – presumably because the Germans are running short of raw materials to run their remaining power stations. That half-light is another sign that the Nazis have been beaten.

You would think the Germans themselves, the civilian workers and their wives, would be cowed, would show the defeat on their faces. But often they seem delirious. Singing at the top of their lungs. Even singing American songs.

'I can't understand it,' I whisper to Marcellin, as we make a pretence of doing more welding. Often these days we take things apart, just to put them back together again, spinning the work out, making it appear as if we're still busy. 'Why are they glorying in their own country's defeat?'

'You cannot judge them by the standards of others,' replies my brother. 'They disgust me. They always have. They always will. They're little better than animals.'

But the eve of defeat brings its own dangers. There are rumours some of the Russians have tried to mutiny.

There's an execution site at the far end of one of the two parallel main tunnels – Tunnel B.

For some reason, to send us a message perhaps about what will happen if we try to rise up, a group of French prisoners – including myself and Marcellin – are paraded past as the executions take place.

There are nine Russian prisoners, standing in a line in a half-metre-deep trench with their heads uncovered. A piece of wood is locked in each man's mouth, secured by iron wire twisted behind their heads, a little like a horse's bit.

Each man has his own noose made from steel cable. There are nine nooses, attached to a horizontal metal rod. In the centre of the rod, another thicker cable is holding it up.

A group of SS troops is in charge, but it is left to a high-ranking prisoner to put each noose around each of their heads.

The central cable – high above the nine men – coils around the drum of an electric winch.

An SS Sergeant Major – this one is nicknamed Horse Head by us, I can't remember why – gives a signal. Then the executioner switches on the motor.

There's a droning noise, and the nine men, as they are slowly strangled, are raised by the winch until they're level with us – ground level.

As we parade past, we have to look straight into their faces and watch their eyes rolling back into their heads.

But death isn't instant.

They spin slowly. Their bodies spasm.

It takes more than a minute as we slowly walk past.

Nine dead men. All in a row.

I never knew their names. But I will never, ever forget those faces.

14

July 1977
Bezirk Magdeburg, East Germany

Müller had never been to this part of East Germany before. She drove the Lada along straight, virtually traffic-free roads, past the occasional town or village, then kilometre after kilometre of thick dark forest. Nearer and nearer to the state border and the West.

At first, Tilsner had flatly refused to come with her, insisting they were off the case, and threatening to tell Jäger what she was up to. Müller persuaded him not to. She also played on his loyalties.

'Remember what happened that time on the Brocken, when I was separated from you? You're my right-hand man. I need you.'

He relented. But she held back the detailed information about where they were going, in case he changed his mind. All she revealed was that it was in Bezirk Magdeburg: a vast area stretching from the Harz Mountains in the south, to the north of the Altmark – the so-called cradle of Prussia.

As they crossed the Elbe at Tangermünde, Tilsner could no longer contain his frustration about her withholding the destination. He was never a particularly good passenger anyway. Usually he would drive, and normally they would have taken the *Kripo* Wartburg. Müller preferred to be in her own car.

'I know this area,' he said. 'Better than you seem to, judging by the number of times you keep referring to that map on your lap. Here, give it to me. Where exactly are we going?'

Müller considered resisting, but realised it was futile. She let him pick the road atlas up, but instead of consulting it, he just placed it on the dashboard shelf.

'To Estedt,' she said. 'A small village north of Gardelegen.'

'I know it,' said Tilsner.

'I thought geography wasn't your strong point?'

'It isn't. But I've family from these parts.'

Müller turned her heads towards him, while keeping half an eye on the road ahead. 'You never said before.'

Tilsner shrugged. 'They're only distant relatives.'

In Stendal, Müller remembered from the map the quickest way was to continue west along Fernverkehrsstrasse 188, towards Gardelegen. But Tilsner directed her instead along a minor road to the north-west, towards the villages of Steinfeld and Kläden.

She frowned. 'Why are we going this way?'

'It's prettier, and we'll avoid any traffic.'

The coordinates in the message sent to Müller related to a wooded area about a kilometre directly west of Estedt. The village itself lay to the north of Gardelegen, on the main road north towards Salzwedel. It would have been much easier just to go to Gardelegen itself, then drive north. But Tilsner seemed to have brought them a circuitous route down country lanes from the north-east.

When they reached the centre of the village, Müller parked the Lada near the church, and then pulled out a copy of a larger scale map from her briefcase.

'You're being very mysterious, Karin. Where are we going, and what are we doing?'

'We're going for a walk. To meet someone.' In truth, although Müller knew the directions from here, she wasn't sure what to expect. Was it some sort of trap they were walking into? Should they simply have detailed the local police in Gardelegen to make the rendezvous, hoping that whoever it was who wanted to get in touch wouldn't just be willing to talk to Müller herself?

The main road which bisected Estedt was surprisingly busy, with lorries speeding each way. Once they'd dodged the traffic, they found the lane Müller was looking for. It dipped down slightly between ploughed fields on either side, and then became an earth and grass cart track. In winter, they would have needed gumboots – it might even have been impassable. But now – in high summer – they could cope perfectly well in their street shoes.

The two detectives strode on in silence. The only sounds were their footsteps on the dirty track, the crackle of paper from the photocopied map which Müller occasionally consulted, and a background of birdsong. In the hedgerows each side of the track, butterflies danced from plant to plant to gather nectar. It was an idyllic summer scene. Yet Müller felt uncomfortable, wary. She realised she'd been biting her lip almost since they'd got out of the car.

Then, from the direction of the woods they were heading for, a scream pierced the silence.

Müller started to run towards the sound. Tilsner grabbed her arm.

'Careful, Karin. We don't know what's going on.'

She shrugged him off. 'You've got your gun, haven't you? Get it ready.'

Silence settled again.

They ran on, up a slight incline towards the wood, the only sounds their own panting breaths and rapid footfall.

About halfway up the incline, Müller had to rest as a stitch kicked in. She felt her old Caesarean scar pulling. It hadn't been a trained doctor who'd done the initial cuts – although an obstetrician had tried to tidy things up a few months later. Instead, the initial cuts had been made by her one-time childhood friend and his accomplice wife, trying – and very nearly succeeding – to steal her babies away from her.

Tilsner looked hard at her. 'Are you OK? Should you really be doing this?'

She nodded. 'Come on. Something's gone wrong.' The scream, she knew, must have come from almost the exact same place her mystery contact wanted to meet.

At the top of the rise, the surrounding fields gave way to the woods, but the cart track continued on. A hundred metres more, and Müller turned off the track to the north, and suddenly they were in a clearing. Shafts of light penetrated the darkness, as though someone was holding a giant torch overhead. Müller checked the map against the landmarks shown: a fork in the track, a large boulder to one side of the clearing, the diamond shape of the clearing itself.

This was the place, she was certain. Yet no one was here.

Tilsner was crouched to the ground, examining it. 'Footprints. They look fresh, and something's been dragged along—'

A car engine started up, startling them. They ran towards the noise. Through the trees they saw an olive green Trabant Kübel racing away in the direction of Estedt. They ran back to the cart track, sprinting after the vehicle as fast as they could.

'Stop! *Kriminalpolizei!*' shouted Müller.

But it was too late. 'Did you get the registration number, Werner?'

He shook his head. 'There wasn't one.'

Müller's face darkened. Who would be able to get away with driving a vehicle with no number plate in the Republic without being questioned or arrested?

There were very few options.

A high-up in the government? Maybe.

A high-up in the army? Perhaps. Such vehicles were certainly in use with the People's Army, although to be driven on a public road – where that one was heading back to – they would normally have some sort of military registration plate.

The People's Police, Müller's own organisation, was another possibility.

But the most likely scenario was that it belonged to the Ministry for State Security.

The Stasi.

Müller ordered Tilsner to go back to the Lada to alert Gardelegen's People's Police. It would almost certainly be too late as the Kübel would be clean away before they could get any road-blocks in place – probably along the exact same network of country lanes that Tilsner had followed to get them to Estedt in the first place. There would be too many bases to cover. But she wanted them to send a forensic scientist and search team up to the woods – there might be other evidence to find.

Müller returned to the clearing. The sense of foreboding that had first chilled her when they had climbed the gentle incline to the wood now returned even more strongly, despite the summer heat. She found herself biting her nails, fearing she'd let down her anonymous contact. But she and Tilsner had arrived at the time the contact had requested. They'd done all they could. Perhaps she should have got in touch with the local uniform division ahead of time and got them to place a watch on the wood. It was too late now. There was no point worrying about what might have been.

She knelt down in the grassy area where Tilsner had seen the prints. She didn't want to move around too much, and destroy what evidence there was. Then she glanced up towards the large boulder. A darker area glistened in the sun on the rock. She approached it with mounting excitement.

Blood.

Congealing, but not yet fully dry.

She took a plastic evidence bag and her penknife from the pocket of her red jacket.

She carefully scraped a sample of the blood into the bag.

Was it the blood of their contact? She didn't know for certain, but she suspected that was the case.

The question, though, was whether he was alive, mortally wounded, or already dead and unable to pass on to Müller the information that he'd risked his life to give.

15

'What exactly are we looking for, Comrade *Major*?' asked *Hauptmann* Albert Janson, the local police captain, surrounded by dog handlers. The dogs strained at their leashes, panting and impatient to get on with their work.

Müller was sure a crime had been committed; she just didn't know exactly what. She was equally sure it was somehow connected to the murders in Karl-Marx-Stadt and Leinefelde.

She pointed to the boulder and the bloodstain. 'The man who was supposed to be meeting me appears to have been seriously injured here. At least, I assume it was whoever was supposed to be meeting me. If you could get his scent, perhaps the dogs could follow it to work out where he had walked from. Did he come from Estedt itself? Does he live there?'

Janson nodded. 'What makes you think he came from the Estedt direction?'

'What's the other way? Is there another village nearby?'

The captain rubbed his chin. 'Yes. Breitenfeld. But it must be five or six kilometres through the forest.'

'See if the dogs pick up a scent. Maybe he came here by car?'

'We've already had a quick scout around. The only fresh vehicle tracks appear to be from the Trabant Kübel you say you saw. That appears to have approached from Breitenfeld, and left via Estedt.'

'Presumably with our victim inside. Dead or alive.'

'OK,' said Janson. 'I'll set the team to work and see if we discover anything.'

Tilsner walked up close to Müller. He glanced up at the sky through the clearing, at the azure blue dotted with the occasional cotton wool cloud, then held Müller's gaze.

'Of course, our man might not have been the victim.'

'What do you mean?'

'Perhaps he was intending to attack someone. He knew someone was coming here, at a particular time.'

'What are you trying to say, Werner?'

Tilsner took a long breath. 'Let's say this is all linked. Karl-Marx-Stadt, Leinefelde. Perhaps something's happened here too. Perhaps our man didn't want anyone investigating it. Perhaps he knew either you or I would be coming here, answering his call.'

'And?'

'It's in the middle of nowhere. The clearing is off the beaten track – literally. So our contact might presume that any man or woman entering the clearing at the allotted time would be you. What if another woman turned up here, in the wrong place at the wrong time?'

'And what if it had been a man?'

Tilsner shrugged. 'Exactly. Either you or I could have been the real target.'

Müller felt her chest tighten. Tilsner could be right. But the scream they'd heard had been male, she was sure of that. She felt a sudden need to be back in the Hauptstadt, at the Strausberger Platz apartment, holding Jannika and Johannes. And she wanted to hug her grandmother and tell her how much she loved her.

There was frenzied barking and a shout rang out.

'I think we've got the scent,' yelled Janson.

The detectives and uniformed officers followed the female dog handler as she tried to hold the animal back. It strained at the leash, almost pulling her along. They found themselves almost running back along the track towards Estedt, in the direction the Kübel had gone.

'Will it be the scent from something inside the car?' panted Müller as she half-ran alongside the uniform captain.

'No. The scent is of whoever was injured, whoever's blood was spilt on the boulder. It means they must have walked here from the Estedt direction.'

The posse of police officers and dogs moved in a line towards the village. Before they got to the main road, the lead dog directed its handler towards a side lane. About fifty metres down that, the dog stopped and started barking at the driver's door of a light blue Trabant saloon.

Müller looked quizzically at the police captain.

'It must be his car. Shall we break into it?'

Hauptmann Janson gestured to one of his men. After first trying the door to make sure it was locked, the second officer pulled his gun from his holster, used the butt end to smash the driver's window, and then opened the door. He pulled out the car's documents, and then leafed through them.

'Lothar Schneider. Apartment 18, Stendaler Strasse 73, Gardelegen.'

Müller turned to Janson. 'Does that name mean anything to you?'

The captain shook his head. 'But I'll radio back to headquarters now, and get a couple of officers to go round there.'

'No, don't for now,' said Müller. '*Hauptmann* Tilsner and I will do it ourselves. We'll let you know if we need any assistance. What I'd like you to do in the meantime is look for other evidence in the woods, see if you can find any witnesses to where that Kübel came from – if it was indeed Breitenfeld – and perhaps see if your dogs can at least trace the direction the Kübel went after it got to Estedt.'

Number 73 Stendaler Strasse lay on the main road out of Gardelegen towards the east, in the direction of Berlin. It was a two-storey block, with another storey in the roof space, of what appeared to be a turn-of-the-century building. Like many of the Republic's older structures, bullet hole damage from the Second World War was still evident in its brickwork. Müller counted two, three, four places at least where either a bullet or ricochet had blown a chunk off the building.

They rang on the bell for Apartment 18. Nothing happened. Tilsner tried the front door. It was open.

The two detectives ran up the stairs to the first floor, and soon located Schneider's front door. Müller rapped on it. No reply. Then she shouted out: '*Kriminalpolizei!* Is anyone at home?'

The noise clearly alerted other neighbours, as an elderly woman peeked out of her door. 'What's going on?' she asked.

Müller showed her ID card. '*Major* Karin Müller of the Serious Crimes Department in Berlin, and this is *Hauptmann* Werner Tilsner. Do you know where the Schneiders are?'

The woman said nothing for a moment, and appeared to be staring past Müller, at Tilsner. Müller turned. Tilsner had his head bowed, and his collar turned up, almost as though he was trying to disappear into his jacket.

Müller turned back to the woman. 'Well?'

The woman seemed to shake herself out of whatever trance she was in. 'They're both out at work as far as I know. Why? What are they supposed to have done?'

'That's none of your business. Where do they work?'

'He works at the power station. She's a school teacher. It's the school holidays but she still goes in on some days to do preparation work and marking.'

'Which school?'

'Oberschule Geschwister Scholl. In Jägerstieg. About one-and-a-half kilometres from here. It's too far for me to walk, but no problem for you young things.' The woman was squinting again at Tilsner. 'Don't I know you from somewhere?'

Müller looked at Tilsner. He'd turned away. 'I don't think so,' he said over his shoulder. 'I've never been here before.'

The woman shrugged. 'Oh well. All young men look similar to me these days. My eyes are going, dear. Will that be all? I hope they're not in trouble. They're a nice couple, always helping me out.'

'That's very useful. And no, they're not in any trouble. We just need them to help us with something.'

'What was all that about?' she asked as she ran after Tilsner down the stairs.

'What was what about?'

'That woman. She thought she knew you.'

Tilsner stopped and turned to her. 'I told you. I have family from this area. Maybe she saw me visiting them one time.'

'I hope you'll always tell me the truth, Werner. We go back a long way.'

'We do. So it's hardly the time to be believing some batty old dear with bad eyesight rather than me, is it?'

The power station or the school? That was their choice. Müller opted for the power station. If Schneider had been badly injured or even killed, she didn't want to upset his wife before she was sure. Emotional sensibilities weren't, of course, at the forefront of her mind. But it was still a factor.

VEB Energiekombinat Frieden Gardelegen was situated on the edge of the town. Two giant cooling towers dominated the skyline, with mountains of lignite – low-grade brown coal mined from just below the surface – standing alongside. With the steam from the concrete towers and smoke rising from various chimneys, it reminded Müller of their interviews at the Eisenhüttenstadt steelworks the previous year during the Dominik Nadel case.

Müller and Tilsner were asked to wait at the entrance checkpoint while an official was summoned from within the complex.

A besuited, middle-aged man with a balding head eventually appeared and introduced himself, with a shorter, younger man alongside.

'I'm Herman Siskind, deputy managing director of the plant.'

Müller showed her *Kripo* ID. '*Major* Karin Müller and *Hauptmann* Werner Tilsner from the Serious Crimes Department in Berlin.'

'Oh dear,' said Siskind, an inappropriate grin on his face. 'I hope we're not guilty of any serious crimes.'

Müller didn't appreciate the man's levity. 'Not as far as I know, Herr Siskind. However we are investigating a potential crime. We believe that one of your employees, a certain Lothar Schneider, may have been a victim of a crime.'

'How dreadful. Well, before I can talk to you, I've been informed by the Ministry for State Security that I need to see your authorisations. Presumably you have such authorisations to show me?'

Müller frowned. 'As I say, I'm a major from the Serious Crimes Department of the People's Police. I don't require any authorisation from the Stasi.'

The younger man now spoke up. 'I'm afraid you do, Comrade *Major*. I'm the *MfS* liaison officer here. Mirco Jundt. You may not be aware, but because of their importance for national security, power stations come under a special set of rules. For something like this you will need authority from the regional office of the Ministry for State Security in Magdeburg. I'm sure they will help you if they can. Would you like their telephone number?'

Müller sighed. 'Can you at least confirm Herr Schneider works here?'

'I don't think I could have been any clearer,' said Jundt. 'We are not permitted to give out any information until you have the necessary authority.'

After the abortive power station visit Müller and Tilsner drove to the People's Police office in Gardelegen. They were quickly ushered up the stairs to see *Hauptmann* Janson.

'We've some news, and it's not good news for your Herr Schneider. His body was found dumped in a lane near Kalbe less than an hour ago.'

'Where's that?' asked Müller.

'About twenty kilometres north of here. Fifteen minutes' drive away if you want us to take you to look at the scene. Our people from the *Kripo* are out there.'

'Is it murder?'

'I should say so, yes,' replied Janson. 'Unless he decided to cut his own throat.'

16

The bombers are here. Marcellin and I are terrified but excited. Discipline in the camp has broken down. Perhaps we can escape, finally get out of this living hell.

But as the string of bombs begins to fall, we realise survival is everything. We see one group of Russian prisoners blown to smithereens as they try to make a run for it, and others shredded alive by shrapnel, so instead we dive into the nearest bomb crater amid the heat and noise of the explosions.

The bombing grows with intensity. We lie flat on our stomachs in the mud, just praying and hoping that another bomb won't hit this exact spot twice. There's no reason why one shouldn't – but somehow we feel safer on this bit of earth that's already been punished for the Nazis' megalomania, brutality, and utter madness.

As the sound of the aeroplanes and explosions dies away, we hear the terrible wailing of the wounded. We creep on our stomachs upwards to the edge of the crater.

'Should we help them?' I ask Marcellin.

'They're dying, Philippe. There's nothing we can do.'

'Should we make a run for it?' I ask.

Marcellin shakes his head. Then I see he's clutching his arm. He's been wounded. 'It's nothing,' he says. 'Just a flesh wound. But I don't want to run with it.'

'Perhaps we can get to the *Revier*. Get it dressed?'

But as I say this, the camp loudspeakers suddenly come to life. The announcement says that everyone, without exception, must assemble at the roll call area with two blankets each, and prepare for a departure.

The announcement produces a kind of mêlée amongst those fit enough still to run. I can't understand what's happening at first. Then I realise. Prisoners, mostly the Russians, are raiding what's left in the stores, getting what little food they can find for whatever journey lies ahead. By the time we work out what's happening, next to nothing remains.

Another cold night, but that is nothing new. It was always cold when we had to sleep down in the tunnels for months on end, bunk piled upon bunk, with only a barrel for a latrine.

When dawn comes, the remaining *Kapos* try to organise us. We're divided into those too weak to be useful workers, and those judged still capable of physical work. I'd managed to get a bandage and iodine for Marcellin's wound and dressed it as best I could the previous night, but one of the *Kapos* spots the bandage. We're about to be separated. I cannot stand that. I will not stand for that.

'No,' I shout. 'He is my brother. He stays with me.' The blows from the *Kapo*'s baton rain down on my back, but one of his colleagues pulls him off, and gestures with his head to Marcellin, indicating he can get back in our line. Of course, we don't know whether it's better to be judged still fit for work or not. We don't have any idea what will happen to us. But after losing Grégoire I know one thing: we must stay together.

We're being marched somewhere. They won't tell us where we are going. But clearly the days of this camp are over. We don't know whether the bombing has finally rendered it useless, or whether the Allies are too near for it to be safe for the Germans. Many are left behind. Many bodies are still scattered around the smoking remains of the camp. Some are finally succumbing to starvation, but most are dead from untended wounds sustained in the unrelenting carpet bombing. And not all of them are prisoners. We pass an SS guard, still in his bloodied, torn asunder uniform, lying where he fell. His eyes are still open, staring unseeing at the sky.

War is a terrible thing. A terrible, terrible thing. Whichever side you are on.

We march, and march, and march. The only thing keeping out the cold and rain are our two thin blankets, our striped, zebra-like prison uniforms, and our next-to-useless wooden-soled shoes.

'Where do you think we're going?' Marcellin asks.

I sniff. 'I don't know. But I don't think it's good. We'd have been better off staying with the injured and ill at the camp.

I think the Allies will be there soon. That must be why they're moving us.'

'We won't make it, Philippe. We won't get to see the island again.'

'We will. We'll be back on the boat in no time. You'll see. And then chatting up the girls in St Martin.' It's bravado on my part. I don't want to chat up any old girl. I simply want to sit on the sea wall, next to Marie-Ange, running my fingers through her flaxen hair, teasing her that she looks more English than French. And I want to finally say those words: *I love you.* I try not to think what she might have been doing in the intervening years. What she would have had to do to survive. Which German soldier, or soldiers, she might have had to sleep with.

Despite our desperation, he manages a weak laugh. 'That never works. They always smell the fish and run a mile. Anyway, you were always the one with the chat. If I had your way with women, I'd have married that Marie-Ange and whisked her off for a new life in America, before all this hell blew up in our faces.' He doesn't mention his own girl, Violette. They were already going through a rocky time, even before all this.

One of the *Kapos* glowers at us. We fall silent rather than risk another beating.

It's hard to know how far we have walked, or for how long. It feels like several hours, and perhaps twenty kilometres, but in reality is probably much, much less. I know I am exhausted, and I can see the same in Marcellin's face. But it seems as though we've arrived. We're in some sort of railway marshalling yard, with what looks like a bomb-damaged station up ahead. But not everything is wrecked. The steam from a locomotive rises up through the morning air. Behind it there are ten, perhaps twenty open wagons. Usually, no doubt, they would carry goods, or possibly livestock, perhaps even the parts for the rockets we've been assembling for months and months underground. But I can predict what is going to be their next cargo.

Us.

And I'm right.

We're shoved into the wagons. The first of us sit down to rest, hoping things will get better from now on. But more and more prisoners are pushed in, until we have to stand or be squashed. The wagon becomes an almighty crush. Marcellin yelps in pain as someone leans against his wounded arm.

Then I realise: things are going to get worse. Much, much worse.

And I've lost faith that I will ever be able to say those words I should have said to Marie-Ange.

17

July 1977
Estedt, Bezirk Magdeburg, East Germany

The Stasi representative's obstruction at the power plant was simply someone doing something rigorously by the book. But Müller was surprised that there hadn't been a more active attempt by the Ministry for State Security to thwart their continued investigations, since her team had been officially removed from the case.

Lothar Schneider had been confirmed as dead – and the pathologist's initial examination said everything pointed to murder, and that the man had been killed some minutes before his body was dumped. With this knowledge, there was nothing to stop Müller and Tilsner approaching his widow at her school. Nothing except for the fact that Tilsner was now saying he was feeling unwell, and would have to return to the Hauptstadt.

'Can't you hang on until we've interviewed her? It would be useful having a second opinion.'

'Seriously, Karin, I feel as though I'm going to throw up any minute. It must have been something I ate. I want to get back to Berlin and lie down.'

'Are you sure this isn't just an excuse to get back to your new girlfriend, and lie down with her? It seems to be what you've been aiming for since the start of this case – or cases.' Although she was dubious, he was looking pale.

Tilsner just gave a long sigh, as if her question wasn't deserving of an answer.

'And how exactly *will* you get back?'

'I can get the train to Magdeburg, and from there it's easy to get to the Hauptstadt. At least on the train there's a toilet in case I am actually sick.'

Müller felt little sympathy. If things continued like this, she knew she would be recommending to Reiniger that he look for a new deputy for her. A functioning deputy. A deputy who didn't look as though he was going to be ill at the sight of a dead body. Or who put his personal problems, his love life, ahead of the needs of the *Volkspolizei*.

'OK,' she said finally. 'You can get the People's Police in Gardelegen to write you out a warrant for the train ticket.'

Müller set off with *Hauptmann* Janson at her side in the Lada, instead of Tilsner. They drove round the inner ring road around Gardelegen old town, and then turned off Schillerstrasse into Jägerstieg, the road that led to the school where Herr Schneider's widow worked as a teacher.

They'd only travelled two or three hundred metres when, up ahead, Müller saw what at first appeared to be a road closure and diversion. A barrier across the road. But then she saw figures on the pavement each side of the barrier.

As they approached, one of the figures stepped forward.

The man leant down as Müller wound down the driver's window.

'Could I see your documents, please?' he asked.

'I'm from the police. *Kriminalpolizei*. I need to visit the school in connection with a murder inquiry.' She showed her *Kripo* ID.

The man took it, nodded, and smiled. 'I understand. But I'm afraid that won't be possible. We represent the Ministry for State Security. The school is in lockdown under our control. We've been expecting you, Comrade *Major*. But I'm afraid there can be no exceptions, not even for the police.' He took out his notebook, and glanced at it. 'And we have a message for you. Please could you ring or radio through to Keibelstrasse and talk to Comrade *Oberst* Reiniger immediately.'

'It's happened again,' she said as soon as she got through to Reiniger on the radio, having driven a couple of blocks to calm down. Janson was beside her in the passenger seat, but she didn't really care what he overheard.

'I know, Karin, and I'm sorry. But we have to obey this order. You'd better come back to Berlin. There's nothing more you can do in Gardelegen. The Stasi insist the latest death is part of their inquiry, and again linked to the Committee for the Dispossessed.'

'I don't believe it,' said Müller. 'This was very different.'

'I'm not in a position to countermand a Ministry for State Security order, Karin. But I can give you orders, as you work for me. And I'm ordering you back to Berlin – now.'

Müller tapped her fingers on the steering wheel, and shook her head to try to work the stiffness from her neck. After all this, she'd need another holiday in the sun. One that wasn't interrupted this time.

'If you insist, then of course, Comrade *Oberst*,' she said. 'I'll drive straight back.'

'Thank you, Karin. It's for the best, I assure you. There will be other cases.'

Müller replaced the handset, breathed in slowly, then let the air out of her lungs gradually.

'If it's any consolation,' said Janson, 'and I know it won't be, what I hate most about this job is when that happens. I feel for you.'

Müller gave a wry laugh. 'It's not the first time. And it won't be the last. Anyway, before I set off back for the Hauptstadt, I'll give you a lift back to the station.'

After dropping Janson off at Gardelegen People's Police offices, she should – by rights – have joined the main road straight back to Stendal, or headed south to pick up the motorway near Magdeburg.

But she didn't. She decided to do a little sightseeing instead, and headed for Gardelegen's historic centre. After parking the car, she walked to the market square.

There it was in all its majesty. A lovely building, that she guessed dated from around 1600 – possibly earlier. *An historic town hall, ivy clad, with a steep red-tiled roof punctuated by low dormer windows, above a grand-looking first floor which in turn straddled the arches of a colonnade at ground level.* It was exactly how it had looked in the photograph from the 1930s. The only difference: here she was looking at it in colour, and the young couple dressed in thirties fashions – no doubt Nazis like most of the rest – were nowhere to be seen. It didn't matter.

This was the link.

This was where it had all started.

18

We see more prisoners arriving through the cracks in the wooden-panelled side of the open-topped wagon we're crushed into. They look to be in an even worse condition than us, their prison clothes ragged and mud-spattered. It has rained a cold, hard rain overnight. We feel the wagon judder as more freight cars are attached.

We eke out our meagre rations. One loaf of bread and a tin of inedible-looking meat paste for a journey of indeterminate duration to an unknown location. I tear off a piece from my loaf and fashion a blob of the paste onto it. Without water to wash it down, I gag on the mouthful, but try to force myself to eat.

We spend our whole time scanning the skies above, waiting for the next air raid. It's a strange mixture of excitement and terror. Excitement that things might be about to end. That we might be free. Terror that the fighter bombers will see a train as a target – not knowing it contains prisoners from their own side.

Night falls. The temperature is thankfully slightly warmer, as though spring may be around the corner. Our train is marooned in the station. No one tells us what is happening, and there is little talking. Every now and then I see Marcellin wince as someone touches his arm. I worry that it may be becoming infected. I hope he lasts long enough for us to get it properly seen to in a hospital, after their final defeat, which surely must be only days away.

There is no room to lie down to sleep. To go to the toilet, we have to shuffle our way to a corner of the wagon and do our business. For Marcellin, even doing that, I see pain in each movement. The smell is awful, like the worst public toilet you have ever been to – and public toilets in France are awful, I can tell you. We are surely going to die here.

Fitfully, we doze off for a few minutes at a time, standing up, or leaning against the sides or a fellow prisoner. I try not to lean on Marcellin, but let him lean on me. If we do lie down, it has to be on top of each other and for Marcellin with his bad arm, that is nigh on impossible.

Dawn breaks and there is still no movement. We are stuck in this station in the middle of nowhere, wondering when the Allies will finally break through and save us, as they surely will. I still have faith, but as I look at Marcellin's grey face, and sunken eyes, I wonder why. He is the oldest of us three, yet for some reason he always seemed to defer to me, and I became the de facto leader of our little gang of brothers. We liked to think of ourselves as the pirates of the *Celestine*, growing old before our time and taking charge of the fishing boat after Papa's sudden death. Out of the three of us, Marcellin perhaps looked the most like a fisher-man with his ruddy face, and broad smile, inherited from Papa. For some reason, I was the schemer of the group, always coming up with some plan to get us into trouble when we were younger. They said I had Maman's brains. I don't know about that.

The minutes tick by. We're bored, tired, hungry, thirsty and cold.

Finally, after what must have been about five or six hours of daylight, the shouting from the German guards increases in intensity. The wagon rocks. I brace myself and try to hold Marcellin to stop him falling or banging his arm.

We are underway at last.

The relief from the boredom is only temporary. After a few kilometres, the train stops again.

'Where are we?' whispers Marcellin.

I squint through the gap in the wooden planks that form the wall of our mobile prison.

'A station.' I move slightly to see if I can spy a station name. 'Ellrich. Wherever that is. It doesn't look very big.'

'Where do you think they're taking us?' There's a note of desperation in his voice. 'Are they just taking us somewhere to kill us all? I wouldn't put it past them.'

Neither would I, but I don't voice that thought. 'Remember. We were singled out as the ones in the fittest state to work. They wouldn't do that if they were planning on killing us.'

Marcellin glances down at his arm which I've been trying to protect by shielding it with my body. 'I won't be able to work,

Philippe. You know that. I am certain they will kill me. And to be honest, it will be a relief.'

Anger wells up inside me, trying to burst out. But I fight it back. I have lost one brother. I will not lose another.

I take his good arm and squeeze his hand, bringing my mouth close to his ear.

'I won't let that happen, Marcellin. I will never let that happen. Stay strong. Believe. We will soon be free. We will soon see Loix again and you will be back with Violette.' I try to inject the words with as much passion as possible. I see in my brother's eyes that he half believes me.

I hate deceiving him like this.

After our short journey, we seem to be marooned again at this Ellrich – another station in the middle of nowhere. Perhaps the rail line further down the track has been destroyed by Allied bombs? Perhaps Allied troops are already closing in?

We spend another night of hell, not being able to sleep properly, unprotected from the elements. Just two blankets each to keep out the cold. Thankfully one body warms the other.

I must have fallen asleep for an hour or so, because I find myself dreaming of hugging and kissing Marie-Ange. I've tried not to think of her too much, because when I do her face keeps changing in my head until I can't remember her properly any more. But I feel her now; the excitement she arouses in me.

Then someone punches me on the arm and wakes me. I shake myself awake, embarrassed. The body I've been clinging onto so tenderly was another prisoner, thankfully not Marcellin. He looks at me in disgust.

In the evening, there has been more bumping of the wagon yet no movement. I can only assume even more wagons were being attached. It's hard to estimate how many, but looking through the cracks I can see the guards marching up and down for several trucks' worth each side of us. Then at one point, further up the train, hundreds of Jewish prisoners, identifiable by their yellow stars, are herded on board. They look to be in an even worse state than us.

Soon after dawn, we set off again, shivering in our blankets. I try to brace myself to protect Marcellin from the buffeting again, but I have little strength left. I find myself shaking, trembling. I try to stop it. I know it will use up energy. But I can't. I try to work out which direction we're travelling, from looking at the sky. Maybe to the west? But then we seem to change direction, and I get confused. Perhaps we are travelling north now?

Occasionally we see – or hear – a plane overhead. At any moment, we expect one to dive down and attack us. But it doesn't. The train continues its slow, uncomfortable progress.

It's the screaming which alerts me.

Someone has died. We're not sure whether it's from the cold or hunger. It's one of the Poles at the other end of the wagon, near the space we use as the latrine. The screaming comes from the man next to him once he realises. The dead body is simply left there, slumped in one corner. Two of the prisoners lay down on it, using it as a mattress of human flesh. Dead human flesh.

When we stop at the next station, at a place called Osterode-am-Harz, his fellow Poles bang on the wooden sides of the wagon and shout at the guards, until one of them opens it. I think for a moment the Polish prisoners are going to make a run for it, but the SS man has his gun trained on them. They point to the dead body. The guard forces them at gunpoint to simply throw it off the side, and there the dead man lies.

When then train sets off again an hour or so later, his body is still there.

Ignored.

Just left to rot by the side of the platform.

Even the Germans have had enough. They can't be bothered to clear up their own waste. For that is surely what this dead prisoner is to them; simply more detritus of war, another heap of rubbish at the side of the line.

When the fighter-bombers attack, it almost comes as a surprise. We hear the whine of the diving engines first, then simultaneously feel and hear the sound of the explosions and feel the hot air blast towards us. We cover our heads with our hands as debris rains down, praying there won't be a direct hit on our wagon.

Marcellin looks weaker with every passing hour. He tugs at my arm.

'Maybe we can escape under cover of the attack?' he hisses, a frantic look in his eyes.

I look through my gap in the wall boards. It looks like some prisoners have done just that. As the bombers continue to dive down and attack, I see a machine-gun toting German open fire, towards the train.

That's what happens if you try to escape, I think.

In the confusion the guards open the wagons, and we are herded outside like the animals they think we are. I have to help Marcellin down from the wagon. His face is contorted in pain. I've fashioned him a sling from one of my blankets, as much to stop his arm moving and facing more pain than anything else. So he has only one good arm.

I spy some prisoners making their escape and others being rounded up. Others are shot in the back of the head. I know Marcellin won't be able to run. We just have to bide our time.

Once the raid is over, prisoners from the wagons where people have been strafed or killed by explosions or shrapnel are forced to bury their dead themselves, in a common grave by the side of the track.

We sit huddled by the trackside. Up ahead we can see the locomotive, badly damaged in the attack. We won't be going anywhere in a hurry.

Eventually they sort out a new locomotive, we're herded back into our wagon, and we set off again. But we can only have gone three or four kilometres further down the track when there's another air raid warning.

We're allowed off the train to shelter. No attack materialises, but in the confusion, more prisoners try to escape. Some are shot as they try to make a run for it – including the Polish man who discovered the body in our wagon.

His body, like that of his colleague, is left in the open to rot.

I wonder if that will be the eventual fate of Marcellin and me. But for now we are alive. In his case, only just.

19

July 1977
The train from Magdeburg to Berlin, East Germany

Tilsner was slowly becoming aware that he was being watched. At first he'd dismissed it as paranoia. After three killings, he had every reason to be paranoid. He moved carriages. The man moved too.

Perhaps it was a Stasi agent, simply giving him a message that he was being observed. That was one of their tricks. To make you start to doubt yourself. Tilsner knew, because he'd had the training. Thankfully, he'd worked himself a comfortable little number in the criminal division of the police, with a boss who he generally enjoyed working with, and who knew he had divided loyalties. She knew by now he supplied some information to the Ministry for State Security. That was the hold Jäger and others had over him – just as he had a hold over them.

He got out his notebook and pretended to study it, holding it up so that if he peeked over his notebook he could see who was tailing him. In some ways, if it was a Stasi agent giving him a 'message', putting the frighteners on him, then that was the least worst result. What Tilsner really feared was that this was the killer, and that he was stalking his next victim – Tilsner himself. But would the man really be so obvious?

The man behind him suddenly got up from his seat and started walking down the carriage towards him. Tilsner quickly put the notebook away, got to his feet and moved rapidly in the other direction down the aisle. But where could he hide on a moving train? He had his Makarov in his holster anyway, and he was a good shot – even though he hadn't had to use it since firing it in anger on the slopes of the Brocken more than two years earlier.

He saw the toilet between the carriages was free, dived into it and locked the door. Then he flattened himself against the wall, pulled out the Makarov and released the safety catch.

He felt his finger trembling on the trigger. *Don't do anything stupid. Don't fire until you are certain. Otherwise you'll be serving, at the very least, a long jail term. It would be the end of everything. And – if he is a Stasi agent – the Stasi would surely liquidate me for doing away with one of their own.*

He waited, and waited. Nothing happened. Slowly his heartbeat started to settle. Maybe he *was* imagining it after all. This had all affected him badly. First, there had been the shock of seeing the face of Ronnebach, after more than thirty years. Then there had been the same shock about the man living as Ingo Höfler, although that wasn't the name Tilsner knew him by. And there was now the man known as Schneider – who, even worse, had been killed where it all started. The old woman recognising him had been the final shock even though he didn't recognise her. She'd even mentioned the 'estate' where he used to work as a teenager.

Everything, everything was unravelling.

Suddenly, there was an urgent rap on the door. Tilsner gripped the gun more firmly. He would have to confront whatever it was head on.

He unlocked the door.

A man in uniform stared at his gun in horror. Without lowering it, Tilsner got out his *Kripo* ID with his other hand. '*Kriminalpolizei*,' he hissed, sotto voce. 'Who exactly are you?'

'I'm the train guard,' said the uniformed man. 'Could I see your ticket, please?'

Tilsner lowered the gun, clicked the safety catch back on, and replaced the weapon in his holster. He started laughing to himself.

The guard looked at him severely. He clearly didn't get the joke.

20

Müller decided to take Reiniger up on his earlier offer to use the remainder of her leave. It would mean she could help Helga out before the twins went back to their crèche at the start of the new term. It also gave her a chance to spend some time with her family.

Being taken off a case – especially one as intriguing and bizarre as the current one – for the second time in the space of days left her reassessing her future. She'd been reluctant to take this role to start with. It was the chance to try to solve interesting homicide cases on the ground that had persuaded her. Well, that and her new apartment.

Helga was obviously out taking the twins for a walk by the time Müller got back. She made herself a coffee, and then wandered over to the lounge window. It was a side view, but she could see part of the impressive Strausberger Platz fountain from here, and then the majesty of Karl-Marx-Allee. Müller knew she was fortunate to have acquired an apartment here, especially one so large. When she'd separated from her doctor boyfriend Emil, the father of the twins, he had moved back into his hospital apartment. Yet she'd still been able to keep a three-bedroom apartment. And this was all due to her promotion to the head of the Special Crimes Department.

But other than that one case in Senftenberg, Guben and Eisenhüttenstadt – at the very eastern border of the Republic – the job had resulted in frustration after frustration. She knew that if she quit she would lose this apartment. She might not even be able to stay in the *Kriminalpolizei*. But she couldn't carry on being undermined and overruled by the Ministry for State Security. On top of that, her deputy Werner Tilsner appeared to have undergone a personality transplant. And the new Tilsner wasn't someone she liked. If she resigned, she would miss Jonas Schmidt, and feel slightly guilty about letting him down. She couldn't say the same about Tilsner. Not in his current mood. He insisted it was because of his nebulous 'new girlfriend troubles', but Müller wasn't so sure.

The sound of a key turning in the apartment front door lock immediately lifted Müller's mood. She felt a lightness in her limbs and rushed to greet her little family.

Jannika was first in the door, running on her tiny legs with a plastic flower windmill in her hand. Müller gathered her up and smothered her faces in kisses. Her daughter wiped her face.

'Silly Mutti. Look flower.' The girl offered the windmill toy to her mother, then her face fell and she immediately wanted it back.

Helga then wheeled the double pushchair in, with Johannes still strapped inside. When he saw his mother, he started excitedly clapping his hands. 'Mutti. Mutti.'

Müller gently placed Jannika down on the floor, ruffling her blonde hair. The girl's face looked as though tears might begin. Müller lifted Johannes and kissed his face, then crouched down to talk to Jannika. 'Mutti loves both of you equally. She has to be fair.' Johannes started tugging her hair. 'Ow! You're getting too strong, young man.' She prised his hand away and got a slap in the face for her trouble.

'He's lively today,' she said to Helga. 'How have they been?'

'Well, it will be nice when the crèche starts again after the summer,' laughed her grandmother. 'You're back earlier than we expected.'

'Earlier than I expected, too. I think my time as a policewoman might be drawing to a close.'

'That bad? Do you want to talk about it?'

Müller shook her head. 'Not now. Perhaps later. Do you want a coffee?' Then she sniffed the air. 'Actually it smells like someone – possibly two someones – need changing. I'd better do that first. You go and put your feet up. I'll prepare supper tonight.'

When Müller had cleared away the dishes, and read a picture book story to the twins before turning their light out, she joined Helga in the lounge.

Her grandmother had put a bottle of *Sekt* on ice.

'As you've got a few more days' holiday, I thought we could celebrate.' The popping of the cork startled Müller. Its echo around the cavernous room sounded almost like a gunshot. Perhaps it really was time to consider a new career. 'And then,' continued Helga, 'we could be really naughty and watch *Tatort*. If you're serious about leaving the police force, you won't be getting into as much trouble for watching western television.'

Müller grinned. 'All right. But I hope I can actually watch it this time.' The last time they'd both sat down with a glass of sparkling wine to watch the popular West German crime series, it had been interrupted by a newsflash about a bombing. The victim had been a politician deeply involved in the first case for Müller's Serious Crimes Department.

Helga tuned the TV in and they sat down to watch.

Müller wagged her finger at her grandmother. 'And remember. I'm only agreeing to this as long as you don't go telling tales on me.'

The evening's relaxation was followed by a deep sleep, and then at breakfast both the twins were in fine form. It started Müller's day off on the right foot, and when Helga took the twins out to the park, she had a chance to tie up some loose ends. One of which was catching up with Jonas Schmidt. She'd last seen the forensic scientist in Karl-Marx-Stadt, but he would now be back in the lab at Keibelstrasse assisting on other matters. Even though they were now officially off the case, there was nothing to stop her getting him to bring her up to speed with his work. One of the things she'd asked him to do was to pinpoint which town was shown in the black and white photograph of the Höflers. In the confusion of the visit from the Stasi, she'd taken the photo from the frame when Frau Höfler had answered the door to Jäger, photocopied it at Leinefelde police headquarters, and then posted a copy to Schmidt at headquarters. She already knew the answer to the question. She'd seen the building with her own eyes. But it would do no harm to double check that Schmidt had reached the same conclusion.

'Did you get back from Karl-Marx-Stadt safely, Jonas?'

'Yes, of course, Comrade *Major*.' Müller had never managed to persuade her *Kriminaltechniker* to drop the 'Comrade this', 'Comrade that' honorifics, despite her best intentions. 'And I have the results of those things you asked me to check.'

'Oh yes. What about that photo? Did you manage to find the town?'

'Of course, Comrade *Major*. It's Quedlinburg.'

Müller nearly dropped the phone in surprise. It wasn't like Schmidt to make a mistake, but she was sure he had. She'd seen the town hall with her own eyes. It was Gardelegen. She was sure she wasn't mistaken.

'You're certain of that, Jonas?'

There was silence for a moment at the end of the line. 'Y . . . y . . . yes . . . Com . . . Comrade *Major*.'

'What about the voice recordings of Herr Ronnebach and Herr Höfler? Have you had chance to study those, and compare them with regional accents?'

'Yes, of course,' said Schmidt, almost snappily. To Müller, he sounded out of character. But perhaps it was the fact that she was talking to him over the phone, rather than face-to-face. 'Both voices have inherited the regional characteristics of where the subjects were living for several years. So Herr Ronnebach's is typical of the Karl-Marx-Stadt area, and Herr Höfler's of Eichsfeld – the mainly Catholic area surrounding Leinefelde.'

'So there was nothing to link the two men – no area where they'd both been living?'

'Well, yes, there was, Comrade *Major*. There were traces of the distinctive accent of the northern Harz mountains.'

Müller knew enough to be aware that Quedlinburg could be considered the northern Harz, although it was right on the edge. The only problem was she knew that Schmidt was mistaken about the location of the town hall. If that was the case, why did the voice analysis point to the same area? Either Höfler and Ronnebach didn't – as Müller had initially suspected – have a link to the Gardelegen area. Or, and she found this hard to believe, Schmidt had made two separate mistakes. Three if you counted each of the two voice analyses. Either she was wrong, or he was wrong about something.

'Look, Jonas, I'm on leave at the moment, but I was planning to pass by Alexanderplatz later. I'll pop in to discuss things with you in person.'

'A . . . a . . . as you wish, Comrade *Major*. But I thought our team had handed over to the Ministry for State Security? And you are on leave.'

'We have handed over to the Stasi. That's true. And I am on leave. I just want to stop by for a chat. I'll take you out for lunch. Now that's something you don't usually turn down, do you, Jonas?'

Schmidt was silent for a moment on the other end of the line. 'You know me too well, Comrade *Major*.'

21

Jäger had summoned Tilsner to this meeting with a message delivered by a motorcycle messenger, no doubt a Stasi minion, thought Tilsner.

The meeting place was a wooded area on the banks of the Havel river, near Töplitz, itself not far from Potsdam. Near enough the Hauptstadt for both of them to get there easily by car. Far enough away and quiet enough to hopefully deter prying eyes. That was what Tilsner assumed, anyway.

The incident on the train – if indeed that was what it was – had unnerved him. Had he been followed and tailed? Now he wasn't so sure that it was just his own paranoia.

Jäger had chosen a meeting place at the end of a wooden boat jetty. Tilsner would have to make sure he never turned his back on the man, and he was ready to get the Makarov out at the slightest provocation. The guard on the train had been petrified when he'd done that in the carriage toilet.

He was a few minutes late. He could already see Jäger standing at the end of the jetty, silhouetted by the setting sun. It would be very tempting to creep up behind him and simply push him in. The man had brought Tilsner – and Müller – nothing but trouble. They'd never really been friends. They were just bound by history, by circumstance. Tilsner chuckled to himself about Müller's first experience of the Stasi colonel – then a mere lieutenant colonel – in the cemetery in Mitte, by the Wall, or as Karin preferred to call it, in her oh-so-correct fashion, the Anti-Fascist Protection Barrier. He'd had to hide the fact that he and Jäger were already well acquainted. He'd also hidden the fact that he'd been planted in Müller's team, specifically because she was young, green and malleable. Jäger had certainly tried to mould her – but Tilsner guessed he'd been surprised that the young murder squad head was tougher, and savvier, than he had assumed. At the beginning she *was* green – that couldn't be denied. In this latest case, she'd been getting far too near the heart of the matter, until the Stasi had intervened.

'Hello, Werner.' Jäger greeted him before he turned round. He'd obviously assumed it was Tilsner from the feel of his footfall on the wooden jetty.

'Klaus.'

Jäger turned to meet his gaze, a serious look on his face. 'I think someone has it in for us. Both of us.'

This wasn't what Tilsner wanted to hear. He wanted reassurance. He wanted to know Jäger and his team were covering his back. He felt his pulse thundering in his ears.

'You've got it under control, though, haven't you?'

'I thought so. Until I got to the fourth or fifth set of traffic lights on the way here. And pressed on the brake pedal.'

Tilsner balled his hands into fists, and clenched them until his knuckles turned white.

'It's not very pleasant sailing through a red light when you're expecting to brake. Luckily I was going slowly. The brakes were working when I set off, otherwise I'd have noticed. Someone must have sawed part-way through the brake lines, knowing they would fail sooner or later. But not be obvious to the driver straightaway. A professional job. The sort of job my agents do.'

If this incident wasn't so serious, and if Tilsner didn't feel himself to be a target too, he might have laughed. A Stasi officer nearly killed by one of his own methods, and possibly by one of his own staff.

'So what can we do?' asked Tilsner, aware of the quiver in his voice.

Jäger sighed and then sucked his teeth before answering. 'I thought that keeping it quiet, letting it all blow over, might be enough. I've changed my mind. Someone, possibly more than one person, is out to get us.'

'For revenge over what happened?'

'Perhaps. But there is another possibility.'

Tilsner held his breath. He wasn't sure he wanted to ask the question. He wasn't sure he wanted to find out.

'I think someone is trying to get rid of the witnesses. The people who knew what went on. In a sense, that is more dangerous for us. We weren't at the centre of things, really, although I accept that we share some guilt by association.'

'But we helped some of them.'

'One of them, Werner. We helped one of them. That's all. One out of more than a thousand.'

22

Mieste, near Gardelegen, Nazi Germany

At some point, the train has turned east. We can tell by the sunrise. A main line, running west to east. If I hazarded a guess, I would say that they are trying to take us to Berlin. Perhaps they hope we will help in the last defence of their capital.

Then we stop.

Each time we stop, new fears enter my head. I worry that this is the new labour camp, that the full extent of Marcellin's injury will be discovered, and that he will be despatched to some sort of sanatorium from which he'll never return. Last night I took a look at the wound. It's not healing properly, despite my treatment with the iodine before we set off. The redness – set against his deathly pale skin – is extending further up and down his arm. The wound itself is angry and weeping. I don't know what to do. If I alert the guards, they will probably take him away and shoot him.

All of a sudden, there are a series of shouts in German. From what little I can understand, it seems the rail tracks a few kilometres ahead have been destroyed in an air raid. We can't go any further. So this wasn't meant to be our final destination, but it seems to be by default. It's another sign that the endgame is here. If the Germans had the resources and the will, there is no doubt that this main rail line would be repaired. It doesn't seem as though they have. They're a defeated nation. Perhaps they will now set us free? Hope springs in my heart. Then I hear the shouts of '*Raus, Raus*'; guards urging prisoners to get out of the wagons. The crack of gunshots reverberates and brings me to my senses. They may be defeated, but in defeat they will be at their most dangerous.

Marcellin is half-slumped against another prisoner who doesn't seem to be moving or breathing. I'm not sure if my brother is unconscious or asleep.

'You need to try to pull yourself together,' I whisper urgently in his ear. 'The train's stopped and cannot go any further. Some of the prisoners are being taken out and shot.' It will be the weakest, I know. Those unable to carry on on foot. I have to make sure Marcellin is not judged to be one of them. 'We need to look strong. Stand straight. No matter how you are feeling.'

His eyes stare straight into mine. I can still see my brother in there. The strong pirate of the *Celestine*, riding the waves. But he is fading fast.

The side of our wagon is opened, and a gun-toting guard is now ordering us out. Behind him, I see other prisoners in their zebra uniforms already sitting on the embankment by the trackside, huddling together for warmth. Earlier in this nightmare journey an incident like this would have led to escape attempts – but now it looks as though no one has the energy left to make a run for it.

Everyone helps each other down from the wagon. I get another prisoner to help me with Marcellin, hoping the guard isn't paying too much attention to the shrivelled, injured man who cannot help himself.

We shuffle over to the embankment and sit with the others. Sitting down helps, but the nausea from extreme hunger and dehydration pulses from deep within me.

I see some of the men grabbing handfuls of grass from the embankment and stuffing it into their mouths. This is what we are reduced to.

The locomotive has been detached from our train, and steams off in the opposite direction: further evidence that this is our last stop. But our captors seem uncertain about what they are supposed to do next.

I doze off for a few minutes, and the next thing I know another prisoner is urgently tugging my arm. Marcellin and some others have managed to drag themselves to a ditch at the side of the track. I see him scooping up handfuls of ditchwater with his good hand, feverishly slapping it into his parched mouth. I want to go over and tell him not to, but instead thirst drives me to copy him.

The three brothers – now just two – once the princes of the sea, riding bravely over the waves in our little fishing boat are now reduced to eking out our lives drinking from a filthy ditch.

Hunger doesn't gnaw at us, it tears at us. At one point, a German housewife from the village leans across the fence with a sheet filled with raw potatoes and freshly baked rolls. Marcellin isn't quick or strong enough to get there before the woman is chased off by the guards. Some of the others managed to grab a roll, all I manage to get is a couple of potatoes.

I hand one to Marcellin. First, he looks at it in disgust. Then something clicks in his addled brain, and he starts to frantically gnaw at it. I do the same. The bitter taste with a slight hint of sweetness isn't too unpleasant. It's no worse than the awful tin of meat paste that I finished – along with the bread – days ago. The prisoners who failed to get any food eye us murderously. I suddenly feel guilty. With about a quarter of it eaten, I offer it to the prisoner next to me – a Hungarian, I think – who takes a few bites and in turn passes it along the line.

We do nothing but sit all day, shivering in our damp blankets. It's not particularly cold, but we have no flesh left on our bones. I find myself half hallucinating about spring days on the island, lying in the sun with Marie-Ange in the cornfields, our bicycles resting on the ground alongside us. Then reaching over and caressing her face. A clear vision of it appears in front of me now – more clearly than she's appeared for days. I reach out with my arm to touch her face.

Marcellin shrugs my arm away, and looks at me pityingly.

Later in the day, word gets round that one of the buildings is a grain store. A group of us set off under the cover of darkness to see if we can break in. It's a desperate plan, but we are desperate.

There are about fifteen of us, with the ringleaders at the front. I am weaker, slower than the others, and I find myself lagging behind.

I'm just about to try to climb into the compound after the others when I hear the shots and shouts of the German guards. We've been discovered.

I stop and back away, my whole body trembling, gasping for air as I start to hyperventilate, trying desperately to control my breathing so I'm not found.

Later, I learn that eight prisoners – those at the front of the group – were shot dead in cold blood by a group of Luftwaffe soldiers. That could have been me. Perhaps it should have been me.

I was stupid, reckless, to join in. It was a betrayal of Marcellin. Without me, he has no chance of survival. With me, he may have no chance of survival either. But at least we would be together in death.

Although hunger and thirst tear at our insides, outside of the wagon we can sleep more easily. The night, however, is punctuated by the distant rumble of artillery fire and a firework show from the tracer bullets of anti-aircraft guns – the last futile attempts by the Germans to repel the advance. From what little we can glean from whispered conversations between the guards, it's the Americans who are nearest. They will be our saviours, if anyone. Part of me wishes we can be liberated by my own side, the French. But any freedom will do. But then I chastise myself. We still have to survive to become free, and that is getting more difficult by the day.

The next morning, I see bodies being dragged off by the guards; prisoners who've died during the night, from hunger, thirst, illness or all three. In a panic, I shake Marcellin, fearing he is dead. He wakes, but there is a look of almost hatred in his eyes as though he wanted to sleep on into oblivion.

'Leave me alone, Philippe. I just want to sleep and never wake up.'

'Don't be stupid,' I hiss. 'Violette is waiting for you back home. It's nearly over. We'll soon be free. But you don't want to be taken for one of the dead. They will drag you away, they will shoot you.'

I shake him awake despite his protests. 'Don't lie to me, Philippe,' he says. 'I don't want any hopes. I don't want any dreams. We were on the point of breaking up anyway. Now she's probably been fucking one of these German pigs – even now, she's probably giving birth to one of their bastard Boche babies.'

At some point, later in the day, a murmur of excitement echoes around us. The rumour passes down the line that a meal is being cooked for us in the cement factory that lies to one side of the marshalling yard. As the smells waft over, I start to salivate – despite knowing that will waste more precious water from my body. And I know the food will be shit, and it won't be enough. I dream of my mother's marsh mutton casserole that she used to make for us as boys if the *Celestine* had found a particularly rich shoal, and my parents had the money to put a decent meal on the table. Or a bouillabaisse or soupe de poissons with fresh sea herbs picked from the marshes that very day. Or dressing in our finest suits for weddings or funerals even, special occasions when the best meats and recipes were prepared.

It will be nothing like that, I know. But the thought of any food almost has me breaking down in tears. I glance at Marcellin. He's half-dozing again. The whiteness of his pallor has now turned grey. As though he's rotting from the inside out. I must rouse him and make him eat, even if I have to force it down his throat.

We stand in line, patiently at first. I prop up Marcellin with the help of another prisoner. If you are too weak to stand and wait, you will not get fed. And if you don't get fed, you will die. It is a simple equation, one that in his befuddled, fevered state, Marcellin doesn't seem to understand.

As we move nearer the front of the line, fighting starts to break out amongst us desperate prisoners. The one who was helping me prop up Marcellin leaves to join the throng. I fear we will not get anything.

I see the German guards to the side, laughing at our desperation. Laughing at the state they've brought us to, that we will fight each other for what scraps we can get. Somehow, I manage to get us to the front of the line. Those serving look dubiously at Marcellin, as though it's not worth wasting their precious food on him.

One of the servers, a woman, shows some pity, and while I hold Marcellin, she fills two tin bowls with a weak broth that smells of meat and potato but appears to have little of either in it. She scoops to the bottom of the tureen to get more solid matter – a last act of kindness before we're hurried along the line. The sight of the food seems to suddenly rouse Marcellin and he finds new strength from somewhere. He holds his own tin bowl as we shuffle along, allowing me to balance mine and collect two mugs of coffee for us at the same time. This is our first meal in more than a week, other than that loaf of bread and tin of disgusting meat paste we were given before the train set off from Niedersachswerfen.

We know that we are walking skeletons. We wouldn't recognise ourselves if we looked in a mirror. I only recognise Marcellin because I see him every hour of every day, growing weaker and weaker.

We make our way to the embankment and sit down to eat and drink. Occasional fights are still breaking out – the stronger stealing food from the weaker. Men reduced to the morals of dogs by a race that has morals lower than dogs. A race I will always detest until my dying day.

I just hope that day does not come too soon.

The only way of staving that off is to eat. Marcellin seems to understand that too. Perhaps we are both pretending this disgusting, overcooked mush is really a sumptuous shellfish casserole, that the watery coffee is a glass of the finest Burgundy.

The meal – such as it was – is soon over.

The salivary glands kick in again.

'I'm still hungry, Philippe,' Marcellin cries, almost with a note of pain in his voice. 'So very, very hungry.' It's a desperate plea, but I try to take it as a good sign.

A will to eat is a will to live. Perhaps we will survive after all.

23

The fine summer weather continued, and Müller decided the best place for her lunch meeting with Schmidt was sitting outside at one of the temporary cafés in Alexanderplatz, a short stroll from the Keibelstrasse People's Police offices. She asked Schmidt to bring with him the details of the voice analysis, and the reference book from which he'd identified the town hall.

Müller ordered a quarter broiler and fries for each of them, with sauerkraut as a side dish, and then went to the bar and collected two beers, before sitting down on one of the beer barrel seats as she waited for her forensic scientist. School-aged children thronged around, boys teasing girls and vice versa, a hubbub of noise and summer jollity. The depressing murder cases in Karl-Marx-Stadt, Leinefelde and Gardelegen which she'd just been removed from seemed a world away from this.

She watched Schmidt as he approached across the Platz to their prearranged meeting place. The *Kriminaltechniker* hadn't bothered, or had forgotten, to remove his trademark white lab coat, and with his portly appearance he looked as though he might be on the way to start his shift on a fast food stall – if it wasn't for the briefcase he carried under his arm. Fast food probably was on his mind, thought Müller – but the eating of it, not the serving of it.

When she raised her arm to beckon him over, he failed to smile, as if something were troubling him. Normally Schmidt was enthusiastic, jolly even, although he had a propensity, as Tilsner regularly pointed out, of using three or four words when one would do, so that conversations – and especially forensic explanations – could get a little wearying. The troubled look on his face was one she'd seen more of the previous year when his son had gone missing – caught up in the big murder investigation involving a rogue scientist near the Polish border.

'Over here, Jonas,' she yelled. Schmidt scurried along, his eyes trained on the ground.

'Sorry I'm a little late, Comrade *Major*. Comrade *Hauptmann* Tilsner has been working on another matter.' Müller briefly wondered what that was, but then banished the thought. She was supposed to be on holiday. She was making an exception for the matter she was meeting the forensic scientist about – but she didn't want to get dragged into other work issues until her leave ended. In any case, this wasn't really work any more, now that they'd been removed from the case. It was simply a question of satisfying her curiosity.

'Did you bring the things I wanted to look at, Jonas?'

'Yes, of course, Comrade *Major*. Although I must say I'm a little baffled as to why you want to go through it all again. The conclusions are straightforward.'

'Quite. I'm sure they are, Jonas. It's just something I saw the other day which has been preying on my mind. Could you show me the reference book first, please?'

Müller noticed that Schmidt's face, florid at the best of times, seemed even more flushed than usual. He reached into his briefcase, and pulled out a single piece of paper.

'I thought I asked you to bring the book itself, Jonas?'

'I . . . I . . . I'm sorry, Comrade *Major*—'

'Please stop all that, Jonas. Karin is fine. I've told you this before. And I'm on holiday at the moment. I really don't want to be called Comrade *Major* this and that when we're just having a friendly drink and lunch in the sun. By the way, I got you a quarter broiler and a beer. I trust that's OK, even though you're strictly speaking on duty?'

'I . . . I . . . I'm sure I can have one, Com . . . , sorry, Karin. I'm sure I can have one, Karin.'

Müller took the proffered piece of paper and examined it. The photograph showed the exact same town hall she'd seen in the photograph in the Höflers' farmhouse – and the same one she'd seen with her own eyes. In the central square in Gardelegen. Yet here it was in the centre of a piece of text which, she had to acknowledge, spoke about Quedlinburg, a town more than a hundred kilometres further south.

She gave a long sigh, then stared hard at Schmidt. 'Could there be two town halls in the Republic, of exactly the same historic design?' As she said this, she reached into her jacket pocket and pulled out her notebook and pen, and wrote down the name of the reference book this photocopy had been taken from. *A History of German Architecture from the Middle Ages to the Modern Day.*

'I ... I ... I ... doubt it, but I suppose it's possible, Karin. I'm not really an expert in historic architecture.' Schmidt took a large bite of his grilled chicken, and then washed it down with a mouthful of beer from the throwaway plastic beaker.

Müller tapped her pen on her notebook. 'What about these voice analyses? You're certain about the results?'

'Y ... y ... y ... yes, Com ... um, Karin. As I said on the telephone, the principal regional characteristic related to the towns and cities in which the two subjects now live, or rather lived, until ...'

'Hmm. But you said there were other underlying characteristics?'

Schmidt reached into his briefcase again, and this time brought out a number of pieces of paper. Each one had graphicised voice waveforms depicted on them. The waveforms had been highlighted at particular points with coloured pen markings.

'This is an analysis of Herr Ronnebach's voice,' said Schmidt, pointing to the sheaf of papers on the left. 'And this is Herr Höfler's.' He tapped the pile of graphs on the right-hand side. Then he took one sheet from each, and placed them alongside each other. 'We can look for certain words which occur in both men's speeches. "Comrades", "the Republic", "Honecker". There are three for example.' Schmidt pointed out various peaks and troughs on the graphs – and with his thumb and forefinger measured the gap between each. 'We can examine the length of each vowel, the stresses within the words, that sort of thing. Anyway, that's what we did at some length.' Schmidt delved into his briefcase to retrieve more voice graphs. 'And then we compared them to control samples from various regions, which are shown here. We can look at the same words. It's a long-winded process, but reasonably accurate.'

'*Reasonably* accurate?' Müller took a bite of her own lunch, savouring the sweet, herby flavour of the grilled chicken and the sharpness of the sauerkraut.

'Yes. It can't be one hundred per cent accurate, because each voice is a melange of various accents the subject will have picked up over the years, influenced by those he or she works with, makes friends with, and so forth. But your formative years tend to have the most effect on any accent you carry, so, what you learnt as a child from your mother, your father, your school-teachers. But even a short period – as little as a year – spent somewhere else with a strong accent can leave an indelible impression on the subject's voice.'

Müller took a slow drink of the cold beer. If she closed her eyes, she could imagine herself still on a beach somewhere hot, with a hunky waiter in front of her, rather than a rotund, sweating forensic scientist. 'So how confident are you about your northern Harz assertion?'

'Very confident, Karin. That will have been ingrained in the nurturing phase, in the subject's first ten or fifteen years of life.' He brought out a chart headed 'Nordharz' and another titled 'Sudharz'. Then he began comparing them to the charts of the late Herr Höfler and Herr Ronnebach. 'Look. You can see all the similarities. Here . . . and here . . . and here.'

Müller's eyes followed Schmidt's pointing finger. What he said seemed to be borne out by the evidence in front of her eyes. She was no expert, but perhaps she had been hasty. Perhaps the mistakes in all this weren't Schmidt's. Perhaps she had been leaping to conclusions, something a detective should never do.

The lunch continued in a convivial fashion, and although Schmidt declined the offer of a second beer, he did accept Müller's offer of the uneaten half of her snack. Over the course of the meal, his nervousness seemed to dissipate – even if his appetite remained as strong as ever. By the end of it, he had convinced her. It was she who must have made the mistake. Perhaps the town halls at Gardelegen and Quedlinburg were very similar and she had simply seen what she wanted to see when she was in the first town. Nevertheless, after saying their goodbyes, Müller decided to double-check at the library before travelling on the U-bahn back to Strausberger Platz to take up the childcare reins again.

At the reference library, she quickly found the book in the architecture section. She took it to a desk to consult, and looked in the index for an entry for Quedlinburg.

Turning to the page, Müller wasn't exactly surprised by what she found. But she was shocked. Shocked because it indicated Jonas Schmidt had tried to deceive her.

She consulted the index again, and this time turned to the page for Gardelegen town hall. There was more written here. It was a Hanseatic building. Interesting, but not what she was looking for. She wanted to see the accompanying photograph.

STASI 77 | 136

The town hall in Quedlinburg was similar to that at Gardelegen at first glance, it was true. She leafed between the two. Both were double-storey affairs, with voluminous, steeply sloping roofs, in which – judging by the dormer windows in each – there was another floor. Both were covered in ivy, and had a series of regular windows on the first floor. But it was on the ground floor where the difference lay.

The photograph for Gardelegen matched exactly what she'd seen with her own eyes, and the Höflers' photograph from the 1930s. She remembered how she'd described it in her own mind: *An historic town hall, ivy clad, with a steep red-tiled roof punctuated by low dormer windows, above a grand-looking first floor which in turn straddled the arches of a colonnade at ground level.*

That was the most striking difference.

Quedlinburg town hall did not have a colonnade.

Schmidt must have taken a photocopy from the book, but carefully attached a photograph from Gardelegen to substitute the correct entry.

He had deceived her.

She had gone out of her way to help him the previous year when his son, Markus, had disappeared. Markus had been a victim of a rogue scientist's experiments. For Jonas Schmidt to betray her now was almost unthinkable. Someone must have been putting pressure on him to lie.

24

When the twins were finally down for the night, Helga had expected another evening of the two of them relaxing in front of the television. Müller had other ideas. She asked her grandmother if she'd mind if she popped out for an hour or so.

'You go ahead, dear. I'll be fine on my own. I think we managed to tire them out at the park. They'll sleep like stones.'

Müller waited until she knew he'd be back from work. Then she drove the Lada out to Pankow, and to the apartment she'd last visited in the run-up to Christmas.

Frau Schmidt opened the door to her.

'*Major* Müller. What a lovely surprise. Jonas will be pleased to see you.' Schmidt's wife seemed oblivious to the fact that for Müller to turn up at his home address, it probably wasn't good news. She was pleased the atmosphere in their apartment was so much better than it had been just a few short months ago. Unfortunately, she was about to ruin all that. 'Jonas is in the bedroom working on something. I'll just go and get him.'

'I'll need to talk to him in private, Frau Müller. Is there anywhere we can go?'

'Of course. You two can be in the lounge. I'm just doing some baking in the kitchen anyway, and Markus is out with his friends. Did you hear his news? He's been accepted at a university. After all that trouble last year, we thought it would never happen.'

Müller smiled at the woman, still feeling guilty she was about to rob her of her happiness. 'Jonas did tell me, yes. How wonderful.'

'Anyway, you sit yourself down in there. I'll just get him.' Müller showed herself through, and then sat at the dining table.

When he entered the room, Schmidt wouldn't meet her eyes. *He knows full well what this is about*, thought Müller.

'Sit down, Jonas. I'm sorry to have to deal with this in your own home, but it couldn't wait.'

Schmidt sat opposite her, his head cradled in his hands, his forearms resting on the table. Still he refused to meet her gaze.

She leant down, and pulled the book out of her briefcase. The library assistant had initially refused. To take a reference book away – even for the one night – was out of the question. Only the sight of her *Kripo* ID and a warning about failure to cooperate with a police inquiry had changed her mind.

'You know what I'm going to show you, Jonas, but I'm going to show it to you anyway, and then you can explain to me exactly what is going on. Your explanation had better be very good indeed.'

She knew Schmidt could see the cover title. *A History of German Architecture from the Middle Ages to the Modern Day*. It was probably the exact same copy he had used to fabricate his photocopy with. She'd already bookmarked the relevant pages, so quickly turned to the entry for Quedlinburg town hall, and then rotated the book so it was the right way up for Schmidt.

'Can you tell me the difference, Jonas, between this original entry for Quedlinburg town hall and the photocopy you showed to me?'

Schmidt took a long sigh, drawing his hands down across his face. His eyes were still closed. He opened them and finally held her gaze.

'You will have my resignation in the morning, Comrade Major.'

'It's not your resignation I want, Jonas. Although I will admit your job is at risk, and I never thought it would come to this. You lied to me. You didn't just lie, you fabricated evidence. I assume the voice analysis report was fabricated too?'

Eyes cast down at the table, Schmidt nodded.

'Well, not only are those both sackable offences, they are criminal offences, Jonas. You could be looking at a jail term. You imagine the consequences then. Markus's university place might get taken away.' Müller wasn't trying to frighten her forensic scientist. She was simply stating the facts. If the process of prosecuting him was started, she wouldn't have any control over the outcome or the consequences. And the families of those convicted of criminal offences often suffered along with the criminals themselves.

'No,' wailed Schmidt. 'Not that, please.'

'Well then, start talking. Explain to me everything that has happened. I want the complete truth. Did someone put you up to this?'

Schmidt sighed, then nodded. Behind his thick, wire-rimmed spectacles, Müller could see his eyes glistening.

'Who?'

'Jäger.'

Jäger? Now Müller was alarmed. If Jäger was getting involved at the level of corrupting People's Police forensic scientists then perhaps what they were facing was something even more serious than Müller had imagined.

'Did he bring pressure to bear on you?'

'What do you think?' There was almost a note of malice in Schmidt's reply. It was totally out of character for the normally mild-mannered man. 'Do you think I would do something like this and throw my job away for a mere trifle?'

'Don't start getting clever with me, Jonas. We go back a long way. If I can help you, I will. But not unless you tell me the whole truth. Not unless you prove to me that I *can* rely on you. The most upsetting part of this for me is that you've let me down, you've deceived me, and you've disgraced yourself. The only way back from here is to be absolutely truthful and tell me everything you know.'

Schmidt nodded reluctantly. 'Jäger contacted me soon after you left Karl-Marx-Stadt. He insisted on knowing what I was working on. At first I refused to tell him, but then he claimed that he'd already asked your permission.'

'You know what to do in that situation, Jonas. You must always contact me. Your loyalty lies with the People's Police, not the Ministry for State Security. At least I hope it does.'

'Of course it does, Comrade *Major*. I'm deeply ashamed about what I've done.'

'So in what way did he put pressure on you?'

'He said what you've just said. That Markus would lose his university place unless I cooperated.'

'And what did that cooperation involve?'

'I had to make sure that none of my research showed any link to Gardelegen whatsoever.'

'So you doctored the photocopy of the architecture book?'

Schmidt's shoulders slumped. 'Yes,' he whispered.

'And you fabricated the voice analysis?'

'Yes.'

'I don't really need you to tell me what the analysis of the two murdered men's voices really showed, Jonas, but just for the record, let's hear it from your own mouth.'

'It's as you suspected, Comrade *Major*. I'm one hundred per cent certain both men grew up in the same region, and lived a substantial amount of their time there.'

'And that wasn't the Nordharz. So where was it, Jonas?'

'The Altmark.'

'Which is a fairly sparsely populated area. But one of the main towns in the Altmark is what, Jonas?'

'Gardelegen, Comrade *Major*. Gardelegen.'

25

Müller was tempted to drive straight to Gardelegen, get in touch with the People's Police captain Janson and begin house-to-house searches, to discover the link between Ronnebach, Höfler and Schneider. Off the case or not, a burning desire to uncover the truth and to stop further killings, drove her forward.

But now it was absolutely clear that Stasi colonel Klaus Jäger was determined to stop her. Had he been the one who'd forced her off the case too? She would have to tread carefully. Rather than go straight to Gardelegen, resume her inquiries, and face arrest, she needed to try to piece this together better. There were loose ends back in Karl-Marx-Stadt, where all this started. She wondered if she could trust Elke Drescher to bring her up to speed without the younger detective alerting the Ministry for State Security. If not, she would have to come up with another reason to return to the south of the Republic and look further into the Ronnebachs' background. His widow had given the impression she would have cooperated, if the Stasi officer hadn't been sitting in the corner of the room. Frau Ronnebach had – after all – given her the information about the country cottage. And there they'd found the women's underwear, the watermarked envelope that perhaps suggested Martin Ronnebach had been conducting an affair with a French woman. New leads had meant they hadn't really followed that up properly.

Müller also wondered if there would be anything to gain from visiting Ronnebach's hunting club. Maybe someone there knew who his secret mistress had been – if indeed there was one. If so, how did that connect with this apparent link to the small, rural town of Gardelegen, hundreds of kilometres further north?

She was sure that one ally in her continued investigations would be Jonas Schmidt. The forensic scientist was a broken man. He had disgraced himself, and would have difficulty living with it. But the only person who knew that – other than Jäger – was Müller herself. She needed an ally. Before leaving his apartment, Müller had promised Schmidt that if he cooperated with her, if he dedicated himself to seeking the truth like she was, then she would defend him. He had already done enough to get himself thrown off the force, but only she could make that happen. He had nothing more to lose. The best way of protecting Markus's education now was to cooperate fully and utterly with Müller – even if that meant being in direct opposition to Jäger and the Stasi. It was a dangerous game to play, and she felt a passing wave of guilt about forcing the forensic scientist into this position. But he had brought it on himself.

Back at the apartment in Strausberger Platz, she outlined her plan to Helga.

'We need to keep the children occupied somehow, as well as making sure we get some rest and relaxation. So I'm proposing we go back on holiday for the rest of my leave. I've got some money saved up. My adoptive family in Thuringia would love to see how the twins are getting on now. Sara and Roland still feel like a brother and sister to me. And I've always wanted to visit Saxon Switzerland. We'll combine that with my adoptive home town of Oberhof. Perhaps do a little tour. I'm sure we'll find things for the twins to do.'

Helga smiled. 'I'd love to. I've never visited the area either. Could we perhaps go via Leipzig on the way, or on the way back? I'd love to show off Jannika and Johannes to my old friends there.'

What Müller hadn't told Helga was that it wasn't the beautiful natural sights of Saxon Switzerland she was interested in. The place she wanted to go to lay a little to the west near the village of Hermsdorf, close to the Czech border. Where Herr Ronnebach had had his weekend cottage and was a member of the hunting club. The trip from there to Oberhof would take them right past Karl-Marx-Stadt, and she would be making a surprise call on Herr Ronnebach's widow to see if she could get her to speak without the interference of the Stasi. And while Leinefelde wasn't exactly directly on the way back to Berlin, if she claimed she wanted to spend a night in the Harz Mountains, she might just get away with it.

There was another reason she wanted to take Helga and the twins with her. On her own, the Ministry for State Security would certainly take an interest. If they did detail an agent to tail her, once he saw she was on holiday with her grandmother and the twins, with luck the Stasi might get bored and leave her to her own devices.

'I am going to go away for a few days for the rest of my leave after all, Comrade *Oberst*,' she told Reiniger in a phone call. 'But I'm taking the Lada. If there is anything urgent, you will be able to get in touch via the car's radio receiver. Although we're going to the mountains, so the reception may not be good.'

'It sounds lovely, Karin. And certainly very sensible. I'm sure we'll have a new case for you by the time you're back. I'd rather like some rest and relaxation in the mountains myself. Whereabouts are you going?'

'We're starting in Saxon Switzerland and going via Leipzig where my grandmother used to live. She wants to show off her great-grandchildren to her old friends.'

'She has every right to be proud of them. And it's a lovely area. I can recommend it. You have a good time. I wouldn't worry too much about listening out for radio messages. I'll try very hard not to interrupt things this time.'

The visit to Leipzig was a huge success. Müller had included it to try to get in Helga's good books – so that she wouldn't complain too much when Müller had to go off piste and revisit the case she was supposed to have been relieved of. Jannika and Johannes both behaved well and attracted glowing praise from Helga's old friends.

It meant that when Müller wanted to make inquiries amongst Ronnebach's hunting colleagues, and asked for a little time to allegedly visit an old friend of her own, Helga was all too willing to look after the children on her own.

As a young girl, Müller had always thought of her adoptive family's bed and breakfast in the winter sports resort of Oberhof as a fairy tale house. Now, it seemed more like a witch's house, given the strained relationship with the woman she'd thought for so long was her natural mother. This building in front of her was more like a witch's castle, with its brooding exterior of dark-stained wood cladding. The sharp-pointed turrets of its towers could be witches' hats – the bright red shutters reminded her of tempting poisoned apples. Rather than a hunting lodge in a socialist republic, it looked more like somewhere Hitler and the Nazi high-ups would have gathered to plot their next mad, murderous scheme.

She soon discovered that most of the building was no longer given over to hunt gatherings. The sign over the door was the giveaway – *FDGB-Heim Hermsdorf Ernst Thälmann*. It was a trade union holiday home named after the former Communist Party leader, who had been executed towards the end of the Second World War; something she knew about from both history and socialism lessons at school.

So where was the hunting club? Her confusion was allayed in a few seconds at the reception.

'You'll find it round the back. There's the clubhouse – well, it's little more than a bar really – and the gun store and workshop.' The young receptionist glanced up at the clock. 'You'll only find the members here at the weekend, but the technician might still be there.' She rattled off a series of directions and pointed out a side door to Müller. 'It'll be quickest if you go through there.'

The route took her round the outside of the hotel, through a yard, and then round a corner. She spotted the door to the club, adorned with two pairs of antlers on each side of the doorway. She tried the door – it was open. Immediately, the contrast with the hotel reception assailed her senses. There, everything had been modernised and sparkled, in what seemed like a deliberate attempt to glue a veneer over the capitalist history of the lodge. The smells were of new plastics, cleaning fluids, polish. Here, her nose was hit by a mustiness, an earthiness, a maleness. This was the preserve of men, and despite the prominent notices proclaiming the egalitarian nature of the *Volksjagd* – the People's Hunt – Müller suspected the members here were the privileged few, perhaps police officers like herself, though male. Or Party high-ups, such as Martin Ronnebach. And, of course, Ministry for State Security officials. The club would be monitored by the Stasi – but how actively? She glanced around, looking for security cameras or listening devices. There was nothing obvious. But there wouldn't be. Just like it hadn't been obvious at the Strausberger Platz apartment, until Johannes had thrown his toy car at the wall, and the damage had exposed the hidden microphone wire.

The place seemed deserted. But if it was, why was the front door unlocked? She gave an involuntary shiver, and felt her scalp prickle. Was she walking into a Stasi trap, designed to expose her continued involvement in the case? She stood stock still and listened.

Nothing.

Just the ticking of the antique wall clock, outpaced by her fast-beating heart.

She was tempted to shout out, asking if anyone was there. Then she spied what appeared to be a membership list pinned to the green baize of the club notice board. The date indicated it had been updated two months previously. Her eyes scanned to the 'R's – *Ronnebach, Martin*. That told her nothing new. She glanced through the other names, starting with the 'A's and working through the list. None seemed familiar. She reached the 'R's again, past Ronnebach, and then the 'S's.

She breathed in sharply.

Strobl, Ole.

The Stasi officer who'd prevented her from questioning Frau Ronnebach properly.

As her mind tried to digest the significance of this link, she heard a sound. A rhythmic, metallic, banging noise.

She followed it through a door. The noise grew louder, sharper, and the smell of musty maleness was replaced by the tang of metal and cordite.

The technician looked up in surprise, stopping work on what was – presumably – a gun part he'd been hammering back into shape.

'Can I help you?' he asked, a note of annoyance in his voice.

Müller hadn't really thought things through. If she announced she was a police officer, that would get back to the Stasi, no doubt within minutes of her leaving. She needed another tactic.

She tried to affect a catch in her voice, and make her face look upset.

'I hope so,' she said. 'But . . . it's . . . it's personal.'

The man laid down his tools, looking confused.

'Are you sure you're in the right place?' he asked. He had an almost Nordic appearance, and looked like the sort of man Müller could have easily fallen for in different circumstances. If he felt the same way, hopefully she could use that to her advantage. She sat down on a chair in his eyeline, hitching her skirt up slightly as she did. His gaze followed the movement, and when he raised it again to meet hers she could tell he'd realised he'd been caught looking.

'It's slightly awkward,' she said, with what she hoped was a smile full of hidden possibilities. 'My boyfriend's a member here.'

'Oh yes. Who's that?' The man had taken a chair opposite her, in front of his workbench. He settled into it with a proprietorial air, his legs spread wide, as though he was inviting Müller to admire them in the same way he'd been ogling her.

'Can I trust you? I don't even know your name.' She angled her head, with a small smile. And pushed her bottom forward a fraction in her seat, her skirt rising by that same fraction. The man's eyes gave away that he'd noticed.

'Berndt Siekert. I'm the gun technician here. And yes, you can trust me.' He glanced down again at Müller's legs, still tanned from the curtailed holiday on the Black Sea coast. Then his eyes were fixed on hers again. 'But can I trust you? It's not every day I get a visit from a gorgeous woman.'

Müller bit her bottom lip at the same time as fashioning a smile. Such a blatant come-on would normally be met by her with an icy stare. But she had started this game – he was just continuing it. What she said next was a gamble. It was time for payback.

'My boyfriend is Ole Strobl.' She hadn't liked the way the Stasi officer had so coolly blocked virtually every question of importance she'd tried to put to Martin Ronnebach's widow.

The man tried to suppress a half gasp. Did he know Strobl was a Stasi officer?

'Well, well,' he laughed. 'And does Ole's wife know about you?'

'No. Ole keeps me well hidden. He's also tried to keep his other girlfriend hidden – that's what I wanted to talk to you about.' Müller had no qualms about trashing Strobl's reputation – although she had a sneaky feeling that within the confines of the hunting club, a reputation as a lothario might be seen as something to admire rather than revile.

'Another girlfriend? Ha!' The man slapped his outstretched thighs as he laughed. Müller tried to affect a hurt look.

'It's not a laughing matter,' she said. 'I think he's been led astray by his friend, Martin Ronnebach.' It was a stab in the dark. It also conspired to move the direction of their strange conversation to what she really wanted to talk about – the murdered deputy Party head from Karl-Marx-Stadt. 'I hear Ronnebach's a bit of a one too.'

The man looked puzzled. 'I didn't realise Martin and Ole were friends. I never saw them together much.'

Müller nodded. 'Ronnebach has a weekend cottage near here. But I hear he uses it as a love nest. For his French lover.' She thought of the women's black knickers. The watermarked

French envelope. Were they really evidence of an affair? And did it have any relevance to the other killings – all of which seemed more to be linked with the history of Gardelegen?

Siekert blew out his cheeks. 'Pah! I'm not sure about that. Martin certainly used to play the field. But as far as I know, all of those he was involved with were German girls.'

'So more than one?' asked Müller. She felt her mouth drying with excitement. She was getting somewhere.

In an instant, Siekert's features changed, and suspicion cast a shadow across his face. He shuffled uncomfortably in his seat, pulling his legs together, hugging his arms in on himself. 'This is getting horribly like an interview I had with another blonde woman a few days ago. She was asking similar questions.'

'Oh yes?' asked Müller, innocently. But she had a good idea who that person was. People's Police detective Elke Drescher. But she didn't reveal that, and instead continued the charade. 'Do you think she was another of his mistresses?'

Siekert coughed, rose from his chair, and made his way back to his workbench. 'No. She was a policewoman. You do *know* what's happened to Martin Ronnebach, don't you?'

'No,' lied Müller.

'Hmm,' said the man, lifting up his hammer again. 'Let's just say he won't be going hunting any more.' With that the man started fashioning his metalwork again. The rhythmic clanging told Müller all she needed to know.

The conversation was over.

26

Once she had been reunited with Helga and the children, Müller headed towards Karl-Marx-Stadt. She hadn't learnt a great deal at the hunting club, but at least she hadn't given her real name away. There was a chance Siekert might relay the contents of her conversation to the club high-ups, and they in turn might report it to the Stasi. But the technician really shouldn't have been gossiping himself. That might give her some protection – for his own sake, he might consider it better to forget all about his flirty chat with a woman who'd identified herself as 'Ole Strobl's mistress'. And Müller had at least established one thing – Martin Ronnebach *had* been unfaithful to his wife. According to Siekert, on more than one occasion. That might provide a motive for his murder. It might even point the finger of suspicion at his widow. But it didn't tie up with the deaths of Ingo Höfler at the Leinefelde cotton mill, or of Lothar Schneider near Gardelegen.

Soon after entering Karl-Marx-Stadt, Müller spotted what she took for a Stasi car tailing her in the rear-view mirror of the Lada. She'd been expecting it – but as far as she knew it hadn't followed all the way from Hermsdorf.

She didn't alert Helga or the twins, not that Jannika and Johannes were old enough to understand. Instead, she found a children's play area and tried to smoke the Stasi man out. The capacity of Jannika and Johannes to entertain themselves in a sandpit was almost limitless. When Helga suggested it might be time to leave, Müller insisted there was no rush. The Stasi man, observing from a distant park bench, eventually looked down at his watch and sauntered off. Perhaps he'd been told to follow her for a certain amount of time. Perhaps he'd simply been attracted by the Lada's Berlin number plate and followed her on spec. Whatever his instructions, it left her free to visit Frau Ronnebach – hopefully, this time, without a spy in tow. Although it took a little persuasion to convince Helga to spend yet more time in the play area, Jannika and Johannes needed no convincing.

On returning to the Lada, Müller opened the boot and took out an evidence bag she'd brought with her. It was one of the items she'd taken from the Ronnebachs' country cottage. She'd already handed the blue envelope to Schmidt for tests – he'd managed to get some fingerprints from it and established that it was, indeed, manufactured in France as she thought. She'd kept the other item from him for now – the pair of black western women's knickers. Should she confront Frau Ronnebach with them? That's why she hadn't handed them to Schmidt yet. Snapping on protective gloves, and glancing round to check no one was watching, she opened the bag and took the underwear out. As she did, a piece of oval fabric fluttered out into her lap. She picked it up and examined it. It didn't make much sense.

On the fabric was what looked like two irregular yellow straw bales – one larger, one smaller – surrounded by a ring of lighter coloured straw. The stitching was terrible, naïve. Then she realised. What she was looking at was the back of the stitched pattern. She turned it over, with a mixture of excitement and foreboding. Now the design was clear. A golden bird of prey in mid-flight, swooping down at a forty-five-degree angle, its talons poised for the kill. Her excitement turned to revulsion as she looked more closely.

It wasn't the bird's clenched talons beneath it.

It was a golden swastika.

Frau Ronnebach seemed surprised – but not displeased – to see her.

'I wondered if you'd try to get in touch again. I wanted to say more last time, but – you know – it was difficult.'

'I don't want to put you in any danger, Frau Ronnebach. Comrade Strobl was most insistent we shouldn't meet again unless he was present. But I do have a few more questions. And I suspect, if he was here, he wouldn't let me ask them. Are you willing to talk to me?'

'Up to a point. There are things I can't say, but I will try to help as much as I can. Would you like a coffee?'

Once the coffee was made and poured – the real thing again, noted Müller – they sat in the lounge, Müller with her pen and notebook poised at the dining table, Frau Ronnebach perched on the end of the sofa, just like the previous occasion.

'Some things have come to light since my last visit that I wanted to ask you about, Frau Ronnebach. Firstly, I believe you and your husband didn't always live in this area, did you?'

'That's correct. We used to live nearer to Magdeburg – further north. That's where we met.'

'Gardelegen, wasn't it?'

'That's right.'

'Did you or your husband know a man called Ingo Höfler? Either when you were living in Gardelegen, or after you moved to this area?'

The small, bird-like woman cocked her head, and paused before answering. With her bright green blouse and electric blue skirt, she almost looked like a parrot.

'Höfler. The name does sound familiar. I think there may have been a Höfler family in Gardelegen. Were they bakers?'

Müller shrugged.

'The trouble is,' continued the woman, 'though it's a small town, it's not that small – if you know what I mean. There must be – what? – twenty thousand or so people who live there. So there might be people I knew to say hello to in the street, but I wouldn't necessarily know their names. But I think there was a Höfler family that owned a bakery.'

'And your husband didn't have any dealings with an Ingo Höfler later, through his relationship with the cotton mill at Sachsenburg?'

'I wouldn't say he had a relationship with the mill. His only link – as far as I'm aware – was that he was involved in the decision to nationalise the mill. But really, locally, he would simply have been rubber-stamping decisions made by the Party in the Hauptstadt.'

'What about Lothar Schneider?'

'Sorry?' The woman looked perplexed.

'Did you know a Lothar Schneider – or a Schneider family – in Gardelegen?'

The woman's eyes darted to the left, as though she was checking something through the window. Then back to Müller. 'No, sorry.'

'Do you have any theories about your husband's murder, Frau Ronnebach?'

'No, well . . . perhaps.'

'Perhaps?'

'I got the feeling the Ministry for State Security officer was most insistent that I shouldn't talk about anything from the past, as we've been doing today. As that's the case, I'm sure that's where the answer must lie.'

'And you're sure your husband wasn't having an affair?' Since her last visit, Müller now had an advantage over the woman. She *knew* – unless what the hunt club technician had said was simply bluster – that Martin Ronnebach had been unfaithful, and not just on one occasion or with one woman. 'Did he have contact with anyone in France, for example?'

'*France?*' echoed the woman, frowning. 'Not that I know of. You seem very insistent about this line of questioning.' Frau Ronnebach stared hard at Müller. 'Perhaps you know something that I don't.' The widow's face took on a momentary look of wistfulness – as if she were remembering past times, when she and her husband had been happy with each other. When they'd enjoyed that first, thrilling rush of love and lust. Then her look hardened. 'If Martin was having an affair, then as I said before, he would have had ample opportunity when at the hunting club or weekend cottage. As I suggested before, you should concentrate your inquiries there.'

'I already have,' said Müller.

'And?'

'That's not really for me to say, Frau Ronnebach.' Although she was stonewalling, Müller tried to convey in her tone of voice and expression the answer the widow was really seeking – confirmation of the suspected infidelity.

'Ah. Well then, if anything like that led to his death, well . . . I can't say I'd wish it on him, because I wouldn't. I certainly had no part in his murder, if that's what you're implying. But if that was what he was doing, and that was the end result, well . . . it was rather his own fault, then, wasn't it?'

Müller let the woman's answer hang in the air for a few seconds, almost inviting her to say more. When she didn't, Müller produced what she hoped was her trump card. She'd decided confronting Frau Ronnebach with the black lingerie was a step too far, and had left the underwear in the Lada's boot. Instead, Müller took out the fabric badge and showed it to the woman.

Immediately there was a look of recognition.

'I found this hidden in a drawer at your cottage,' the detective said. 'Your husband was a member of the Nazi Party, wasn't he?'

The woman toyed with the badge, but otherwise seemed unperturbed. 'You do *know* what this is, don't you?'

'I know what the emblem at the bottom of the design is.'

'All such badges from this period would have included that,' said the woman, coolly holding Müller's gaze. 'It is simply a *Fallschirmjäger* or paratrooper badge. Gardelegen had a *Fallschirmjäger* barracks – my husband was a young officer stationed there. That's how I met him. I was involved in amateur dramatics – it was my passion. We put on a show for the paratroopers.'

'That's all very well, Frau Ronnebach. But the fact is your husband was a Nazi, wasn't he?'

The woman dropped her eyes, and initially didn't answer.

When she raised them, there was an icy coldness in them which made Müller shudder.

'I'd like you to leave my apartment now, please. Immediately.'

Müller tried to ask more questions, but any trust had been broken. The woman just shooed her out, reminding her that a call to the Ministry for State Security would land Müller in hot water if she failed to leave. Her assertion about the answer lying in the past seemed to be borne out by the fabric paratrooper badge, despite the question mark still hanging over her husband's apparent hidden love life, and whether that might have provided a motive for his murder. Nevertheless, Müller's own view was that the connection between the victims *was* something historic. Probably something to do with the Nazi period, although Frau Ronnebach had succeeded in placing a doubt in her mind about her husband's Nazi affiliations.

27

Mieste, near Gardelegen, Nazi Germany

All the time we've been here, we've watched the skies, expecting an air attack to come at any moment. It came the day after our misery was partially relieved by the insubstantial meal.

There is no air-raid warning. We hear the drone of the planes first, then the whine of the bombs, and we scatter – running as fast as we can away from the train. Marcellin and I dive into the ditch to take cover. He's been partially revived by that one meal. We flatten ourselves to the bank. I see Marcellin's wounded arm has been soaked with ditchwater. That can't be a good thing.

The prisoners run in all directions. One of the bombs scores a direct hit on the railway yard, sending dirt and debris flying into the sky. It rains down on us like a dirty hailstorm.

Some prisoners try to escape. I think it's some of the Russians. I watch them running across a cornfield, willing them to reach the cover of the trees. I know Marcellin cannot run like that. He cannot run at all. The will to live gave him the adrenalin to escape into the ditch, but it hasn't done him any good.

Then comes the sound of automatic gunfire.

We watch the Russians mown down, one by one.

Two of them are still running. One reaches the woods, and safety.

The other gets tangled in a fence, and we watch the bullets shred him apart.

Life is like that. One minute you're there, the next you're not.

I don't believe in the afterlife. I never have. So no matter how desperate our situation, I want to survive.

The *Kapos* and guards round us up again, and we're soon sitting back on the bank where we have been for days, slowly wasting away. But something has changed. There are frantic shouts among the guards. One of them has heard the Americans are nearly here. Little more than ten kilometres away.

Surely now we are safe?

Surely the Germans will now lay down their arms and give up?

We are being moved, that becomes obvious. We're divided into three groups of a few hundred people each. At one point, it looks as though Marcellin will be taken on the horse-drawn carts with the others who are unable to walk any more. I plead with the guards to let me stay with my brother. For some reason, my pleas are listened to. But instead of both going on the carts, we are pushed into one of the marching groups. I immediately regret my actions. I should have let Marcellin go with the carts. He will not be able to walk far, and if he collapses, that will be it. They will shoot him. I've seen it too many times already.

One group leaves, a picture of abject misery. They are human skeletons in rags, with thin blankets wrapped around their shoulders. It is beyond shocking what man can do to man in times of war. I must survive, we must survive, in order to tell our story – to make sure that this can never happen again. But over the years, despite what terrible acts have been committed, people forget. They want to forget. It's human nature.

We are in the second group. We're marching north, not east as I expected, as we head for the woods down a narrow lane.

Suddenly, out of the skies, Allied aircraft bear down. Machine guns open fire, scattering us into the fields. I'm half-running, half-dragging Marcellin. Is this finally our chance to escape?

Flat to the earth, I scan the horizon. The woods aren't far. If I can help Marcellin, we can get there.

'Leave me, Philippe,' he says. 'I won't make it. Save yourself.'

But I cannot do that. I force him with what little strength I have in me to try to hurry. I am weak, he feels so, so heavy, but I know that he is not. There is little flesh left on his bones.

A shot rings out over our heads.

We freeze and put our hands up, but for Marcellin, that is just one hand. He cannot raise his other arm.

I brace myself, expecting the next shot through my back. Expecting it all, finally, to be over. There is little liquid left in my body, but what there is is expelled now down my trousers.

The shot doesn't come.

Instead, there is shouting in German. Someone in civilian clothes, armed with what looks like a hunting rifle, prods us back towards the column of prisoners, now reformed after the air raid. The man isn't a soldier and isn't a *Kapo*. He's just a farmer. All of them are doing their dirty work together. But I suppose we should be thankful; at least he didn't shoot us.

From the other sounds of gunfire we heard, others weren't so lucky. We see the evidence first-hand, their bodies piled by the side of the road.

We reach a village; Breitenfeld, according to the road signs. Here, we turn off the road and are marched due east through the woods again. If the Americans are advancing, if they are only a few kilometres away, surely they will reach us soon?

At some point, possibly because Marcellin cannot keep up with the others, we become separated from the main group. At first I think it's just us two, then I look behind us and realise that there are perhaps a hundred or so of us, the weakest. Then I realise something else. There are no guards. We are free. We are free, but we have no food, no shelter, no water. And no idea where to go or what to do.

Someone makes a decision. We will wait here and camp for the night. Wait, and hope that by morning the Americans will be here, and we will be saved.

The next morning, we're on the move again. Still without guards, still all together. We're going east. I try to tell the others we should go the other way, towards the Americans, but they won't listen. Most of them are Poles. Perhaps they are under the mistaken belief they can walk all the way back home. None of them will make it.

I have a decision to make. Do Marcellin and I strike out on our own, or is there safety in numbers? I chose the latter. It's a decision I will always regret.

Just outside the village of Estedt, a German car overtakes us. Nine soldiers get out. German soldiers. *Fallschirmjäger* – paratroops. Once the elite of the German fighting force, now about to be defeated. But before their final defeat, they are going to deal with us. Their eyes look murderous. This is different. These are not *Kapos*. These are trained soldiers out for revenge.

For some reason, they march us back to the west, towards Breitenfeld, up the same track we've already been down when we were on our own, without guards. On the way it was easier, downhill. On the way back, it is more of a struggle as we are going up the incline, towards the woods where we camped overnight. One of the other prisoners who still has some strength left helps me with Marcellin. Otherwise he would not make it. And I know the *Fallschirmjäger* troops will have no mercy.

We reach a clearing in the woods, just to the north side of the track. The sun has come out, and it shines like a torch, highlighting the grassy area. On one side of the clearing is a giant boulder moved there by some force of nature thousands, perhaps millions, of years ago.

We are all told to strip naked.

I know now what I suspected when the car overtook us on the road, and these troops – with their evil, wolf-like eyes – took us under their control.

We are not leaving this clearing alive. None of us.

Six of the stronger-looking amongst us are handed shovels that I now realise the troops brought with them. This was all planned.

At gunpoint, we're ordered to dig a trench.

Out of the corner of my eye, I see one Polish prisoner prostrate himself in front of a German guard, kissing his boots, begging him not to shoot him. I want to feel disgust, but I cannot. If I wasn't having to wield a shovel at gunpoint, digging what is certainly my own grave, I might do the same.

Life is a precious thing. I have enjoyed it, despite these last couple of years.

When the trench is little more than a metre deep, we're told to stop, and lay our shovels aside.

We are told to stand back. We're not going to be the first.

Instead, a group of weaker prisoners are lined up facing the trench, the guards behind them. One of the prisoners is Marcellin.

The guards raise their weapons.

'No, no!' I shout. 'He is my brother. Please let him live.'

The guard turns his gun on me. 'Silence,' he barks.

I see his gloved finger resting on the trigger, about to squeeze.

But my mind is back on the *Celestine*, sailing out of Loix's tiny harbour, with Marcellin and Grégoire riding the waves. Then lying with Marie-Ange amongst the vines, with the sun beating down in a blinding white light. Her caresses on the side of my face. The exquisite taste of the fresh herbs in Maman's marsh mutton casserole.

My life is over, but I have memories to cherish, and they flicker like a well-worn newsreel in front of my eyes.

28

By the time they neared Oberhof – the large village, or town Müller had grown up in and the next leg of their family tour – Jannika and Johannes had started to fret about the journey. Müller had needed to stop a couple of times so she and Helga could calm the twins' crying. Nevertheless, Müller took a short detour so that they approached Oberhof from the north. She wanted to be reminded of the magnificence of the Interhotel Panorama, the modernist structure whose two main buildings were supposed to look like twin ski-jump slopes, echoing the winter sports theme for which Oberhof was famed. To Müller, in the summer, it looked more like a giant ocean liner that had broken in two and was slowly sinking beneath the waves. Today, in the bright sunlight, its multitude of windows glittered with reflections – much as they had on her last visit to see her adoptive family some two years previously. It had been a turning point in her life. She'd finally discovered the reason why she'd always felt 'different' from her brother Roland and younger sister Sara, and why the woman she'd always assumed was her natural mother had seemed – to Müller anyway – to treat her less favourably. It had been the visit where she had finally discovered that she was adopted, nearly thirty years after the fact.

The anger she'd felt at her adoptive family had dissipated now that she'd met Helga, now that she had a real family of her own. She knew she wanted to at least stay friends with them. She owed it to her adoptive brother and sister – and, yes, even her mother – to let them be a part of the twins' lives, if only peripherally.

She took one last look at the hotel in the rear-view mirror, and the top of Haus One – where she and Tilsner had climbed up to challenge her childhood friend, and save her baby son's life. She glanced at him in the mirror. He was oblivious now, finally asleep again with a bottle of juice lolling from his mouth. One day she would take him up there, and tell him the story.

Müller pulled up in front of Bergpension Hanneli, killed the Lada's engine, and then – for a few moments – let the thoughts and memories wash over her. Her last visit had been almost exactly two years earlier, in the summer of 1975, while she was working on the missing babies case in Halle-Neustadt.

Then, as now, she'd felt a level of apprehension, a tightening in her stomach when confronted by the gloss-red painted log cladding of the lower floors, and the black slate of the sharply sloping eaves containing the guest rooms above. It still had the look of a witch's house – almost like the little sister of the witch's castle of a hunting lodge in Hermsdorf. The window boxes in the lower floors were still filled with golden hyacinths – the gold of the flowers, red of the logs and black slates above mimicking the colours of the German flags, both the Republic's and that of the West – the BRD.

Müller turned to survey her passengers. They were all asleep. She'd been careful to bring the car to a gentle halt so as to try not to wake them and to give herself a few moments to collect her thoughts. She looked at Johannes. He was such a cute boy. So unlike his namesake, Johannes Traugott – the childhood friend she'd felt she'd abandoned. The awkward, bespectacled boy who'd turned into a half-deranged man, and nearly robbed her of her happiness at being a mother. She was never going to let that happen again, never let her own job put them in danger. If anything like that ever happened again, she knew what she would sacrifice. Her career. Never her children.

After playing up earlier in the car journey, predictably Jannika and Johannes were both as good as gold for Rosamund Müller – her adoptive mother – her sister, Sara, and brother, Roland. Perhaps they'd been refreshed by their long sleep.

'They are darlings, Karin,' said Rosamund. 'I'm so proud of you.'

The genuine joy on Rosamund's face brought tears to Müller's eyes. She'd have liked to hear the words *I'm so proud of you* a little more as a child herself. She always felt Sara and Roland got more favourable treatment – although at their last meeting Rosamund had denied it. She felt more affection for her mother now, however. The woman who had given her a home and raised her, despite the fact she wasn't her natural child.

'I can see both of you in Jannika,' said Sara, after hugging her adoptive sister. 'She's got your eyes, Karin, but more of your face, Helga.'

Müller could see Helga's eyes watering. 'She's the spitting image of her mother, really, Sara. I so wish you could have met my daughter, and that she could have seen her grandchildren.'

Müller tenderly laid her hand on Helga's forearm. 'Don't get yourself upset.'

'No,' agreed Rosamund. 'Now, Karin tells me you used to do a bit of flower-arranging when you were living in Leipzig, Helga. I wanted your advice on an arrangement I'm putting in for the town show.' She dragged Müller's grandmother away to try to distract her from her sad memories, which seemed to have been prompted by which toddler looked like whom.

'You're looking well, Sara. You've lost weight too,' said Müller to her adoptive sister.

'Ha!' laughed Roland. 'That's because there's a man on the scene, now isn't there, Sara?'

Sara blushed. 'We've not been going out that long.'

'Who is it?' asked Müller. 'Anyone I know?'

'Tomas Jollenbeck.'

'Tomas the butcher's son?'

'That's right.' Müller pictured the boy – round-faced, happy, always helping out his father in the shop. Not exactly handsome, and certainly not Müller's type.

Sara got a photo from her handbag and passed it to her adoptive sister.

The round-faced, spotty boy that Müller remembered had flowered into a strapping, hunky man, who towered over Sara in the photograph, his arms clasped round her as if protecting her. As a boy, Müller wouldn't have spared him a second glance. As a man, she suddenly felt a pang of jealousy.

'I'm so pleased for you, Sara. You look so happy together.' It was what she'd imagined for herself and Emil – until everything had gone wrong.

'He's asked her to marry him,' said Roland. 'I don't think he realises what he's letting himself in for.'

'Shh, Roland. I wanted to tell Karin myself.'

Müller stood up, and smothered her sister in another hug. 'Oh Sara, Sara. I'm so thrilled for you. When's the wedding?'

'Oh we haven't set a date yet. We wanted to save up a bit more first. But get your glad rags ready. I expect it will be next spring or summer.'

Müller was overjoyed for Sara, and the two women moved into the snug to discuss the wedding and reminisce over their childhoods, as Roland entertained the twins, playing peek-a-boo and roughhousing around. When Sara said she had to check on something that was simmering away in the kitchen, Müller took the opportunity to slide away for a moment, and began to climb the stairs of the guesthouse, past the guest rooms on the first floor, right up into the eaves.

She'd half-expected the room to have been redecorated, perhaps put into use as another room for paying guests. After all, she was – in effect – no longer Rosamund's daughter. The fact that it hadn't been, the fact that it had been left almost as a shrine to the teenage her – as a time capsule, with the fading Beatles poster carefully reattached to the wall – brought a rush of affection towards Rosamund in Müller's heart. Perhaps her adoptive mother did love her after all. Perhaps she always had. Perhaps it had simply been Müller's own perception, her own selfishness, which had meant she'd perceived herself being treated less favourably than Roland or Sara.

She'd done this two years earlier: reached to the top of the wardrobe for her 'secret' key. It was still there, and the layer of dust she disturbed suggested that Rosamund had left things well alone. Once again, she used the key to open the desk drawer and pull out her old diary. It still smelt the same; musty paper mixed with Casino de Luxe – one of the Republic's perfume brands which had been popular with girls of her age. It probably still was, for all she knew. Things changed slowly from year to year in this country. Brands stayed the same, prices stayed the same, leaders stayed the same. But nothing is permanent, she knew that.

This time, she didn't look through the diary entries. She knew what was in there: the account of the day when she'd been a young girl of five, and – overnight – almost all of Oberhof's guesthouses had been nationalised, their owners and families bussed out, hundreds of kilometres away. One of those had been her childhood friend, Johannes. And she had witnessed it with her own eyes, as he'd remonstrated with the soldiers.

Instead, she moved the diary aside, and took out one of the envelopes underneath – a letter she'd received from some boyfriend or other, probably met at a summer holiday camp, or when she'd been a promising schoolgirl ski jumper, even though women's ski jumping had never been allowed in the Olympics. It still wasn't.

She turned the envelope over and over in her hands. It was white turned browny yellow with age, not the blue of the French envelope in Martin Ronnebach's weekend cottage. She was convinced that was a red herring, that Ronnebach's affairs were red herrings. She was looking through a window into the past now – in this room. That's what she needed for the deaths of Ronnebach, Höfler and Schneider. Three murdered men – two of them killed with exactly the same method. All three of them with links to the past, in the small town of Gardelegen. That was what she needed to crack in this case – a window to look into their pasts. Because she was sure that was where the answer lay.

Helga seemed to have genuinely struck a bond with Rosamund. The meeting of the two had been something Müller was apprehensive about, but her natural grandmother and adoptive mother had been a good fit. They were a similar age, Helga having been a teenage mother herself when giving birth to Müller's natural mother, while Rosamund and Müller's adoptive father had at first thought they couldn't have children – and Rosamund only conceived with first Roland, then Sara, later in life.

'Thank you for taking us to meet them, Karin,' said Helga, as they drove out of Oberhof towards Gotha, through the forested low mountains of Thuringia. 'It can't have been easy for you, but

I'm sure now we've met we'll stay in touch. I'd like to, anyway.'
Müller was of the same opinion. She'd enjoyed the reunion,
brief though it was. She knew that from now on, she would keep
in touch more regularly and make her adoptive family a larger
part of her life.

The fact that Helga was enjoying their touring holiday made
it easier for Müller to persuade her grandmother to allow her
another couple of hours off when they arrived at their next
stop near Nordhausen. Müller had chosen it for an overnight
stay ostensibly because it was a good base to tour the Harz
mountains – or at least the part of the Harz which lay in the
Republic. Her real reason was that it was less than an hour's
drive to Leinefelde.

Frau Höfler was more suspicious about Müller's motives than
her fellow widow in Karl-Marx-Stadt. At first she stood on her
kitchen doorstep, unwilling to invite Müller inside. It was only
when Müller mentioned the possibility of her being arrested for
obstructing a police inquiry that she relented.

'I thought it wasn't a police inquiry any more. Hasn't the
Ministry for State Security taken over from you?'

'In some respects, Frau Höfler, yes. But there are still a few
matters I need to clear up from my end for my report, when I
hand the file to the Stasi. So it's in your interests to cooperate.
Otherwise . . .'

The woman shrugged, opened the door, and gestured to the
kitchen table. Müller pulled out a chair and sat down.

'By the way, I have something for you.' She reached into her briefcase, and pulled out the 1930s photograph of the Höflers as a young couple outside Gardelegen town hall.

'I assumed the Stasi had taken it. I only noticed it had gone the other day. I didn't really like to ring them and ask them what had happened to it.'

'I'm sorry, Frau Höfler. I needed to check where the photograph was taken.'

'Gardelegen, of course. It's where we met and grew up.'

'That's what I'm interested in,' said Müller. 'Your time in Gardelegen. Particularly any connections that you or your husband may have had with a Martin Ronnebach and a Lothar Schneider.'

'That's past history,' said the woman. 'Best left well alone. Do you think all the great and good of the Republic were all in jail for opposing the Nazis during the war? I can tell you, they weren't. So you can use your own imagination to work out what they were doing.'

Müller sighed and leant her arms on the table, fingers steepled together and thumbs under her chin. She held the woman's gaze. 'I can get a warrant to search your house if you'd prefer, Frau Höfler. But it would be easier for you to tell me everything I want to know. Less mess to clear up afterwards, too.'

The woman looked away from the detective, and rubbed the palm of her hand across her brow. Then she seemed to come to a decision.

'Come into the living room. I want to show you something.'

Müller followed her. Unlike the bird-like Frau Ronnebach, Ingo Höfler's widow gave off an air of strength and resilience. For her age, she still had a good figure, with curves in the right places – as though she'd made a point of trying to keep herself fit, rather than succumbing to middle-age spread.

She went over to the side table, and picked up a photograph which Müller hadn't spotted before and handed it to the detective. It was a black and white photograph of a dancing girl, one leg kicked high, showing off stockings and suspenders. The rest of the outfit was almost as risqué: a bustier-style top showed off much of the girl's ample breasts, and between that and the stockings, what looked like ruffled knickers. Müller eyed the girl's face, then compared it to Frau Höfler's. Pear-shaped, jolly, yet sensual. Yes, the features had sagged a little, were more lined, but it was the same person.

'I was in demand, you can imagine. That's how Ingo and I met – he was in the audience one night. But most of the time, in those days, as you can imagine, we were dancing for Nazis.'

Müller tried to hand the photograph back, as if it were tainted.

Frau Höfler snorted. 'What do you think happened in this part of Germany after 1945? Where did all the Communists suddenly come from? The trouble with you youngsters is you don't question things enough. Everyone from that era has skeletons in the cupboard. It was unavoidable.'

Things were starting to come together in Müller's mind. 'What were you and your husband's skeletons, Frau Höfler?

What did he do in the war? Surely he was of fighting age. Yet he survived. Why?'

'He was of fighting age, that's true. But Ingo was never sent to the front. He'd had a terrible motorcycle accident as a teenager. He always walked with a limp, and in those days the pain was even worse. So no, he didn't fight. But he played his part in the last few months of the war. In the *Volkssturm* – the home guard. As for skeletons, well, they're the same as everyone's in Gard . . .' The woman paused. 'What's that noise outside? Do you hear it?'

Müller listened. She couldn't hear anything.

'There it is again,' said the woman. This time Müller heard it. It sounded like a radio conversation. The woman opened the kitchen door, and Müller realised the noise was coming from the Lada. She'd left her police radio on in case of emergencies, and someone was trying to get in touch.

'I'd better respond to that, Frau Höfler. I'll be back in a moment.'

She climbed into the car, picked up the receiver, and pressed the button to speak.

'*Major* Karin Müller, *Kriminalpolizei* Serious Crimes Department.'

'Ah, Karin, at last.' It was Reiniger. 'We couldn't get a signal for a couple of hours. I'm terribly sorry; I said I wouldn't interrupt your holiday. But I'm afraid there's something that needs your attention. Whereabouts are you? You said you might be going to Oberhof.'

'We've left Oberhof now. We're in the Harz area.' It was a small lie. Reiniger could no doubt check her location if he wanted to by tracing which police station had patched through the call. She was hoping he wouldn't bother.

'Well, that's not too far away, either. A pathologist has got in touch from Eisenach – you know, where the castle is, and where they make the cars. Wartburgs. Anyway, there was a death in the factory. Something that wasn't widely advertised, obviously. This pathologist reckons he's found something strange about this death that seems to undermine the official account of an accident. As you can imagine that's a little sensitive, and he wouldn't go into details. He said he knew you and wanted to talk to you directly. Although don't rock any boats. We don't want to disrupt production or endanger targets at the factory.'

'Of course, Comrade *Oberst*. I'll treat it sensitively, and get on to it right away.'

Reiniger gave her the pathologist's phone number and she noted it down.

'Did he leave his name, Comrade *Oberst*?'

'Ah! No, sorry. It was Truda that took the message. If you do decide it's worth you going to see him, and if you need any help getting your family back to the Hauptstadt, be sure to let me know. I feel very bad about doing this twice to you in such a short space of time.'

Müller noted down the details, ended the conversation, and then returned to Frau Höfler's kitchen door and knocked on it again.

The woman opened it, but blocked the doorway with her body and looked at Müller stern-faced.

'While you were out there I thought I'd better put in a call to the local Ministry for State Security,' she said. Müller rolled her eyes. 'You can imagine what they said about you asking me questions. You're not supposed to be still on this case. They'll be over here in a few minutes to talk to you.'

Müller turned on her heels without saying goodbye to the woman. The Stasi might be travelling out to the farmhouse to talk to her, but she wasn't going to stay around to talk to them.

29

Müller found a public call box sufficiently far away from Frau Höfler's house that if Stasi agents came to visit, as Frau Höfler intimated, they would hopefully not see her. She dialled the number Reiniger had given her. The voice on the end of the line sounded familiar.

'You may not remember me, Comrade Müller, but I was involved in a case with you a couple of years ago, in the Harz area. I'm Dr Rudolf Eckstein. I'm now semi-retired, and have moved to be nearer my daughter here in Eisenach.'

'I remember you, Dr Eckstein, yes.' He'd been the pathologist who'd examined the body of Matthias Schmidt – one of the reform school teenagers. The murdered boy had been the boyfriend of the teenage girl found mutilated at the foot of the Anti-Fascist Protection Barrier. At the time, Müller had thought Eckstein had already been wheeled out of retirement, given the white hairs sprouting from his ears and nostrils.

'Well, I saw a small piece in the newspaper about you investigating a death in Karl-Marx-Stadt at an industrial plant, and I saw you were in charge of a new Serious Crimes Department. I didn't really know who to talk to, but I thought you might be able to help.'

'Help with what?'

'It's a little sensitive. I told your police officer in the Hauptstadt that I'd rather not discuss it on the phone. Could we meet? Here in Eisenach?'

'When?'

'Well, it's a little late today if you're coming from the Hauptstadt.'

'I'm not, Dr Eckstein. I'm currently near Leinefelde looking into another matter. So you're only just over an hour's drive away from me.'

'Ah, good. Well, in that case, shall we say in two hours' time?'

Müller made a mental calculation. She would have to ring Helga and persuade her to take the twins back to the Hauptstadt on the train. It wasn't the easiest of journeys, via Leipzig – but perhaps Helga could break the journey there and stay with her friends who they'd met earlier in the trip and who'd been so taken with the twins.

'I just have to make one other phone call to sort something out. But that should be all right. In the hospital mortuary?'

'No. As I say, this is rather sensitive. There's a parking space halfway up the road from Eisenach to Wartburg Castle. That would be a good place.'

'All right. Let's assume I'll be there in two hours' time. If it looks as though I may be late, I will ring you.'

Müller knew this had to be followed up immediately. The information that the bird-like Frau Ronnebach and one-time dancing girl Frau Höfler had given her were more pieces of the puzzle. First, that Martin Ronnebach had been a paratrooper – and very possibly an active Nazi. Secondly, that Ingo Höfler had a disability so couldn't fight yet had joined – or been conscripted into – the home guard when the Nazis faced imminent defeat. But how did it all fit together?

Müller was fortunate to catch Helga having lunch in the hotel when she rang. Her grandmother was clearly disappointed their little break now looked to be at an end, but the Harz area had been their last stop anyway.

'We've had a nice little tour,' said Helga. 'And I knew you would have to go back to work sooner or later. If you had a normal job, you wouldn't need me living with you in any case. We'll be fine on the train. And as you say, if I wanted I could always break the journey in Leipzig.'

The white hairs in Dr Eisenach's nostrils and ears looked even wilder than they had before. He hadn't said if he was still married, but if he had been then Müller imagined his wife would have nagged him to pay more attention to his personal appearance.

He'd joined her in the Lada, and sat in the passenger seat, with a sheaf of papers in his lap. He seemed to have trouble bending his limbs to sit down. 'You can see I'm getting on a bit, Comrade Müller. But every time I try to retire, there's a shortage somewhere or other and they drag me back in. I could say no, of course, but then what else would I do with my time? It's very hard letting go when you enjoy your work.'

Müller hadn't given the first thought to her own retirement. But the way things were going, she doubted very much that she'd ever get that far. There had been so much interference from the Ministry for State Security recently that a much more likely outcome would be her handing in her *Kripo* ID card voluntarily – perhaps in the not-too-distant future.

'Anyway, here are some things to look at.' He pulled a couple of black and white photographs from the pile of papers. He handed one to her. It was a naked body of a male – but it didn't look much like a body any more. The face had been mangled or crushed beyond all recognition. The upper body, too, appeared to have suffered severe crush injuries.

Eckstein handed Müller a second photo. In this the body had been photographed in situ at the scene, crushed under the half-built shell of a Wartburg 353 – the current model favoured so much by the People's Police. The car, somehow, seemed to have fallen off an inspection pit ramp.

'On the face of it, this seems to have all the hallmarks of an accident,' said Müller. 'Who is he, or rather who was he?'

'His name was Heinz Unterbrink and he was the quality control manager of VEB Automobilwerk Eisenach. It's perfectly feasible that he might have been checking under the cars, although normally one might expect someone in a managerial position to delegate that work.'

'And why are you of the opinion that this wasn't an accident?' asked Müller.

'It's not an opinion, Comrade Müller. Dead bodies are a little like printed books. You can't easily undo what has already been printed in black and white. And they can be read like books. Yes, the body has been crushed under the car. Yes, clearly such trauma would be sufficient to cause death, and of course – unless you could prove that the inspection ramp or the car itself had been tampered with, or that Herr Unterbrink had somehow been forced under the car before it fell – then you would conclude that he died in an unfortunate accident. And that is indeed what the factory and the People's Police here in Eisenach have concluded, and they don't seem to be interested in anything which disagrees with that conclusion.'

'But nevertheless you *do* disagree?'

'Far be it for me to question our esteemed People's Police or indeed the management of the Wartburg factory itself. However, the *facts* disagree, Comrade Müller. Herr Unterbrink couldn't have been crushed to death.'

'Why?' asked Müller. She wasn't sure why she asked the question, as she already knew the answer. It simply seemed the way Eckstein preferred to explain things.

'Because he was already dead.'

Eckstein wanted to show her the scene of the accident before he would say any more. Müller wasn't clear why, and had some reservations. Although the car factory was unlikely to deny her access in the way the power station in Gardelegen had, it would still alert the local police – and almost certainly the local Stasi – that someone had rumbled that the so-called 'accident' was, in all probability, anything but accidental.

Müller chose not to mention the Serious Crimes Department, and decided to show her *Volkspolizei* ID to the factory officials, rather than her specific one relating to the criminal division.

That way, she hoped, they would assume she was from the local People's Police office.

'I'm new in Eisenach,' she half-lied, 'and Dr Eckstein here simply wants to show me how the accident happened.'

The junior manager who met them didn't even refer the matter upwards, taking what she said at face value.

The row of inspection bays were to one side of the main factory buildings, where car production had got back into full swing, judging from the crashing of metal and general hubbub of mechanical noises.

'I'll leave you to it, Comrade *Major*, if you're happy with that,' said the manager, sweeping back his greasy black hair from his forehead. 'We're not using this bay until it's been established exactly what went wrong, and we've got a deadline to meet on a new order from Hungary. Our cars are very popular with our socialist neighbours.'

When the manager had departed, Dr Eckstein started to examine the car and the bay. 'This is the first time I've had the chance to be here since the initial examination of the body when it did indeed look like a straightforward accident.'

Müller saw that the car had dropped several metres from the platform to ground level. The failed platform was still in place.

'What do you think happened?' she asked.

'I'm not really an expert in mechanics; I was just curious, to be honest. If it really was an accident, there must have been a catastrophic failure of the platform. Given he was already dead, it must have all been staged. So any failure of the platform was deliberate.'

'You still haven't said how you came to the conclusion that the death occurred before the crushing.'

Eckstein came out from under the platform, shaking his head. 'Very strange. I can't see anything obviously wrong with it.'

Müller raised her eyebrows, and repeated the question. 'Why are you so convinced that this man was already dead before his body was crushed beneath the car?'

The pathologist looked to his left and right, then up into the ceiling void. Then he frowned.

'I don't want to talk too much about it here. Why don't you take me back to my car at the parking space and we can discuss it there.'

When they were back at the parking space, Eckstein turned to her.

'My view is that the crush injuries he received were caused post-mortem, rather than ante-mortem, and indeed several hours after his actual death. Possibly as many as twelve hours. I couldn't understand initially why the time of death I estimated didn't tally with when the body was found, and when the accident is alleged to have occurred.

'There were a number of signs. The abrasions from the crushing were yellowish in colour with defined borders. If those injuries had been sustained ante-mortem they would have been reddish brown in colour, with undefined edges. This is due to the inflammatory reactions which would have occurred. The edges of the injuries should have been gaping and swollen. In fact, they were either closed or curled inwards. There was no loss of elasticity of the tissue, which there should have been if the injuries had been ante-mortem.'

'All right, so he didn't die as a result of being crushed by the car at the factory. What did he die from?'

'Well, I dissected the lungs and found carbon particles in the terminal bronchioles, and cyanides were present in the blood.'

'Cyanide? So he was poisoned?'

'No, no. Decomposition of a body can produce cyanide naturally. However, the type of cyanides, carbon particles and the soot I found at the back of the pharynx—'

'Mean that he died of smoke inhalation.'

Eckstein furrowed his white brows. 'Yes.'

'And was there any sign of isolated burn marks on his wrists?'

Eckstein shook his head of white hair. 'That's a very strange question. And how did you know about the smoke inhalation?'

Müller didn't answer. So it was the same method of death – yet disguised by someone, or some organisation. She could imagine who. Meanwhile, she frantically leafed through Eckstein's documents from the post-mortem. 'Is his address anywhere here? Was he married?'

The pathologist nodded, and picked up the sheaf of papers, riffled through them, and found a sheet with Unterbrink's address. He handed it to Müller. A block in Eisenach-Nord. Müller had seen the road signs on her way from Leinefelde – a satellite town of concrete slab apartment blocks, presumably specially built for the workers at the car factory.

She restarted the Lada's engine, and reached over Eckstein to flick the passenger door open. The man looked a little put out that their discussion was at an end.

'You've been very helpful, Dr Eckstein, and I want to ring you or meet again to go over all this in detail. But I need to interview his widow as soon as possible. I'm going straight there.'

30

Müller considered attaching the magnetic blue emergency light to the Lada's roof to cut through Eisenach's traffic more quickly. But she didn't want to draw unnecessary attention. The Stasi had tried to thwart her so far. Was it too much of a stretch to think they could have been behind the faking of the cause of death of Herr Unterbrink?

Instead, she drove quickly but carefully, obeying the rules of the road and all traffic signals, until she drew up outside the modern block that – according to Eckstein's documents – housed the apartment where the Unterbrinks lived, or at least where Frau Unterbrink now lived.

All the time, Müller was trying to work out what was going on. Had Reiniger known what Eckstein had revealed to her – that this was another 'fire' death, where a common denominator was the inhalation of smoke, rather than death through burning? Was it Reiniger's way of once more circumventing the Stasi's insistence that they should take control of the case? And what did the lack of wrist burns mean? Perhaps – if Unterbrink's hands *had* been lashed together – he had somehow managed to free himself another way before being overcome by smoke.

She also had no idea where the fire that killed Unterbrink had been set – or where his body had originally been found, before the cause of death had been faked at the car factory. There were so many loose ends. And – in effect – she was having to work on her own. To draw in Tilsner would risk him telling the Stasi she was back investigating the cases. Common sense dictated they must be linked: Ronnebach, Höfler and Unterbrink all being despatched by the same method. Then Lothar Schneider apparently being ambushed, his throat cut. Müller assumed that was because he was about to blow the case wide open by telling her some vital information about the killings.

She looked up at the block. Apartment 210 – presumably the second floor. Would Frau Unterbrink know what connected these four dead men? More importantly, would she be prepared to tell Müller, without first alerting the Stasi?

The woman who opened the door to the apartment was considerably younger than Müller had been expecting. Pretty, too, with an almost elfin face, framed by straight black hair cut in a fringe, with bangs each side.

'I'm *Major* Karin Müller of the People's Police.' Again Müller deliberately chose not to mention the *Kripo*, and she showed a standard *Vopo* ID. 'I'm sorry to disturb you but I wanted to talk to Frau Unterbrink. Is that you?'

'No. It's my mother you want. Is it about my father's accident?' Müller nodded.

'You'd better come in.' Then the woman lowered her voice to a whisper. 'As you can imagine, she's not taken it too well.

So please treat her gently. I've been staying with her since it happened. She's sitting through here in the lounge. Can I get you a coffee or anything?'

'Please. A little milk, but no sugar.'

Frau Unterbrink's daughter showed her through. The mother was sitting, staring into space, nursing a hot drink in her hands.

'Mutti. This is *Major* Müller from the People's Police. She wants to ask you a few questions about the accident.'

The woman looked confused. 'Why? The police seem to know more than we do anyway. They should be down at the factory asking them questions.' She sniffed, and Müller detected redness around her eyes as though she'd recently been crying. 'How could something like that happen in this day and age? That's what they should be asking.'

'I'm sorry, Frau Unterbrink. I'm sure my colleagues will be doing just that. We're taking it very seriously. May I sit down?'

The woman shrugged. Müller took it as a 'yes', sat at the dining table, and got out her notebook and pen.

The daughter smiled at her. 'I'll just go and sort out your coffee.'

'Use the *Kaffee Mix*, Sabine. We've not got much left of the other. And I'm sure as a member of the authorities, the lady policewoman would like to help the State by using the type of coffee the high-ups want us to use.'

'I'd be very grateful for whatever you can give me, Frau Unterbrink.' Müller picked up her pen and clicked it into the writing position. 'As part of our investigations into the accident,

I want to get a sense of your husband's life. Would it be all right to ask a few questions about that?'

'His death tells you all you need to know. The factory was up against ridiculous targets – they seemed to grow each year. Heinz felt under pressure to do more and more. He wasn't happy in his work any more. It's obvious they must have been taking short cuts. Why else would an inspection ramp fail?'

Müller felt slightly guilty that she was unable to reveal the truth to the widow. But Unterbrink was dead. There was nothing she could do to turn back time. Her duty was to try to find out why, and to catch the killer before he could strike again. 'I'm sure that's something my colleagues will look into.' The lies were coming too easily. 'So your husband was under pressure at work. Was he under any other pressure at all? Had anything from his—'

She was interrupted by Sabine Unterbrink returning with her coffee. The younger woman placed it in front of Müller, and the detective breathed in the rich aroma. It certainly smelt like the real thing. She took a sip, expecting to be disappointed by the weak ersatz taste. Instead, her taste buds revelled in the crisp sharpness, the acidity, the chocolatey aftertaste. It *was* the real thing. Out of her mother's eyeline, the daughter gave Müller a little conspiratorial smile.

'Sorry, Frau Unterbrink. I was just asking whether anything from your husband's past life had recently raised its head. Anything that might have disturbed him, affected his concentration?'

The mother's face took on a severe frown. 'What a strange question! What on earth has that got to do with my husband's accident?'

Müller tried another tack. 'Have you and your husband always lived here?'

'These flats were only built a few years ago, so obviously not.'

Müller tried to ignore the open hostility the woman was showing. 'And had he always worked in the car industry?' she continued.

Frau Unterbrink gave a long sigh, as though the question almost wasn't worth answering. 'He'd always been interested in mechanics, but in the early days only as an amateur. He used to be in the fire service.'

'The fire service?' *How odd.* Someone involved in fighting fires caught up in a murder investigation where fire and smoke had been used as a means of murder. Was that just coincidence, or something more?

'That's what I said, didn't I? He changed career, but he'd always been technical – there would have been transferrable skills.'

'Why did he change career?'

The woman snorted. 'Why would I know that? And if I did, why would I tell you?'

Sabine, alongside her mother, rolled her eyes. 'Mutti, this policewoman's only trying to help. You know that you haven't always lived in—'

'Be quiet, Sabine. I will answer the questions as I see fit, but only,' she turned to Müller and fixed her with an angry glare, 'if they are directly about the accident. Otherwise you can get out of my apartment, now.'

Müller frowned herself now. 'Frau Unterbrink, I *am* trying to help. I simply need to fill in a few details about your husband's past. I'm particularly interested to know if you or he ever lived in Gardel—'

'No!' shouted the woman. 'Get out of my home. I said I would only answer questions about the actual accident. Get out, now.'

'Frau Unterbrink, obstructing a police—'

The woman picked up a glass ashtray, and made as if to throw it at Müller. 'I won't tell you again. I won't be responsible for my actions unless you leave now. Do the Ministry of State Security know you are here?' Something in Müller's face must have betrayed her subterfuge. 'No, I thought not. They told me not to answer any questions, not from the police or anyone. I wasn't very happy about that; I thought they were just trying to cover up what happened. But I can see that perhaps they were right after all. Sabine, see this lady out, please.'

Müller gathered up her pen and notebook, and replaced them in her bag. It had been another less than satisfactory attempt to interview a victim's widow. In fact, this had been the least productive so far, just when Müller had glimpsed a possible breakthrough.

She didn't bother to say goodbye to the woman, even though, perhaps her erratic, angry, behaviour was understandable, as a recently bereaved woman.

Sabine gave Müller a small smile as she was seeing Müller out of the door, and beckoned her closer. As the woman prepared to speak into her ear, Müller could smell her perfume. The floral-citrus tones seemed to set her even more on edge, bouncing on her toes, hoping this was the moment.

'You were asking if anything from my father's past life had raised its head?'

'Yes,' whispered Müller, matching the still-lowered tones of Sabine.

'I might be able to give you some further help on that,' said Sabine. 'But it would be better if we didn't talk here.' Müller felt a sense of mounting excitement. She didn't know if she could trust Frau Unterbrink's daughter not to tell her mother if they did have another meeting, and she thought it was highly likely the mother would be alerting the Stasi in any case. But what did she have to lose? 'It's all right, you don't have to say anything,' continued Sabine. 'If you want to know more, let's meet tonight. Eight p.m. in the Schlossbar, in the centre of town.'

31

12 April 1945
Gardelegen, Nazi Germany

How many times can you stare death in the face before it comes to claim you?

We're marching down the road, with some of us – including Marcellin – barely able to shuffle. I still try to help him, but my strength is failing too.

At the last moment, a car arrived up the track from Estedt to the woods, and the clearing where we had dug our own graves. It was hard to understand what was going on, other than that a messenger had arrived with some sort of change of plan, which was handed to the German paratroopers. We had been spared, at least for the time being. The see-saw between life and death was too much for one Russian. He fainted on the spot. His reward: a bullet in the back of the head.

We have been ordered to march from Estedt to Gardelegen, where apparently we must assemble in the cavalry school compound. There – we are told – there will be shelter and food. None of the German troops escort us, but we seem to have lost our will to rebel or think for ourselves, numbed by hunger, thirst, and dashed hopes of being saved by the advancing Americans. A Czech prisoner urges us to go in the other direction, to try to meet up with the Allied forces. But most of us just want to stop walking. If the underground rocket factory was Hell, then what is this march? Perhaps it is a march to our deaths.

We trudge on for what seems like hours towards the town. We try to find food in barns, in fields, but armed villagers chase us off.

At one farm, a woman comes out and tries to offer us some raw potatoes. It would be something to fill the emptiness in our stomachs, to dull the pain. She's chased off by an armed youth with a Nazi armband.

When we enter the town limits, I notice Marcellin and I are lagging behind again.

'You go on, Philippe. Please, I beg you. I am finished. I just want to lie down and die. Or be shot. I don't care.'

As if someone's heard his words, a shot does ring out, then a few pitiful screams from behind us, then silence. We look round. We hadn't been the last of our column. Some twenty metres behind us, the prisoner who had been limping at the end has been downed by a bullet. His arm gropes towards us in his death throes. Marcellin makes a move to limp back towards him. I grab my brother.

'No. There is nothing we can do. We need to catch up. We need to save ourselves. We are sitting ducks in these uniforms.'

Suddenly, every townsperson, many of them armed, seems to be our enemy. Soldiers with guns are haring round on motorcycles, like cowboys from the Wild West that we saw in those American films just before the war started, and in the early days before the Germans came.

We reach the town centre. It's a pretty town in the middle, despite the evidence of war. If I close my eyes, I can almost imagine myself in a market town in France. At least these German pigs will have been driven out of my homeland by now. If the Allies are just a few kilometres away from here, that must be the case. My country must be free – I just hope that Marcellin and I will get the chance to see it again, to breathe in the salt air from the sea wall path between La Couarde and Loix. To smell my home.

Grégoire will never do that again.

We are excited now. There is a rumour Gardelegen has been declared a hospital town. We're going to be handed over to the Allies. I feel a sudden rush of joy through my whole weakened body. I start to tremble from the inside and have to fight back tears. Marcellin's face, though, is greyer than ever. He is barely clinging on.

When we reach the cavalry school, we see most of the horses being led out. Presumably the Germans want to keep them out of Allied hands if they can. We are ushered into the stables the horses have vacated.

Being treated like animals – worse than animals – seems appropriate, somehow. Now we are living where the animals lived. But I'm not complaining. There is straw to lie on, and the smell of food being prepared.

Out in the cavalry ring, we line up to receive our meagre rations. A loaf of bread each, and a bowl of thin soup. It's nothing more than flavoured water, with a few bits of old potato in the bottom.

But it's the first meal for days. The first liquid we've drunk other than stagnant water from ditches and pools by the roadside.

Once we've eaten and we are back in the stables, lying down uncaring about the stink of horse shit, I start to feel sleepy. I try to keep myself awake to watch over Marcellin. I worry that when he sleeps he may not wake up. But finally, I drift off into the land of dreams. I am full of hope now, that we *are* going to be saved.

32

Müller arrived fifteen minutes early to the bar to meet Sabine. She'd already rung Helga to talk to the twins, to say that she loved them, and to ask them to be good for Oma. Not that they were old enough to really understand her entreaties. But she at least got some kissing noises in return and shouts of 'Mutti, Mutti' down the phone line. Being good for Oma wasn't strictly accurate anyway. Helga was really their *Tick-Tock Oma* – their great-grandmother – but neither Helga nor Müller wanted to complicate the toddlers' lives with that distinction at this stage.

Sabine Unterbrink turned the heads of the mostly male drinkers when she finally turned up, around five minutes late. She was an attractive young woman, little more than a girl really, thought Müller. There was no doubt that if Tilsner had been here, he would have been trying to chat her up.

She saw Müller in the corner seat and sat down next to her. Again, she smelt the same waft of perfume. Müller was trying to place it – then suddenly she did. When she'd made the brief foray into West Berlin in the middle of the graveyard girl case more than two years earlier, she'd had to shop for a list of items at Jäger's behest. She had indulged herself by trying a few perfume sprays on the back of her hand. This was one of them. She was sure.

'Chanel Number 5,' said Sabine.

Müller looked startled.

'I could see you sniffing the air outside the apartment door when we were talking, and then again just now. My grandmother's in the West. She sent it as a present.'

'It's lovely,' laughed Müller. 'I went on assignment to West Berlin a couple of years ago. I tried a tester then.' She gave a small laugh. 'I couldn't afford to buy any, though.'

'I didn't think they allowed police officers from the East over to the West. I thought it was only pensioners.'

'It is, usually. As I say, it was a special assignment. Anyway, we're not here to talk perfume. What was it you wanted to tell me?'

Sabine cocked her head, considering the question for a moment. 'I will tell you as much as I know – which probably isn't everything you want or need to know. But first, I want you to answer a question.'

'Go on.'

'You're not really investigating the accident, are you?'

Müller frowned. She wondered how much she could tell this young woman, who she barely knew. She might just be genuinely curious – it was her father who had been killed, after all. She might something else entirely – an agent for the Ministry for State Security. But she was the one who'd volunteered information in the first place, and who had asked for the meeting. Sometimes you had to take things on trust – whatever the risks.

Müller looked around, then lowered her voice so that only Sabine would be able to hear. 'I *am* investigating the accident – but I'm not one of the official investigators, if that makes any sense. I'd be very grateful if you'd keep that information to yourself.'

Sabine nodded, and grinned. 'Of course. So who do you work for – is it really the police, or is it the Stasi?' There was a breathless excitement to the question – almost as though this was all a game to the young woman.

Instead of answering, Müller got out her *Kripo* ID, the new one with her rank, *Major*, and the fact that she was the head of the Serious Crimes Department.

The schoolgirlish grin was wiped from Sabine's face. 'So there *is* something more to this. It wasn't an accident, was it?'

Müller sighed. 'It's me who's asking the questions, Sabine. Now tell me about this thing from your father's past.'

'Sorry, yes, of course. There isn't much, I'm afraid, but I didn't want any chance of my mother overhearing.' Müller nodded, encouraging her to continue. 'About a week before my father was killed, I was round their apartment while my mother was out. I took a phone message from someone calling himself Lothar Schneider.'

Müller tried to hide the excitement from her face, but she could see that Sabine realised the name was significant.

'What was the message?'

'Well, first he asked if he could speak to my father. I explained he was at work, and even gave him his extension at the car factory. But he didn't seem to want to ring Vati at work.' For the first time, Müller noticed Sabine's eyes glistening. She'd shown no signs of grief so far; clearly, remembering this felt significant to her.

'Then I remember his voice became sort of strange. It sounded like he was excited, or frightened or something. He was speaking quite quickly. I was having to get him to repeat things. He wanted my father to meet him. He gave me an exact time, and even some grid coordinates.'

'Grid coordinates?' Müller began to get alarmed. This sounded exactly like the message to her at Keibelstrasse. 'Can you remember what they were?'

'I can do better than that,' said Sabine, reaching into her handbag. 'I made a copy for myself as well as for my father.'

'Why on earth did you do that?'

'I could tell it was something strange. Something dangerous.' A single tear had started to fall from Sabine's eye. Müller offered the girl her handkerchief, after she'd drawn a piece of paper from the handbag.

'Here you are,' she sniffed.

Müller opened the folded piece of paper. She was almost certain she knew what the coordinates would be, and she was correct.

52°34'26.3"N 11°20'55.3"E

It was the exact spot in the woods near Estedt where she had been summoned to. But it was the date and time which made her grip the paper so hard, she found her knuckles turning white.

Saturday 29 July at 1 p.m.

It wasn't just the exact place. It was the very time that Müller and Tilsner had heard the scream in the woods, then found the blood in the clearing, and seen the 4x4 racing away, presumably with Lothar Schneider inside.

On his way to his death.

33

'Are you all right?' asked Sabine.

'Yes, yes. Of course.' Müller tried to gather herself. 'This is very useful. Can I keep this piece of paper?'

'By all means.'

Some of the possibilities ran round inside Müller's head. Had Schneider been intending to reveal what this was all about, getting Unterbrink to provide corroboration? Or – as Tilsner had alleged might be the case – had Schneider been trying to lure both Müller herself, as well as Unterbrink, to their deaths – but instead had met his own? And was his death linked to this message? Had the phone been tapped, and the message intercepted by the Stasi? Or – as Müller had already wondered – was the young woman sitting next to her a Stasi agent, currently playing Müller to see exactly what she knew? Whatever the truth, for the moment Sabine still seemed her best source of information.

Finally, Müller framed another question. 'How did your father react when he got the note?'

'His face went white as a sheet. Like someone had walked over his grave.' Müller knew what she meant – she remembered seeing the exact same look on Tilsner's face at the start of this mystery, something her deputy had tried to explain away as 'girlfriend troubles'. 'Vati tore the note up, but as he did so I noticed that his fingers were trembling. He saw that I noticed. When he looked at me, his eyes weren't just full of fear – there was an awful sadness there. As though he knew something terrible was about to happen.'

Müller sighed, and took a sip of her beer.

'I couldn't resist checking on a map where the grid reference was,' continued Sabine, 'and then it made some sense to me. You know where it is, don't you? You were asking about the same place until my mother refused to answer any more questions.'

'Yes. I know where it is. I still don't understand the full significance.'

Sabine stretched her arms above her head. 'Even before he received that contact from this Schneider person, I could tell Vati seemed troubled.'

Müller frowned. 'In what way?'

'He started letting himself go. Women notice those things more, I suppose. Forgetting or not bothering to put on deodorant, not cutting his fingernails or toenails, not washing his hair, that sort of thing. In some ways, when I heard about this accident – though I don't believe it was an accident, and I suspect you know full well it wasn't – I wasn't entirely surprised, because his mind was elsewhere. In those circumstances it's easy enough to make a mistake.'

'It wasn't a mistake,' said Müller.

'Can you tell me what really happened?'

'I don't know the full story, Sabine. And what I do know, I'm not at liberty to tell you at present. What I promise you is once my investigation is complete, I will give you the full facts – I owe you that for all the help you're giving me.'

'Thank you,' said the woman, her voice catching with emotion. 'There is some more. As I say, I could tell my father was troubled. I thought perhaps he – or my mother – had been having an affair. I've always felt closer to Vati, so I asked him.'

'Go on.'

'He told me he'd been involved in something awful during the war, where he used to live. He claimed that he hadn't instigated anything himself, and that he was simply following orders – and indeed tried to resist those orders, and help the victims. I asked him outright: "Were you a Nazi?"'

Things were starting to become clearer to Müller. She felt her stomach tingling – was that what this was all about?

'And was he?' she asked.

'He didn't answer directly at first. He simply said: "You didn't live through those times, Sabine. Almost everyone who did had some sort of stain on their character." He said he was little more than a boy when Hitler came to power. It soon became all but compulsory to join the Hitler Youth movement – my father claimed you couldn't avoid it. By the end of the war, he was still in his early twenties. He told me: "Terrible things happened, things I can't forget, but at the time we believed we were doing what we did for the best. Even if our own eyes told us differently."'

Sabine paused, wiping her eyes.

'So you believe your father was involved in something terrible? Involving the Nazis?'

She nodded sadly.

'But you don't know what it was?'

She shook her head. 'That was pretty much all he would say. I did manage to find out one more thing.'

'What?'

'My father said that at some point – in order to live on safely in the Republic – he had to start again elsewhere.'

'What do you mean?'

'He constructed a new life here in Eisenach, at the car factory. To hide his past during the war in . . .'

Sabine had paused, as though she herself was unable to contemplate what had gone on. What her now dead father may have been responsible for.

But Müller could complete the sentence for her. 'In Gardelegen. What he'd been responsible for in Gardelegen.'

Sabine held her head in her hands, as the tears fell, a transformation from the earlier meeting at the family apartment when she'd eagerly offered to tell Müller more.

They were tears of shame, Müller assumed, shed on behalf of her murdered father.

Müller had intended to stay the night in Eisenach, but she knew she couldn't do that now. She had to piece this puzzle together – to solve the murders of those who'd been killed so far, and to catch the killer before he struck again.

So she drove north, some 250 kilometres. As fast as the Lada would travel, without endangering herself or breaking the law. It would take her more than four hours, even if she didn't stop for a break. But she had to get there. She had to know.

It was after midnight by the time she reached the edge of the town, and it took another five minutes to reach number 73, Stendaler Strasse. She'd been checking her rear-view mirror Every few minutes, expecting at some point to see someone from the Stasi tailing her. So far, they didn't seem to be. After parking the car, she rang the entry phone for Apartment 18. There was no answer. She tried again, and again. Eventually, a woman's sleepy voice answered. 'Who is it? It's after midnight. You'll wake the whole neighbourhood.'

'It's the *Kriminalpolizei*, Frau Schneider. We need to talk to you urgently.'

Frau Liselotte Schneider had her nightgown wrapped tightly around her. She seemed almost to shrink in on herself, illuminated by a single table lamp so that her thin face was shadowed in a sinister way. She didn't offer Müller coffee – no doubt hoping she could get her out of the door as soon as possible.

'I'm sorry to disturb you and rake up bad memories, Frau Schneider.'

'It's all right. I've got some preparation to do, but otherwise it's the summer holidays. What did you say your name was again?'

'Karin Müller. *Major* Karin Müller of the Serious Crimes Department of the *Kriminalpolizei* in Berlin.'

The woman frowned. 'Ah. I think you were the one Lothar . . .' She broke off and choked back a sob. 'Weren't you the one Lothar wanted to meet?'

'He did try to set up a meeting with me, yes.'

'When?'

'On the day he was killed, I'm afraid.'

'You didn't tell anyone about the meeting, did you? Could that be why he was killed?' The woman got to her feet, and had moved across to a writing bureau. She switched on a desk lamp, and then began rummaging around without saying what she was looking for.

'I didn't, no. The only people who knew, as far as I'm aware, were myself and my deputy.' As she said the words, it felt like her blood seemed to freeze in her veins. *Tilsner*. Had he betrayed Schneider to the Stasi? But then she remembered – she hadn't actually given him the coordinates or details until they reached Estedt.

'Anyway, perhaps he had some sort of premonition about it. Perhaps he knew he would never get to talk to you in person.' She handed Müller an envelope with her name on it. 'He entrusted me with this, to give to you – and only you – if anything should happen to him. I put it away in the drawer. I'm sorry, I should have tried to contact you to give you it before now. But the Ministry for State Security insisted I should talk to no one but them.' The woman gave a weak smile. 'They also told me to contact them if you should ever come round here asking questions. But I think I'll forget about that part.'

Müller mouthed a 'thank you' to the woman. She recognised Schneider's handwriting from the note he'd sent her – the one with the coordinates for his chosen meeting point in the wood to the west of Estedt. The one where he met his death.

She was almost scared to open the envelope. Finally, she breathed in deeply, and tore it open.

Dear Major Müller,

If you are reading this, it almost certainly means that our intended rendezvous did not take place and that I have been arrested.

One other person has tried to thrust all this out into the open before. His name is Ernst Lehmann. If I have not been able to speak to you, I suggest you go to talk to him, if you can reach him. As far as I know, he is in the Stasi jail in Potsdam. But my information may be incorrect.

With friendly greetings,

Herr Lothar Schneider

Frau Schneider was trying to peer over her shoulder. But Müller's mind was racing. She needed to speak to this Ernst Lehmann – and quickly. Further questioning of Schneider's widow would have to wait.

Somehow she had to get access to this Stasi prison in Potsdam.

34

Transcribed and translated interview with Hitler Youth member Günther Palitzsch, conducted by Captain Arthur T. Wagner of the Ninth Army War Crimes Branch on 25 April 1945, at 1100 hours

Wagner: Now, Günther, I want to turn our attention to the events of the 12th of April. I believe you were at that time working on the Isenschnibbe estate, near Gardelegen.

Palitzsch: That's correct. I was a groom.

Wagner: You looked after the horses on the estate. Was that all you did?

Palitzsch: I was a member of the Hitler Youth movement too.

Wagner: Describe the atmosphere for us on that day. How did it feel? Were you frightened? Afraid of what would happen after the town surrendered?

Palitzsch: Yes, but it wasn't only that. We were afraid of the prisoners too – the Zebras. We'd heard what had happened at the village of Kakerbeck. That's about fifteen kilometres north of Gardelegen. There were various stories of the prisoners escaping, running amok, raping women and children and looting homes. Everyone was afraid that would happen here, in Gardelegen, too. Everyone was scared that as soon as the Americans arrived, the prisoners would be set free, and they would take their revenge on us. The SS and the *Fallschirmjäger* were saying there needed to be a solution. My boss was throwing a party for all the departing soldiers that evening.

Wagner: Your 'boss' being?

Palitzsch: Frau Bloch von Blochwitz. She's the owner of the estate. The lady of the manor. She's getting on a bit. Must be in her eighties, I think. I hope you're going to interview her too. She's got a lot to answer for.

Wagner: I'm sure we will. But that's not your concern. You say there was going to be a party?

Palitzsch: There *was* a party. You'd have thought the troops would be out fighting on the front line. But lots of them were at Isenschnibbe. I was one of the waiters for the evening so I saw what went on.

Wagner: I thought you were a groom?

Palitzsch: I am. I was. Well, I don't know what will happen now. But whenever her ladyship held events, I had to help out as one of the waiting staff. So I saw everything that went on. I heard everything that went on. I always say you should keep quiet and listen. You can learn a lot that way. Anyway, there was lots of drinking going on. I felt a few of them shouldn't have any more, and I told her ladyship that. Some of them were blind drunk. I suppose they knew defeat was inevitable. They were drinking away their sorrows.

Wagner: And you say these were SS and *Fallschirmjäger* officers?

Palitzsch: Mainly. The ones I recognised, yes. But I think there were also the SA, *Wehrmacht* people, and local leaders of the Nazi Party. It was hard to tell, though, because many of them were already in civilian clothes. The clothes they hoped to flee to safety in. Then after a couple of hours the *Kreisleiter* of Gardelegen, Gerhard Thiele, bursts into the sitting room. He's very agitated, and I don't think best pleased that so many of the officers are drunk. He says: 'Here I am with a thousand criminals on my hands. The Yankees are just down the road. They'll be here in a couple of days. What on earth can I do?'

Wagner: And that's when you say Frau Bloch von Blochwitz said the words you claim she said.

Palitzsch: I don't claim it. She did say it.

Wagner: But you don't have a note of it?

Palitzsch: Why would I have a note of it? I was a waiter for the evening. Serving drinks. I overheard it, but those were her exact words.

Wagner: All right, Günther. I'm not questioning your recollection. Let's take a short break.

35

Müller was thankful she'd filled up the Lada at a filling station on the edge of Eisenach – she doubted she'd find one at this time of night in the wilds of Bezirk Magdeburg.

It was now after one in the morning. There seemed no point in driving on when she had little faith in her ability to talk her way into a Stasi prison, major in the People's Police or not. The guards at the prison would simply refer her request upwards, and at that point there would be a big red flag against her name at Stasi headquarters in Normannenstrasse in the Hauptstadt.

Instead, she found a forest track off the main road, drove a few metres down it, then pulled to the side in case any early morning forestry workers needed to get through. She opened the boot of the Lada, brought out the blanket she kept there in case of emergencies, and then stretched out as far as she could on the back seat of the car, using her jacket as a makeshift pillow.

Sleep wouldn't come easily. She knew she'd made mistakes in this inquiry, but she was still technically on her annual leave – and had been taken off the case. It had only been the fortuitous intervention of the white-haired Dr Eckstein, aided and abetted it seemed by *Oberst* Reiniger, that had pushed her to get back on the case. But her biggest mistake had been not consulting the history books. Something had happened in or near Gardelegen during the war. She should have looked into that as soon as she saw that photograph of the Ronnebachs – or at least as soon as it was confirmed that the photograph was of Gardelegen town hall. It was a job for Schmidt. She'd get some sleep and then phone him first thing in the morning. He owed her one anyway. She still hadn't decided how to proceed with what had been a very serious bit of duplicity on his part.

She woke, aching and cold, just before 6 a.m. when a bird or animal started walking across the Lada, the tap tap tap going backwards and forwards like a hammer on the car's metal roof.

Müller got out and stretched. Her bones and sinews seemed to crack as they were cajoled back into place. Her clothes felt damp from the condensation in the car. Of the summer camps on the Ostsee with Gottfried. Of simpler, happier times. But then she thought of Jannika and Johannes. Was she doing the correct thing leaving them in the care of Helga? Was it fair? After being blessed with children, after so many barren years, shouldn't she now be spending more time with them? She knew she should be. But she also knew she had to see this case to its conclusion.

She drove on for an hour, through Stendal and across the Elbe again at Tangermünde, retracing the journey she'd taken with Tilsner only a few days earlier. Then went south to Genthin.

On the outskirts of the town, she spotted a yellow public call box, parked the car, and then proceeded to ring Schmidt. It was just after 7 a.m. He would probably be up and eating breakfast by now.

On this occasion, his wife was decidedly less cheerful in her greeting of Müller.

'What is it you want this time?' she asked defensively.

'I'd like to speak to Jonas, please, Frau Schmidt. It's nothing to worry about.'

'No doubt you said that to him last time,' said the woman, a bitter edge to her voice.

Müller heard Schmidt remonstrating with his wife in the background.

'Sorry, Comrade *Major*. My wife is never at her best in the morning. What can I do for you?'

'I want you to look up some World War Two history for me, Jonas.'

'Oh yes? That doesn't sound too difficult.'

'What do you know about Gardelegen?'

'Not a lot, Comrade *Major*. I think it's somewhere in Bezirk Magdeburg, isn't it? To the west of here. Isn't it fairly near the state border?'

'It is, Jonas, yes. But what I want to know about is what happened there during the war. I get the feeling it was something fairly momentous.'

'I can't imagine that will be too difficult to find out, Comrade *Major*. It won't require forensic science expertise.'

'I'm aware of that, Jonas. But you're good at research, and it's research I want. And not just on the events. Try to find out about the people, and what happened to them, by any means you can.'

'I understand, Comrade *Major*. Consider it done.'

Müller wasn't looking forward to her next call. First, she fished in her jacket pocket to pull out some more coins. Then she fed them into the slot, and dialled.

'Who is it?' barked Tilsner.

'That's not a very pleasant way to greet your superior.'

'Oh. It's you. What do you want? Aren't you on annual leave?'

'I was. A case came up near where we were holidaying. So that was the end of the holiday.'

Müller could hear her deputy's anger in the silence at the other end of the line.

'Are you still there, Werner?'

'I'm still here, yes. I thought we were a team. Why didn't you send for me to help?'

'It was down in Eisenach. The Wartburg factory. An accident there.'

Tilsner snorted. 'I thought your accident investigation days were a thing of the past. You always said that the Königs Wusterhausen disaster gave you nightmares for years afterwards.'

'It did. It still does. Anyway, I'm ringing you because I need a bit of help now. You know that watch I always tease you about?'

Müller could almost envisage the grumpy frown that would have settled on her deputy's face. He sighed loudly down the line. 'Not that again. I've told you before, change the record.'

'Just listen to me a moment. Let's say for a moment I was right in my suppositions about the wa—'

'Give it a rest, Karin. I've said I don't want to talk about it.'

'Wait a moment. Don't get angry. Just imagine I was correct. If I was, do you have an ID that goes with the membership of that organisation?'

'What? You expect me to tell you that over an open phone line? Have you gone completely mad?'

'You don't have to tell me if I'm right. You don't have to answer the question. But – if it's true – I want you to bring the ID with you, and meet me at the junction of Hegelallee and Lindenstrasse in Potsdam in an hour-and-a-half's time.'

'And what it if it's not true?'

'Still come and meet me, and I'll bring you up to speed.'

36

Müller wasn't certain that Tilsner would turn up. So she was delighted to see him parked up near the junction, sitting in the Wartburg. She found a parking space as near to him as possible, and reversed the Lada into it.

By the time she'd turned the engine off, and collected her jacket and bag, Tilsner was already leaning over the driver's door.

'You summoned me, madam, and I am here to do your bidding.'

'Good. Let's take a walk first. I'll show you some history.'

Their 'walk' was just a few metres to the impressive Jägertor – the preserved city gate from Old Potsdam, dating back to the eighteenth century.

'I hope you're not taking me on a guided tour of Potsdam's sights,' grumbled Tilsner. 'I hate sightseeing. I'd much rather go for a coffee.'

'I just wanted to talk where we couldn't be overheard, or at least where we can see everyone who's approaching.'

'OK. Why all the secret squirrel stuff?'

'Did you bring the ID?'

'Look, I've told you I'm not getting into all that.'

Müller cocked her head in what she hoped was a coquettish way. 'Pretty please?'

Tilsner punched her on the arm. 'I'm not discussing it. But I heard what you said on the phone. You can draw any conclusion you want from that.'

'All right, let's assume you've got your ID.'

'I'm not saying anything.'

'Would it get us in to see someone at 54 Lindenstrasse?'

'What?! The Stasi prison?'

Müller nodded.

Tilsner gave a long, drawn-out sigh. 'If one had such an ID, I would assume it might get you into the reception. It might get you into the office to speak to an officer. Was that what you had in mind?'

'No.'

'No, I thought not.' He shook his head slowly. 'Sometimes, I just think you're lucky.'

'Why?'

'I have a couple of mates who work there. There is the off-chance I might be able to get in; we may even be able to interview a prisoner. I assume that is what you want. But I will do it via my *Vopo* ID. Nothing else. I have nothing else. Do you still have that old *Vopo* ID you had from when you were an *Unterleutnant*?'

Müller hunted through her bag, and found it. 'Yes, it's here. Why?'

'Because, dear Karin, for once in your life to make this work you are going to be my deputy. Comrade *Unterleutnant* Karin Müller. It has a much nicer ring to it than *Major*, don't you think?'

37

13 April 1945
Gardelegen, Nazi Germany

Each time Marcellin is given some food, it seems to revive him a little. But every time he moves, I see him wincing. The wound on his arm is starting to smell. I can't bring myself to look at it any more. Every time I do, it looks worse. It is not healing.

'Surely the Americans should be here by now?' he whispers to me. I can see the desperation in his eyes. I take it as a good sign. He still has a little hope in his heart.

There is indeed some activity this morning. When we arrived here in the cavalry school barracks, the SS guards had begun looking for new *Kapo* guards amongst us – to replace, presumably, other German guards who'd fled in the face of the American advance and the impending surrender. It was the Germans they wanted – communists, criminals, anyone who'd fallen foul of the Nazi regime and ended up in a labour camp like us. Around twenty-five of the prisoners stepped forward to volunteer. Most of them were indeed Germans, but there were also a few Poles. None of us French. They knew we hated them and would never do it.

At the underground rocket factory, the *Kapos* had never been armed, save for the batons they wielded, which they had smashed into mine and Marcellin's back with regularity. If I ever get to inspect myself in a mirror, I expect the bruises will still be there, if there's any flesh left.

But sometime around midday, the SS come into the stables and gather the *Kapos* together. They ask which of them can fire a rifle. Just under twenty of them raise their hands, and are led away, the others are returned to the barracks. I wasn't particularly worried by this – if the Germans are preparing an operation to hand us over to the Allies, they will probably need to guard us on the way, given some of the antipathy some of the townsfolk have shown towards us 'zebras'.

A few hours later, there is more activity. The *Kapos* who were led off are now back, armed with rifles and ammunition. Together with the SS, they start forming us into groups of about a hundred prisoners each. Something is happening. It looks like – finally – we are being marched out to be handed over to the Americans. I find myself biting my lip, saying 'please, please' to myself under my breath. I feel almost tearful through joy.

It doesn't surprise me that Marcellin is judged too weak to walk. There are three carts, two being pulled by horses, one by a tractor. It's clear the weakest will be taken to the Americans in the carts. I don't want us to be separated. I plead with one of the SS guards, even though I know that doing so is a risk. If he loses his temper, he could simply shoot me dead on the spot.

The guard laughs. 'Of course. Why not? Brothers should never be separated. It'll be like a taxi ride for you both.' His tone is mocking. I know he regards us as worse than pieces of shit. But I will put up with the humiliation in order to stay with my brother.

I chance my luck by asking another question: 'Why are we being moved?'

Again, the mocking laugh. 'It's just getting too crowded in the barracks, that's all. We need to find you some more space.' One of the other guards laughs knowingly at this, and spits on the floor. I just assume this is bravado – soldiers of a defeated nation not wanting to admit when they've been beaten. They would never acknowledge to us that they're about to surrender.

We're led towards the north out of the cavalry school. The first group of several hundred – perhaps three hundred – marches off as we wait in the carts. I find myself fidgeting, eager to get on with it, excited about what the American troops will look like. Do they even know about us? Did they know about the secret underground factory? Presumably they did, and that was why it was bombed to bits in those final days before we were moved out.

There are a surprising number of guards. Not just the twenty or so armed *Kapos*. There are at least as many – if not more – SS men, some of them with dogs.

Finally, after three groups of prisoners have been marched off, we are underway. But after a kilometre or so the convoy stops, and the other groups of prisoners have come to a halt too. Perhaps there is some confusion about the handover to the Americans, but my hope's not dimmed. We see a tractor passing, towing a trailer with various goods on it and what look like ammunition boxes and fuel cans. Presumably as part of the surrender, the Germans have to hand over their arms.

The walking groups begin to march again, and eventually we follow. After another kilometre along a farm lane, we reach a large masonry barn on a gentle hill. I turn my head and can see all the way to Gardelegen, where we've just come from. Presumably beyond that is Mieste, where the train stopped, and to the north Estedt, where I came within seconds of losing my life. Now I'm about to be freed. It feels good.

Suddenly we see an Allied warplane circling overhead. The guards usher us into the barn, the weakest from the carts going first. Inside it is empty, save for a bed of straw on the floor. At least we will be able to gather that together to make ourselves beds.

'I don't like the look of this, Philippe,' says Marcellin. 'What's that smell of petrol?'

It's true, there is a strong smell of fuel. But I seek to reassure him. 'It's a farm building. Machinery will have been stored here too. They've got to put us somewhere. Stay strong. By morning we will probably be free, and we can finally get that arm looked at.'

He smiles at me then, and for an instant, in the half-light of the barn, I see the old Marcellin. The fearless Marcellin of the band of three brothers. The pirates of the *Celestine*. And I feel my heart fill with love for him.

38

While Müller waited in the public reception room at the Stasi jail, she found herself crossing and uncrossing her legs. Then picking at her fingernails as she wondered if Tilsner was actually doing what he said he would try to do – gain access to Ernst Lehmann for her. Or whether he was even now on the phone to *Oberst* Jäger at Stasi headquarters.

After a few minutes, Tilsner returned with a Stasi officer. A captain, like her deputy. Müller could tell from the four gold stars on his grey-green uniform epaulettes. A thought flashed in her brain: *He's here to arrest me.*

But he wasn't.

'This is *Unterleutnant* Müller,' said Tilsner. 'She's a trainee detective on attachment from the uniform division assisting me with our inquiries into the robbery.' Tilsner grinned at Müller, out of sight of the Stasi captain. He was enjoying this.

The captain nodded slowly. 'And why do you think Lehmann can help you?'

'He was friends with one of the ringleaders who at the moment isn't talking,' answered Tilsner. 'We think Lehmann may have information that will help us to get him to talk. To reveal where they stashed the money.'

'And why do you think Lehmann will talk to you, a *Kriminalpolizei* detective, when he hasn't responded to our . . . *methods.*' As he said this, the Stasi captain was looking at Müller's chest. She realised her lightweight bra and thin blouse was probably showing too much. She adjusted it self-consciously. *Little does he know I slept in these clothes last night in the car. They probably stink to high heaven.*

Tilsner cracked his knuckles: his right hand, then his left. It sounded like the snap of a bone breaking. 'We've got our own methods. Don't worry. *Unterleutnant* Müller here may look like butter wouldn't melt in her mouth, but take it from me, you wouldn't want to get a kick in the balls from her. Lehmann won't like it either if he doesn't cooperate.'

The captain smiled at Müller as he jiggled a set of keys in his hand. 'Intriguing. I'd like to see that.'

'Maybe one day, Hans, but this time we want him on our own if that's OK. We won't need more than about ten minutes.' He cracked his knuckle again to emphasise the point.

The Stasi officer shrugged, pressed a button and then spoke into the intercom, before leading them into the inner sanctum of the prison.

When they looked through the spyhole into the cell, Müller could see the prisoner – Lehmann, she presumed – sitting on a stool in a corner of the bare room. As they entered, he immediately got up and seemed to be about to say something to Tilsner. But her deputy rushed over, and yanked Lehmann's arm high up behind his back, producing a yelp of pain.

He brought his mouth right up to Lehmann's ear. Müller couldn't hear what he was whispering – and couldn't even lip read as he'd manoeuvred his body between her and the prisoner, blocking her eyeline. After he'd finished whispering what Müller assumed were instructions as to how this would play out, he stepped aside.

Lehmann nodded as though accepting Tilsner's instructions, but remained tight-lipped.

Tilsner started to speak aloud. 'OK, I think Herr Lehmann understands what's required of him. *Unterleutnant* Müller here and I will be asking you some questions about a robbery, Ernst. I'm sure you're going to help us with our inquiries, aren't you?' The man's brow creased in confusion. Tilsner yanked his arm again – provoking a louder scream – then got up close to his ear once more. He resumed the whispered conversation – Müller could only assume that Tilsner had seen a hidden listening device, or had taken it as read that there would be one, and that the Ministry for State Security would be listening in.

'Ouch, OK, OK,' shouted Lehmann. 'I understand.'

Tilsner pressed his index finger against Lehmann's lips. 'Remember,' he mouthed silently to the man. Then he sidled over to Müller and whispered very quietly in her ear. 'OK. I think he understands what to do. You and I will need to ask him some questions about a robbery – we can just make it up as we go along. In the pauses – while he's silent or refusing to answer – you can whisper your real questions to him and he will whisper back the answers.'

'OK. So you're taking it as read that there are listening devices here. Are you sure there aren't cameras too?' asked Müller, matching Tilsner's secretive hushed tones, and cupping her hands over his ear.

Tilsner shook his head. Then mouthed, and gestured: *There aren't – I've looked around.*

This all had a theatrical feel to Müller, and she was aware that – in his whispered conversations to the prisoner – Tilsner could have been making threats she knew nothing about. She wouldn't put it past him. She might have been mistaken, but she thought she'd seen a flicker of recognition pass between Tilsner and the prisoner when they'd first entered the interview room. So what came out of Lehmann's mouth from now on could be nothing but lies and half-truths. But Lothar Schneider – it seemed – had lost his life trying to give her information about this case. To ensure the story still emerged, he had referred her on to Lehmann via that note found after his murder. She owed it to Schneider, and his widow, to try to make this work.

Speaking out loud, Tilsner began the false interview about the robbery.

'So, Ernst, tell me what you know about Manfred Fuchs – you two go back a long way, don't you?'

'I'm not going to talk to you,' said Lehmann, again out loud.

Müller saw Tilsner silently mouth a 'well done' to the prisoner, and at the same time he waved her forward to begin the real – *whispering* – interview.

As Tilsner droned on in the background, with Lehmann alternating between answering with 'no comment' or 'I don't know about that', Müller drew up close to the prisoner. She cupped his ear with her hand.

'I don't know if my colleague explained everything to you, but I'm interested in what you know about Gardelegen. What happened there in the war – and particularly anything you know about a Martin Ronnebach, an Ingo Höfler, a Heinz Unterbrink and, finally, Lothar Schneider – who I believe is a friend of yours.' Müller used the present tense deliberately – this wasn't the time or the place to be letting Lehmann know that his friend had been murdered, possibly by the same organisation that was holding him captive.

Lehmann nodded to her to indicate he understood. Then he, in turn, cupped his cuffed hands to Müller's ear, and whispered through his thumbs. While he was doing this, in the background Tilsner kept up his monologue about the fictitious robbery and robber.

'I will try to help,' whispered Lehmann. 'But I have one condition. I want to get a letter to my wife.'

Müller nodded her assent. She'd make sure she read any such letter before handing it over.

'Does she live in Gardelegen?'

The man nodded to Müller, as he gave another unhelpful answer to Tilsner's out-loud fake 'interview'.

He cupped Müller's ear again. 'You have to understand that everyone's name was changed. What we did was wrong. But we were schoolboys. You can't hold us responsible.'

Lehmann shouted out another non-answer to Tilsner, then resumed his whispered conversation, as Tilsner droned out another false question. 'Lothar came to see me – he was frightened. We were witnesses. We knew *who* was involved. Some people were given new identities to cover up their crimes, because they went on to work in important positions in the Republic.' Müller thought of Ronnebach, Höfler, and Unterbrink – all of whom had been in relatively important positions, particularly Ronnebach. And she knew that both Ronnebach, as a paratroop officer, and Höfler, as a member of the home guard, were in some way involved in the war in Gardelegen. 'Lothar had been approached by two people. And both approaches had made him very frightened.'

'Come on, Lehmann,' shouted Tilsner. 'You can't just continue this stonewalling.' Müller realised the prisoner had become so caught up in his story, he'd forgotten to vocalise a fake reply to Tilsner.

'I don't know what you are talking about, honestly,' he said aloud. 'I've never heard of this Manfred Fuchs. I've never met him.'

As Tilsner started speaking again, Müller and Lehmann resumed their whispered conversation.

'Who was it who approached Lothar?' asked Müller. 'Did you get a name, a description?'

'A French businessman. Lothar thought he was an industrial spy . . . he said something about the power station.'

'Did he give a description of him?'

'In his fifties.'

'Why did this unnerve Lothar?' whispered Müller.

Lehmann broke off to give another unhelpful answer to Tilsner.

'He was trying to find out about people who were there, and mentioned the other names you mentioned. Then Lothar got another visit.'

'From whom?'

'A Stasi bigwig from the Hauptstadt, who made all sorts of threats. Lothar recognised him as someone who was involved.'

Lehmann broke off again to give another fake answer to Tilsner. As he did so, Müller saw Tilsner tap his watch. *We need to wrap this up*, he mouthed, crossing his arms over his chest to emphasise the point. But Müller had two burning questions – one of which she should have asked all the widows a long time ago, despite the fact that some of them had been deliberately unhelpful. She should definitely have asked Frau Schneider, though.

First, she had her suspicions about the Stasi officer. 'Did Lothar give any description about the Stasi man?'

'He gave me names – current and previous. Back then he was Harald Scholz. A senior member of the Hitler Youth. We were all guarding the march.'

'The march?'

'To the barn! Isn't that what all this is about?' hissed Lehmann.

Behind them, there was a knock on the door.

'OK, we'll have to leave it there, Lehmann,' shouted Tilsner. 'But we'll be back, mark my words.'

For the sake of any eavesdroppers, the prisoner gave an answer out loud. 'I've told you time and time again. I know nothing about this.'

Müller frantically tried to ask further whispered questions. 'What happened at this barn? And describe this Stasi man to me.'

Lehmann looked nervously at the door. They could hear a key turning in the lock from the outside. 'He was in his late forties. Sandy, collar-length hair, looked like that West German news r—'

The door to the room swung open. Lehmann stopped whispering, and Müller pulled back. Their time was up. Lehmann hadn't had time to write a letter to his wife. But she had secured her reply about the Stasi officer: *Jäger*. Although that wasn't even his real name. He was really Harald Scholz. She was shocked, but not surprised. She hadn't had time to learn about what happened at the barn. But even if it wasn't in the history books, it sounded as though there would be plenty of people in Gardelegen who would know all about what had gone on there.

39

Continuation of transcribed and translated interview with Hitler Youth member Günther Palitzsch, conducted by Captain Arthur T. Wagner of the Ninth Army War Crimes Branch on 25 April 1945, at 1145 hours

Wagner: So, Günther, when were you aware that the plan was being put into action?

Palitzsch: Our Hitler Youth brigade was required to attend the cavalry school barracks in Bismarkerstrasse the next day.

Wagner: At what time?

Palitzsch: At 1500, I think.

Wagner: And you were aware of what was about to happen?

Palitzsch: Yes, but that doesn't mean I agreed with it. A few of us thought it was wrong. We'd heard some of the SS leaders were even refusing to take part. There were rumours some of them had run off. I think that's why we were needed as guards. But I'm only fifteen. I wasn't in any position to refuse. I had nowhere to run off to.

Wagner: So you guarded the convoy of those too sick to walk, and the columns of those prisoners walking to the barn?

Palitzsch: That had been the original plan as I understood it. But something changed. They managed to appoint some *Kapos* from amongst the prisoners themselves. These *Kapos* were told that – in exchange – they would get cigarettes and food, and that nothing would happen to them.

Wagner: We'll come to the *Kapos* and what happened to them later. So if you weren't required as guards, why were you there at all? You're not trying to minimise your involvement or lying to me, Günther, are you? That would be a very serious matter.

Palitzsch: I'm telling you the truth. I was ashamed about what happened. Sickened, really.

Wagner: So what I don't understand is why you were at the barn at all.

Palitzsch: It must have been because the SS, or *Kreisleiter* Thiele as it was him in charge really . . . it must have been because they already knew what they were going to do with the new *Kapos*. That they would need guards to replace them. That's all I can assume. Anyway, we were taken up to the barn on a tractor trailer.

Wagner: Did the prisoners themselves understand what was going on?

Palitzsch: No. Everyone just encouraged the rumour that they were being moved from the cavalry school barracks in order to be handed over to the Americans. So although many of them were in a bad way – terrible, really, like walking skeletons, those who could walk – their spirits were quite high. Almost euphoric. They thought their nightmare was over. I understand that now. It's been explained to me. But at the time you have to understand that we kept on being told about the terrible things that had happened when the zebras – sorry, the prisoners – at Kakerbeck turned on the villagers. We were all frightened that the same would happen in Gardelegen.

40

August 1977
Lindenstrasse, Potsdam, East Germany

Müller could tell something was wrong by the expression on the Stasi captain's face as he entered the interview room. He was livid, and wouldn't look Tilsner in the eye. Somehow – despite their precautions – it looked like they'd been found out.

'I'm afraid your interview will have to end now, Comrade *Major*,' he said to Müller. So she was right. The trainee detective ruse hadn't worked. 'I've instructions to take both of you to another interview room. Someone is coming from Normannenstrasse to see you.'

After they were led to the interview room, which was almost identical to the one in which they'd been quizzing Lehmann, they heard the Stasi captain lock the door behind them, and slam close the spy hole.

'I knew this was going to get me in trouble,' said Tilsner. 'Why didn't you just go through the official channels?'

Müller shot him a withering look. 'Why do you think? And please don't make out you're the injured party here. You've got a lot of explaining to do.'

She slumped down in one of the two chairs provided. At least they weren't forced to sit on a stool like Lehmann. But other than this, the room had no more comforts: bare, two-tone cream walls, a single desk, and two chairs. Not even a telephone or intercom. They were – in effect – prisoners themselves, if not in name.

It must have been about an hour before they heard the sound of the door being unlocked again. An hour where they had sat in virtual silence. There was much that Müller wanted – needed – to ask Tilsner. But they knew that whatever they said here would be listened to. It rather limited the options for conversation.

The identity of the man who opened the door wasn't a surprise to Müller. It was Jäger. Stasi colonel Klaus Jäger – the alter ego for the one-time teenage Hitler Youth member Harald Scholz. Müller had always been wary of him – now she saw him in a completely different light. What would he be prepared to do to prevent his past history coming back to haunt him? Could he have killed Schneider? Slit his throat – or at least ordered the slitting of his throat – in the woods east of Estedt? Possibly. Would he have set fires to ensure Ronnebach, Höfler and Unterbrink met lingering deaths? Unlikely, unless it was a double bluff designed to try to point Müller towards the wrong suspect – one she simply hadn't found yet. But there was one thing she was certain about. The Stasi, and Jäger, were capable – if that was what they wanted to do – of disguising Unterbrink's death to look like an accident. She thought back more than two years to the killing of Horst Ackermann by the reform school teenager, Irma Behrendt. That story hadn't suited the Stasi. So they'd changed it. Ackermann – it had been announced in the Party newspaper – had died in a car crash. They had form.

'This is very embarrassing,' said Jäger. 'I've got a young chicken to pluck with you two. And I'm not sure I can help you out this time.'

Müller laughed sarcastically. 'Help us out? When have you ever done that?'

'And you, Werner,' said Jäger, turning to Tilsner. 'I'd have thought better of you.'

Müller sighed. 'It's nothing to do with him. It was my idea. Everything he did, I asked him to do, so if anyone is guilty of anything, it's me.'

'Well, we don't want to make an elephant out of a mosquito. However, I do need to know everything that Lehmann told you, Karin.'

'Or else?'

'Or else it will get very uncomfortable for him here. And for his family back in Gardelegen.'

'You've got to be joking. He told me nothing. We were questioning his relationship to a robber.'

'Who doesn't exist. Anyway, I take it you're content for us to find out what Lehmann told you using our own methods, then?'

Müller felt a momentary stab of guilt – Lehmann had tried to help her. And with the interview being interrupted, she hadn't even had the chance to fulfil her part of the deal – smuggling a letter from him to his wife.

Tilsner breathed in slowly. 'Tell him, Karin. I'd like to know too.'

Müller raised her brows at Tilsner, then turned to Jäger and shook her head.

'Are you arresting me? If not, I'd like to go now, please.'

Jäger opened the door for her. 'Feel free. But I wouldn't want to be in Herr Lehmann's shoes.'

Müller simply glowered at him as she passed. She didn't wait to see if Tilsner was following. She didn't care.

41

Oberst Reiniger gazed at Müller in the manner of an exasper-
ated father trying to talk sense to a particularly troublesome
teenager.

'Whose idea was the trick you pulled in Potsdam, Karin?'

'Does it matter, Comrade *Oberst*? Tilsner was only there
because I asked him to try to get me in to see the prisoner.'

Reiniger leant back in his chair, his hands clasped together
over his bulging stomach. 'Why didn't you go through the official channels?'

'If you mean the Ministry for State Security, they would have
worked out why I wanted to talk to Lehmann, and would have
denied me access. Not only that, they would have accused me of
continuing my inquiry after I'd been taken off the case.'

'Well, they've made sure of that now anyway. The Stasi have
also taken over the investigation of the death of Heinz Unterbrink. However they've asked me to pass on that they're grateful
to you for the evidence you've uncovered that he was murdered,
rather than died accidentally.'

'Surely they can't continue to claim this is the work of the
so-called Committee for the Dispossessed?'

Reiniger stroked his chin. 'On the contrary, Karin. That's exactly what they *are* saying. They just say Unterbrink was possibly not the intended target. They claim it was to do with the passing of Automobilwerk Eisenach into public ownership.'

'But it was a BMW company before the war. A corporation owned it. That's a ridiculous theory. No one could possibly hold a grudge, and the transfer of ownership was a result of the war. It passed into Soviet hands initially.'

'I respect your knowledge of history, Karin. However, it's not part of my role to contradict the Ministry for State Security. I strongly suggest it shouldn't be part of your role either. Otherwise your tenure as leader of the Serious Crimes Department may not last very long. As for the present moment, you may as well simply go back on leave. Until there is another case for which I think you'd be suitable. *If* there is another case.'

Müller hadn't seen fit to reply to Reiniger. It seemed like everything was stacked against her. Tilsner was no longer the loyal deputy she'd once thought. Jäger was revealed as a former Nazi, albeit a junior member, with the Hitler Youth. Even Schmidt had stepped out of line. Thinking of Schmidt, she remembered the historical research she'd set him on to. It was time to catch up. Then she needed to get back to the Strausberger Platz apartment for catching up of a different sort: with Jannika, Johannes and Helga.

Schmidt wasn't at his usual desk in the lab, so she left a message asking him to call her when he had a moment. In the meantime, she sat back in her office desk chair, and tried to think if there was any way she could continue the inquiry without making it obvious. Without breaking the rules. Without getting into more trouble. Delving into the history of Gardelegen with Schmidt was one option. But the other concerned something Lehmann had mentioned: the French businessman. It was unusual enough that a foreign businessman had been prying around in the Republic. Dangerous too, for him. But he would need to secure authorisations, to show passes and papers at checkpoints. The trouble was, she didn't have a name. She didn't really have any dates. And other than that one visit to Lothar Schneider in Gardelegen, she didn't really know his movements.

The likelihood was that her phone was being tapped by the Stasi now, if it hadn't been before. But she only wanted to make one phone call, if the person she wanted to call actually possessed a telephone. It wasn't a given in the Republic.

She picked up the phone and talked to the Keibelstrasse switchboard operator. She gave the woman on the switchboard the Schneiders' address in Gardelegen. 'Can you check for me if they have a private telephone in their apartment?' Müller had visited, of course, but she couldn't remember seeing one, though it had been well after midnight. The room had been in semi-darkness. 'If they have, could you ring them for me and then patch the line through to me on this extension.'

Müller waited for a few minutes, twiddling her thumbs. She was just about to give up and go home, when the extension rang.

'I've got your call on the line now, Comrade *Major*. Go ahead, caller.'

'Hello?' said the woman's voice at the other end. Müller immediately recognised it as that of Lothar Schneider's widow.

'Frau Schneider. It's *Major* Müller from Berlin again. Thanks so much for talking to me last night.'

'That's all right. I'm not sure there is much else that I can tell you, though.'

'What I'm interested in is some sort of meeting Lothar had with a French businessman. Do you remember him telling you anything about that?'

'He didn't need to tell me about it. I spoke to the man myself. On the telephone. Like this.'

'When was this?'

'The first time?'

'The *first* time? He got in contact on more than one occasion?' Müller felt a lightness in her chest.

'Yes. The first time was, let's see . . . it would have been in the spring. April maybe. Hang on. You're lucky. I always write . . .' The woman sighed, loud enough for Müller to hear over the crackly line. 'It's difficult, you know. Believing he's actually dead. It just feels like he's gone away for a few days. I know that's not the case. Anyway, I always used to write messages for Lothar on the wall diary, in case he was doing night shifts at the power station and our paths didn't cross for a day or so. Hang on, I'll go and get it.'

Müller found herself slightly breathless waiting for the woman. This felt like something significant.

The woman returned to the line. 'Here you go. Fifteenth of April. That was the first call.'

'This year?' *April? The timeframe tallied with the killing of Ingo Höfler.*

'Yes, earlier this year. And then he got in touch again very recently.' The woman paused. 'Here it is. The 22nd of July.' *Mid to late July. Martin Ronnebach.*

Müller tried to breathe evenly and deeply, to keep the excitement from her voice. 'What was the message each time?'

'Well, that was very odd. It was just this: *wants to talk to you –* that was Lothar, of course, this was my message to him – *about a farming question.*'

'A *farming* question?'

'Yes. I just assumed he had a wrong number and had mixed us up with some other Schneiders or something. But I wrote it down in case it meant anything to Lothar.'

'And you're sure those were his exact words.'

'Well . . . that might have been my interpretation. Let me think. Oh yes, it was a bit more detailed than that. Something about *the best way to store hay in a barn.* That was it. *A farming question* would just have been my shorthand for Lothar.'

Mention of this 'barn' again. Where Lehmann said he and his Hitler Youth colleagues had escorted the 'march'. What was that all about?

'And did the man leave a name or a telephone number?'

'Yes. Both.'

Müller felt her hands tremble as she held the receiver. 'What were they, Frau Schneider?'

The woman read out a telephone number and a room number – the same phone number for each message, but each time a different room. Müller noted it down. She wasn't sure, but she thought that was the dialling code for Magdeburg. It must have been the hotel where the businessman was staying.

'And the name?'

'Well, I hope I've spelt this correctly. I possibly just spelt it phonetically, but being a teacher I know some French so I think it's correct. His name was Philippe Verbier.'

42

In the space of a ten-minute phone call, Müller had made the first significant breakthrough in the case. A case that had nothing at all to do with the confiscation of private property and its nationalisation by the Republic. That was a smoke-screen from the Stasi. Possibly even directly from Jäger, who clearly had a personal involvement, one she was determine to expose. If no one else was prepared to hold him to account, then she would have to.

She was champing at the bit to get started and phone the hotel in Magdeburg. But she'd already risked one phone call that could easily have been listened in on. She needed to try to find out which hotel it was without ringing. She needed to pay it an unannounced visit.

She also needed – somehow – to be able to check the records of passenger arrivals at Schönefeld from France and elsewhere in Western Europe, particularly French citizens arriving by train at Friedrichstrasse, and for French-registered cars crossing into the Republic on the relevant dates.

There was a lot of legwork to be done, and she would be doing it alone. Although she didn't think Schmidt would betray her again, she wasn't going to risk it. As for Tilsner, she felt very much that his initial reticence – shock, even – about the various smoke deaths, indicated an involvement that was too close. Maybe the doddery neighbour of the Schneiders who thought she recognised him from the 'estate' hadn't got such bad eyesight after all. Perhaps Tilsner's connections with the Altmark and Gardelegen itself weren't just the distant relatives he claimed to have in the area. Perhaps – like Jäger – his involvement was far darker, and went far deeper.

It was still the early afternoon by the time Müller got back to Strausberger Platz, finding a parking space in a nearby side street. She was going to leave ratcheting up the search for Verbier's comings and goings from the Republic until the next day. For now, she wanted to re-integrate herself into family life.

When she let herself in through the front door, she was disappointed the apartment was empty. After her night in the car, and her marathon drives around the Republic, she had been looking forward to a long, hot soak in the bath. As she ran the bath, she stripped off her clothes and examined herself in the full-length mirror. The partially-botched – or at least unprofessional – Caesarean scar was slowly fading. It would always be there, but she was getting used to it. It was almost like a trademark, a brand. She smiled to herself. There would be few children in the world, if any, who'd had as exciting a first few hours as Jannika and Johannes, who had been plucked from her womb, spirited away, and chased in desperation by her and her police colleagues. But they'd survived, she'd survived, and she'd got what she'd always wanted – a little family.

She smoothed her fingers across her face. There was tiredness there, but she'd seen the Stasi captain's looks of appreciation and the same from the Bulgarian waiter. She lifted the undersides of her breasts, first one, then the other. She would like someone to caress her. She would like to find another man. But it wasn't the be all and end all. There was still time.

The steam from the bath had started to cloud up the mirror. She'd run it hot, despite the heat of summer outside the apartment. It was a throwback to her days in Oberhof, when after ski-jump practice as a teenager she loved nothing better than running a bath which was just on the cool side of scalding, then staying in it as long as she could, as her fingers crinkled and the water cooled. She climbed in, and lowered herself into the water.

So she was off the case and had been thrown off – in effect – three times in a row. But this time, she wasn't going to let it stop her. She had something on Jäger now. He wouldn't be the only official in the Republic who at one time had been in the Hitler Youth. But it was certain that he wouldn't want it widely known.

She was almost drifting off in the bath when the sounds of screaming awoke her. She jumped out of the bath with a start, almost sliding and falling on the tiled floor, frightened for an instant. Then she realised it was a young child yelling his head off.

Johannes.

Helga and the children were back.

Then came Helga's voice. 'Jannika, put down the telephone, please.'

Müller came out of the bathroom, wrapped in a towel, to see that her daughter was standing on a chair, pretending to talk into the phone. Her son was still in the pushchair, bawling and arching his back.

'You're back at last,' said Helga. 'I know with the job you can't always warn me when you'll be away longer than expected, but we were getting worried.' Her grandmother pulled her into a hug.

'I'm sorry, Helga. Everything just snowballed. I didn't have chance to ring.'

Helga turned to her great-grandson, with her finger against her closed lips. 'Shush, Johannes! Otherwise Mutti won't give you a hug.' Then *sotto voce* to Müller. 'He's been a little menace today.'

In the mayhem, Jannika had climbed down from the chair and was now trying to pull Müller's towel down. She succeeded. 'Mutti! Mutti!' she cried, shaking her little blonde head in mirth at her mother's nakedness.

'Ooh, you little rascal,' said Müller, pretending to chase her daughter round the hall, not bothering to pull the towel back up. Then she lifted Johannes from the buggy, struggling under his weight, and rocked him till he calmed, singing his favourite lullaby.

'Schlaf, Kindlein, schlaf
Der Vater hüt't die Schaf
Die Mutter schüttelt's Bäumelein

Da fällt herab ein Träumelein
Schlaf, Kindlein, schlaf.'

By the end of the first verse, Johannes was calmed and instead of crying, was trying to grab his mother's breast.

'Typical man,' laughed Helga. 'Can't keep his hands off.'

When they'd eaten, the children themselves had been bathed and Müller had read them a bedtime story, she finally got the chance to talk to Helga.

'So are you still on holiday or not?' her grandmother asked.

'Officially, yes. Unofficially, no. I've got plenty I need to get on with tomorrow. I feel guilty leaving them with you all the time.'

'Nonsense. We have a lot of fun. It's no trouble. I've signed them up for the summer club at Volkspark Friedrichshain for the next couple of weeks, so I'll get a few hours off to go shopping or whatever. Or if you're free, we could go shopping together. To the Centrum in Alexanderplatz?'

'Hopefully one day this week. Not tomorrow, though, I'm afraid. There's something from this last case I need to follow up on.'

The next day, Müller began her search for records relating to this Philippe Verbier – the French businessman.

She tried to find Jonas Schmidt, only to be told the forensic scientist was off ill. That explained why he hadn't returned her call about the history of Gardelegen. Still, she could easily look it up herself in the library when she got the chance. She did ask a favour of another *Kriminaltechniker* who she knew Schmidt was friendly with. She asked him if he could go through all crime reports for the last six months, checking if any unexpected tyre prints of French cars had been found. She knew from the grave-yard girl case that the tyre manufacturers of different countries often used distinctive patterns – and the forensic scientists would keep a pattern book or file.

Her next visit was to the switchboard room. She asked one of the telephonists she knew in passing whether they had any reverse directories for Magdeburg to see if they could match the number Frau Schneider had given her to a particular hotel. Failing that, could they check the obvious ones where western businessmen might stay, to see if they could find a match?

Müller's next task would be more difficult without alerting the Stasi: trawling through the passenger records of trains, aircraft, or cars. She had to decide which mode of transport to check first. What made her mind up was the fact that she and Tilsner had been to the vehicle checkpoints between West and East Berlin before, during the case of the reform school teens. It was more than two years ago, but there was an outside chance that some of the same faces would be there. Many worked for the Stasi, despite their border guard army uniforms. But that was true for the airports and railway stations too. Of course, Verbier might not have crossed into the Republic via the capital. If he'd been involved in the Leinefelde murder, then the border checkpoint at Düderstadt/Worbis would make more sense.

She was shooting in the dark. There was very little chance of her uncovering anything – particularly without sharing the workload with Tilsner. And she didn't trust him enough at the moment to share anything with him.

But she had to try.

43

13 April 1945
Gardelegen, Nazi Germany

Only a few minutes after the barn doors are closed behind us, I realise Marcellin was right, and I was wrong. Two German soldiers enter and start setting fire to the straw in the barn in several places.

Hope turns to terror in an instant.

Suddenly, I feel strong again. We rush round with our blankets, and manage to put out most of the flames. Marcellin is coughing alongside me, slumped to the floor. We try to push the straw to the middle of the barn, in case those same two soldiers return. I start telling myself that perhaps it was some sort of cruel, drunken dare, the last act of bravado by a defeated army.

But then they're back.

This time they don't just have matches, they have signal flares, which are fired at the straw.

Again, we frantically try to smother the flames. We've just about managed it, when the doors open again. This time grenades explode, and there is the sound of machine pistols and the cries of prisoners in their death throes.

Somehow I find Marcellin as the smoke begins to take hold. I cover my mouth with my partly burnt blanket and drag him, half-stumbling, towards one of the walls, pressing ourselves against it to try to gain some protection against the bullets.

This is a massacre, I realise. A cold-blooded massacre.

Through the smoke, on the opposite side of the building I see a group of some fifty or so Russian prisoners barge through the wooden doors. Hope surges as they force them open and flee into the open air.

There's a chance of escape.

Then – in the fading light – we see their silhouettes mown down by machine pistol fire and rifle shots.

By now the fire is completely out of control. The inside of the barn fills with choking smoke. There are cries of panic every-where. Marcellin is shaking in the chaos. I try to protect him – try to cling on.

I start singing 'La Marseillaise' – trying to get Marcellin to join in. Trying to die with dignity. Human torches run around to try to extinguish the flames they're engulfed in, until they drop down dead.

In the mêlée, in the choking smoke, I lose my grip on Marcellin. My brother.

I do not want to lose another.

I try to fight my way back to him, but the crush is too much, as body after body falls on me. I feel the air being squeezed from my lungs like a pair of bellows, and the fire rages around us. I try to wriggle free from under the mass of bodies, but I cannot.

Those flickering images I saw of my life at Estedt are back.

The laughing faces of Grégoire and Marcellin when we were younger.

The games of oyster *petanque*. Running my fingers through Marie-Ange's flaxen hair – the same colour as the straw we first saw piled up in this barn.

The sweet, sweet smell of my mother's marsh mutton – the memory so real I can almost actually smell it.

As I start to drift out of consciousness, I have one last – horrible – conscious thought.

I *can* smell it. It's not my imagination playing tricks.

The smell isn't of marsh mutton.

It isn't ovine meat at all.

It's the smell of roasting human flesh.

44

Müller parked the Lada as near to the crossing point as she dared, without attracting attention. Then she approached. She'd chosen to wear her summer uniform with her major's insignia, even though she was on holiday and a detective who normally wore plain clothes. She wanted to try to make an impression on the person she was hoping to see. It might prevent her being arrested by the Stasi.

Perhaps she was being unrealistic. Around two and a half years had passed. The fellow major she was hoping to meet had probably moved on, or perhaps wouldn't even remember her.

Müller scanned the border guards in the checkpoint. The officer she was looking for was stocky, had messy dyed and permed blonde hair. But – like Müller – she was a woman in a mostly man's world. She needed a modicum of female solidarity. And then she saw her, sitting at a desk going through some paperwork.

One of the other guards tried to stop her getting through, but Müller flashed her ID card. 'I'm here to see the Comrade *Major*,' she said, brushing past him.

'You mean the Comrade *Oberstleutnant*,' the officer whispered to her, grinning. 'I warn you. She's recently been promoted, and likes everyone to know.'

At that moment, the lieutenant colonel looked up from her papers, and frowned. 'I remember you from somewhere.'

Müller held out her hand. '*Major* Karin Müller of the *Kriminalpolizei*. You were very helpful with a case we were working on a couple of years ago. Although I was a mere *Oberleutnant* then.'

'Aha yes,' cried the woman, giving Müller a firm handshake. 'I trust you tracked down who you wanted. I remember your letter of authority.' The woman winked. On the previous occasion, Müller had carried a letter of authority from Jäger, countersigned by the Stasi head, Erich Mielke. It was exactly the sort of thing Müller had hoped the woman would remember. She didn't have a similar letter this time. In fact, if Jäger had known what she was doing, he was more likely to sign something ordering her arrest. 'Anyway, come through into the office. What can we help you with?'

Müller explained what she wanted. The files corresponding to a week either side of Verbier's phone calls to the Schneiders. There would be a mountain of entries to work through – it would probably take her all day – just on the off-chance that the Frenchman might have crossed here.

After an hour of fruitless searching, the lieutenant colonel took pity on her, and popped her head round the door.

'Would you like a coffee? I can get one of the junior officers to make you one.'

'That would be very kind of you, Comrade *Oberstleutnant*.'

When she returned with the drink a few minutes later, she sat down next to Müller. 'Is there anything I can help you with? Last time you had your rather handsome deputy with you, I seem to remember. This time you seem to be struggling on your own.'

'To be honest, I'm working on a bit of a hunch. It didn't seem worth detailing someone else to it. I'm not fully sure why I am.' Müller showed the woman the date ranges she was working within. 'I'm looking for a French citizen crossing from the West within these dates.'

'In a French car?'

'I'm not sure. Possibly. Or he might have flown into the BRD and then hired a car. Or he might not have come by car at all.'

'Well, I can save you a bit of trouble then. It's not a hard and fast rule, but foreigners tend to cross at Grenzübergang Friedrichstrasse. If I were you, I would start there. I know the head of the unit there. I'll put in a call to smooth things along. I can also get someone to leaf through the files here in any downtime, and I'll contact you if we turn anything up. Where's the best place to get you?'

'At Keibelstrasse, Comrade *Oberstleutnant*.'

'Good. Consider it done. And if you need to do any follow-ups here, make sure you send that deputy of yours. He's much prettier to look at than any of my boys.'

Müller half-expected to be double-crossed, despite the genuine nature of the woman, and wouldn't have been surprised if a

Stasi agent had been waiting at Grenzübergang Friedrichstrasse. Instead, she was greeted warmly. The female lieutenant colonel's introductory phone call seemed to have done the trick.

When she'd begun this search, just a few hours earlier, she thought it would be like looking for a needle in a haystack.

But here, in front of her, a junior officer was brandishing a list of French citizens who'd crossed into the Republic at this checkpoint – which Müller knew was the most famous one in the West, featured in many western spy movies, and known that side of the Anti-Fascist Protection Barrier as 'Checkpoint Charlie' – from the designation 'C' the Americans had given it. In the American phonetic alphabet, Charlie was the codeword for the initial 'C'.

The list was a long one. She scanned down it. Most of them would be tourists.

Then – amongst the entries for April – his name suddenly leapt out at her. Philippe Verbier. April the 13th. That tied in with everything. Her eyes widened when she saw the description of his profession. Fire Prevention Consultant. This was him. This was her man.

She quickly scanned the other entries. There were no other mentions, except for his return crossing in April, about a week after he'd entered.

She quickly scanned the more recent entries and found his name again; an entry from ten days earlier. He had been driving a Citroën CX, which rang a vague bell as an executive car she'd seen in a West German television advert. This time, there was no entry for a return. There was a slight chance he could have exited the Republic at a different crossing, but it was unlikely under existing visa rules.

She felt sure Philippe Verbier was still here.

Stalking his next victim.

45

The entries gave her vital information such as his car registration number. In normal circumstances, it would have been an easy job to radio through to the uniform or traffic division, get the car stopped, and have Verbier arrested ready for her to question him.

But these weren't normal circumstances. If she did that, she risked alerting the Stasi. By not doing it, though, she knew she was giving him free rein to stalk his next victim, assuming that was what he was planning.

Instead, she would have to go after him herself. It would put her in danger of losing her life should anything go wrong and he discovered her and confronted her. That was something she'd vowed not to do in this new job, now that she had children. But it was a vow she'd failed to keep during the last big case, on the border with Poland. And it was a vow she knew she was going to break again.

She rang the switchboard at Keibelstrasse and asked to speak to her contact there to find out if she'd had any success with the telephone number. She had. The number corresponded to Hotel

International in Magdeburg. The extension numbers were for rooms there.

Müller watched her hands tremble as she made her next call to the hotel itself. If Verbier liked to follow the same routines, then perhaps he was back in Magdeburg, the nearest big city to Gardelegen, staying at the same venue, in plain sight. It was well known that the luxury Interhotels were used by the Stasi for spying on western businessmen and politicians.

When she got through to the hotel switchboard, she almost didn't want to ask the question for fear of failure. But she did. 'Hello. I'm inquiring after a guest that I believe is staying at the hotel at the moment. A French guest by the name of Philippe Verbier.'

'Could you hold on a moment, madam? I'll just check the register.'

Müller waited, tapping her fingers on the receiver nervously.

The operator came back on the line. 'Yes, Herr Verbier is staying with us at the moment. Would you like me to put you through to his room?'

Müller found herself gulping down breaths, almost unable to speak. 'Y . . . yes. Yes, please.' She racked her brain trying to be clear in her mind what she would say to him. Speaking in the middle of a murder inquiry that she wasn't even supposed to be carrying out, to the man she suspected of being the murderer himself. It was breaking new ground. It was frightening.

The operator was back. 'There's no answer at the moment, I'm afraid. Would you like to leave a message?'

'No. That's all right. I'll try again later. Thank you.'

Müller put the phone down. She had one more call to make. To Helga. She knew the Stasi were probably listening in – let them. They wouldn't learn anything useful from this.

'Helga, I'm sorry,' she said when her grandmother came on the line. 'This is taking longer than I thought. I might even have to stay overnight. Is that OK?'

'Of course it is, darling. You do what you have to do. Ring when you can. The children always like to hear your voice.'

'I will do. I'm sorry, Helga.'

She didn't have a clear plan. Did it make any sense to confront Verbier? Not really. She would be no further forward unless he confessed, and she would have revealed her hand in continuing the investigation, putting herself at risk of arrest. It was better to find out more first.

To follow Verbier.

To watch him.

To piece this all together.

46

Continuation of transcribed and translated interview
with Hitler Youth member Günther Palitzsch, conducted
by Captain Arthur T. Wagner of the Ninth Army War
Crimes Branch on 25 April 1945, at 1400 hours

Wagner: I want you to cast your mind back, Günther, to
what you claim were the words of the lady of the manor,
Frau Bloch von Blochwitz, at the party at the Isenschnibbe
estate on the evening of April 12th. Can you recall them
exactly for me again?

Palitzsch: As I said, she was responding to a question from
the *Kreisleiter* of Gardelegen, Gerhard Thiele, the head of
the Nazi Party in the district. He asked: 'Here I am with
a thousand criminals on my hands. The Yanks are down
the road and will be here within a couple of days. I can't
very well have all these criminals shot in the open country.
What can I do?'

(PAUSE AS CAPTAIN WAGNER CONSULTS HIS NOTES)

Wagner: When I asked you about this earlier, I have a note of that question, but your recollection of it doesn't include the words: 'I can't very well have all these criminals shot in the open country.' Is that something you've just remembered?

Palitzsch: I must have missed that bit out, I'm sorry. A lot has happened. But he definitely said that.

Wagner: So the notion of killing all the prisoners came initially from *Kreisleiter* Thiele? This may be important in respect of future proceedings.

Palitzsch: Yes. Whether he was acting on someone else's say-so, someone else's orders, I have no idea.

Wagner: And can you recall Frau Bloch von Blochwitz's exact response?

Palitzsch: Yes, because it shocked me at the time. I nearly dropped the drinks tray. Other workers who overheard it were shocked too. I talked about it afterwards with Frau Rost.

Wagner: Who is Frau Rost?

Palitzsch: She was one of the servants at Isenschnibbe. A kind woman. She looked after me.

Wagner: Are you sure you are not repeating what Frau Rost said, as opposed to what you heard yourself?

Palitzsch: We both heard it. In reply to *Kreisleiter* Thiele, Frau Bloch von Blochwitz said: 'There is an old barn up there that belongs to me. Why don't you put them inside and set it on fire?'

Wagner: Thank you for clarifying that Günther. Now I want to return to the events of the following day, when you and your Hitler Youth troop reached the barn. Can you continue your account in your own words please?

Palitzsch: Yes. By the time we got there, the zebras were already being herded into the barn. An enemy plane was circling overhead, so I think the guards started to panic. One of them fired at the prisoners to try to hurry them up. At least one of the prisoners was injured then.

Wagner: Did you fire at the prisoners?

Palitzsch: Me? God no! I was sickened by what was happening. I'd already decided that, unless I couldn't avoid it, I wasn't going to use my gun at all. I was only there because I'd been told to be, by both my Hitler Youth troop leader and Frau Bloch von Blochwitz. If I hadn't gone with them, I was frightened she'd sack me. We were just standing to one side, watching.

Wagner: What happened next?

Palitzsch: Once all the prisoners were inside, the barn doors were closed by the SS and wedged shut with rocks and stones. A few minutes after that there was a commotion by the south-west door, and I saw flames. Soldiers seemed to be firing flares in there, I assume to set the barn alight. Then I saw grenades being thrown in, and Panzerfausts – anti-tank weapons – being fired. It was chaos. Scary. Then on the opposite side of the building we saw some prisoners break down the doors. They were machine-gunned down.

Wagner: Were you ordered to open fire?

Palitzsch: Yes, we had machine pistols. *Wachtmeister* Georg Brandt gave the order.

Wagner: And you obeyed it?

Palitzsch: We made as if to obey it, otherwise we might have been shot ourselves. But me and my friend had already decided we were going to shoot to miss, deliberately. No one would be able to tell. I didn't kill anyone.

Wagner: Who was your friend?

Palitzsch: Harald Scholz.

Wagner: Did Harald stick to your plan not to shoot to kill or injure? To deliberately miss?

Palitzsch: I don't know.

(SHORT PAUSE WHILE CAPTAIN WAGNER MAKES NOTES)

Wagner: What happened next?

Palitzsch: I don't like to remember, really. It was horrible. Sickening.

Wagner: We're all sickened by what happened, Günther. One way you can start to make amends is by giving a truthful account. It will help us bring the perpetrators to justice. So please continue. If you need to pause for a drink of water or anything, just let us know.

Palitzsch: You could hear the cries of pain, the shouting, swearing, panic in all sorts of languages. It sounded like some of the prisoners were singing their national anthems as they were burned alive. It was awful.

(GÜNTHER PALITZSCH BECOMES TEARFUL AND ASKS TO TAKE A BREAK)

47

August 1977
East Berlin to Magdeburg

As she joined the motorway network outside the Hauptstadt, the radio suddenly sparked to life. It was Schmidt. Müller asked for him to wait until she'd found the nearest exit, then parked up the Lada and lifted the handset again.

'Sorry not to have been in touch about this earlier, Comrade *Major*, but I was off ill for a couple of days.'

'Nothing serious, I hope, Jonas?'

'No. I think it was just a sickness bug I caught off my wife. I felt awful. I couldn't keep anything down – you know that's not like me.' If Tilsner had been telling the truth about his 'illness' then perhaps Schmidt had caught the bug from him, thought Müller. 'Anyway, I'm fighting fit again now and have looked into those matters regarding the Second World War in the Gardelegen area.'

'Go on.'

'Well, you were correct that something terrible happened. I'm surprised neither of us knew about it. It's a horrific story. In summary, more than a thousand labour camp prisoners – most of them from satellite camps aligned to the Mittelbau-Dora V1 and V2 underground factory near Nordhausen – were herded into a barn and burnt to death.'

Müller tried to swallow but found she couldn't. Was this what Jäger had been caught up in? It just sounded too awful.

'What makes it worse,' continued Schmidt, 'is it happened just days before the Nazis surrendered to the advancing American army in Gardelegen.'

She found herself wincing at the details Schmidt had given. 'Why on earth do that when the war was almost over?'

'It doesn't make any sense to me, Comrade *Major*. The prisoners, as far as I understand it, were being moved by train from the camps in the southern Harz to other camps further to the east and north to escape the advance. Near Gardelegen, the rail track was bombed. The prisoners were stuck for a couple of days. Then they were marched to a cavalry school town. Several of the weakest were shot when they couldn't keep up. There was a smaller massacre of around one hundred such prisoners in the woods near the village of Estedt, north of Gardelegen.'

The woods near Estedt. Lothar Schreiber's meeting place given to her in those coordinates in the anonymous message sent to Keibelstrasse.

'Why?' asked Müller, aghast. She knew the Nazis were capable of terrible evil – but this seemed senseless too.

'The logic – if you can call it that – of killing the remaining prisoners in the barn was that the Nazi leader in the town had frightened everyone into thinking that if they were set free by the Americans, they would attack any and every German person they could find in revenge.'

'Were there any survivors, Jonas?'

'Only a handful I'm afraid, Comrade *Major*.'

'What nationalities were they?'

'Various. Russians, Poles, Hungarians, Czechs . . . and a few French, former resistance fighters.'

French survivors.

Was one of them Philippe Verbier?

Was he back, finally, to take his revenge?

Müller said her thank yous to Schmidt, and gave him a new task: to see what he could discover about the involvement of the Hitler Youth in the massacre, particularly any mention of Harald Scholz. The more of a hold she had over Jäger, the more it would be to her advantage, and the better chance she would have of cracking this case.

She got out of the Lada, and walked around to the boot. She was in a lay-by of a main road just off the motorway, but traffic was light, and there were no houses or apartment blocks nearby. With a little luck she wouldn't be observed. She opened the boot, and rummaged through the various piles of children's paraphernalia, such as plastic buckets and spades. Underneath, hidden by a piece of old carpet, was what she was looking for. Her set of false number plates – acquired by Schmidt for moments like these, when she didn't even want her own employers – the People's Police – to know what she was up to.

Müller waited patiently for a break in the traffic, then clipped the new rear plate over the real one. Then she moved to the front of the car and did the same. If any of her uniform colleagues – or even the Stasi – felt the inclination to check the registration, they would be disappointed and confused.

It was a plate from another Lada of a similar model and colour which had been crushed after an accident.

Officially it didn't exist.

Müller had pulled another item from Schmidt's box of tricks in the boot – a curly-haired black wig. She fitted it in place using the rear-view mirror as she sat in the driver's seat, tucking her own blonde hair under it. Then, from the glove compartment, she brought out the oversized sunglasses she'd bought on the Bulgarian beach trip.

She admired herself. The transformation from just two items was impressive. With the fake number plates and the disguise, she hoped she wouldn't easily be recognised.

The Hotel International in Magdeburg sat proudly on one of the city's main streets. It was a grey giant that glistened with modernity and was in the same chain of Interhotels as the Panorama in the home town of her adoptive family, Oberhof. But while the Panorama was all angular shapes and sharp apexes, the International was rectangular and squat; a concrete cuboid.

Müller parked in the large parking lot on the opposite side of the dual carriageway street, which looked a little like Halle-Neustadt's Magistrale. As she searched for a parking space, she kept an eye out for the Citroën CX, with its distinctive French number plates, and sleek shape.

There it is!

She paused the Lada in neutral for a moment, and checked her notebook. The likelihood of there being two *French* cars, two Citroën CXs in the same parking lot in Magdeburg was virtually non-existent.

She glanced at the registration plate, and the corresponding one in her notes.

153 AAX 17.

It matched.

There was a spare space right next to it, but Müller felt that would be too obvious. She needed some distance.

Instead she found a space almost directly opposite, with a clear view of the car. The problem now, however, was what to do? Should she wait here in the car park until Verbier decided to make a move? Or should she check out the hotel? Try to track him in the building in case wherever he was planning to go next wasn't in his own car. She noticed that the bus station was opposite the car park, and saw a tram rumble past the hotel. There were several transport possibilities here. If Verbier was heading to Gardelegen, surely he would opt to use the car? It would give him more flexibility once he got there. But he wasn't necessarily going to Gardelegen. He was a fire prevention expert. Perhaps he had some genuine business in Magdeburg? She would have to risk going into the hotel first. Hopefully her disguise would offer some protection against the prying eyes of the Stasi. As she approached the entrance, she noticed a flower vendor's stall – an unusual sight in the Republic, but presumably targeting foreign clientele of the hotel, like Verbier. She got out her wallet and handed over a ten mark note for a bouquet.

She nervously approached the reception with the flowers.

'Could you check if Herr Philippe Verbier is in his room, please? I have a delivery for him.'

The receptionist seemed to look down her nose at Müller for a few seconds, without doing anything. It was as though she was sizing Müller up. *She probably thinks I'm a prostitute, with this wig and the sunglasses.* Then she began to dial an extension number. Müller made sure she watched carefully, memorising the digits the woman dialled as they almost certainly formed the room number, *5106*.

The receptionist passed the handset and receiver across. Müller placed the bouquet on the counter, and then took the offered phone.

'Monsieur Verbier,' she gushed. 'I've brought some flowers as a gift for you. I'll leave them at reception.' Before she handed the phone back, she replaced the receiver – cutting the call before the Frenchman could reply. Müller left the flowers with the receptionist, and then swiftly crossed the lobby, choosing a seat that was partially hidden by an overgrown pot plant.

Without being too obvious, she kept a watch on the reception for a few moments, hiding behind both the plant and a magazine she'd picked up from a nearby coffee table.

About five minutes later, she saw the flowers handed over to a man who she assumed must be Verbier. He picked them up, a confused expression on his face as he failed to find any message attached. Müller could see words exchanged with the receptionist, shrugs of shoulders on both sides of the counter, and then Verbier retreated to wait for the lift back up to his room.

As the lift doors opened, and the man she assumed was Verbier entered, Müller walked quickly from her hiding place and got into the lift behind him. Sure enough, he pressed the button for floor five, and then looked inquiringly at Müller.

'The same,' she said, smiling sweetly. 'Are you here on business?'

'Yes,' said the man. But the key thing for Müller was that it was a surly 'yes' tinged with an unmistakeable French accent. This was her man.

'And are those from your wife?'

The man frowned, nonplussed by this stranger who appeared to be chatting him up in a lift.

'No.' He looked a little confused, as he stood back to allow Müller to exit first at the fifth floor. As she scanned the numbers on the room direction sign, working out where room 5106 was, Verbier tapped her lightly on the arm.

He proffered the flowers. 'Would you like them? I think they were sent to me by mistake. They'll just be going in the bin.'

'How kind,' gushed Müller. 'They're lovely.'

Verbier shrugged and started to walk off towards his room.

Müller didn't know why she did what she did next. It was on impulse. The sort of thing you do, and say, in an instant – and then regret for years afterwards. But the words came out of her mouth nonetheless.

'If you're looking for some company, I might be available.' She wasn't even sure of the correct form of words a prostitute would use. It was just a ploy to get into his room – to find out if there was any incriminating evidence clearly on show – before she would have made her excuses and left.

Verbier looked at her with an air of faint disgust at first, but his eyes still travelled over her body. He was thinking about it.

'No. I . . . um . . . I'm very busy at the moment.'

'No problem,' smiled Müller as he opened his room door. She tried to look over his shoulder without being obvious about it. But there was little to see other than a partially unpacked suitcase on the bed. 'If you change your mind, you might find me in the bar later. Bar Juanita. You could buy me a drink . . . to go with the flowers.'

'Yes . . . erm . . . I don't think I'll have time. But thank you. Good day.' With that he closed the door.

Müller felt she'd put on a good performance and acted the part. But it had been nerve-wracking. Her legs were shaking, her heart pounding. It was the first time she'd ever been face-to-face with a man who she assumed was a murderer, whose work was not yet done, and yet she was powerless to intervene and stop him.

All she could do was watch and wait.

She was about to toss the cellophane-wrapped flowers into the nearest bin, when it suddenly dawned on her what a gift she'd been given when he'd handed her the bouquet. It hadn't been her plan. The flowers were meant merely as a ruse.

Verbier hadn't been wearing gloves. His fingerprints had literally been handed to her – by the man himself. Yes, there would be other prints on there. Hers, the flower seller's, the receptionist's. But back in the lab, Schmidt would be able to cross-check against prints found in Karl-Marx-Stadt and Leinefelde. Eisenach was more difficult, as only the Stasi knew where the original murder had taken place. And what about Schneider's murder in the woods near Estedt? She was convinced that was nothing to do with Verbier anyway.

The prints would provide her with enough evidence for an arrest. She took out the spare evidence bag she always carried in her pocket, and – using her handkerchief – carefully sealed the bouquet wrapper inside.

Then she flung the flowers themselves in the bin. They had served their purpose.

Müller found a stool at the bar which had a good view of reception. She ordered a coffee, and then prepared for a long wait. She'd picked up the magazine from the coffee table again, although she wouldn't have a chance to read it. The fashion periodical served two purposes: as something to hide behind to observe the lobby, and as something to discourage would-be suitors or over friendly barflies.

When Verbier finally emerged back on the ground floor, she saw him wander over to reception – presumably so they could guard his key until he returned. She waited a second or two until she followed, allowing time for any Stasi tail – if Verbier had been assigned one – to show themselves. Then she was after him. But when she got out of the front door, she initially couldn't see him. She thought he might have turned left or right, heading for the bus or train station. But then she spotted him, darting between the traffic, heading for the car park. She quickly followed, glancing over her shoulder to make sure no one was following her.

One thing she hadn't thought about was whether the Lada was fast enough to keep up with the Citroën. If Verbier's route lay on the motorway network, Müller doubted it would be, although compared to cars manufactured in the Republic, the Lada was no slouch.

Driving north through Magdeburg, she initially assumed that was where he was heading. But instead of aiming for the motorway junction, he chose a national road signposted to Haldensleben instead.

It was then that Müller knew. He was heading back to the Altmark.

To Gardelegen.

To the scene of the horrific massacre all those years ago.

When they reached Gardelegen, Müller tried to hang back in the car a little more. In a built-up area, there was more chance of him regularly checking his rear-view mirror. She might have been spotted already. She'd nearly lost him between Haldensleben and Gardelegen, and in accelerating to catch up had moved in a little too close. She was further back now, but she had a good idea, from the route he was taking, where he was planning to visit. It was the same place he'd made the phone calls to.

Apartment 18, Stendaler Strasse 73, the former home of the late Lothar Schneider, and still the home of his widow.

She watched him park the car, approach the apartment block, and ring the entry phone. Someone had let him in. She had no idea whether Frau Schneider was at home and had let him in, or whether it was someone else.

Now she had to make a choice. She could wait here, and make sure she was able to follow the Citroën to Verbier's next destination, wherever that was. Or she could enter the apartments herself, and try to overhear what was going on – but that was fraught with danger in case he recognised the 'prostitute' from Magdeburg, as he surely would, given their close-up conversation outside his hotel room.

Or she could wait until he'd left, and question Frau Schneider or whoever else he'd gone to talk to.

None of the options were satisfactory. She had no real idea what to do.

She discounted the idea of going into the apartment block after him – there was too much risk of being spotted.

After about fifteen minutes, her options were narrowed again. Verbier came out, and got back into the Citroën. He started up the car, and began pulling out of the parking spot. Müller fired up the Lada's engine, but – as she had done in the Hotel International – she waited a couple of seconds before moving off, to check she wasn't the only interested party following the Frenchman.

This time she wasn't. She noticed a dark Volvo saloon take off after him. The car was sinister enough. She knew the higher echelons of the Stasi often drove them. But what really sent a flush of adrenalin pulsing through her body was the identity of the driver and passenger she briefly spotted from the corner of her eye.

The driver was *Oberst* Klaus Jäger; his passenger, her own *Hauptmann*, Werner Tilsner.

Müller followed Jäger's Volvo, that was in turn following Verbier's Citroën. It was a procession of murder suspect, secret police, and detectives.

She realised they were taking a secondary road towards the north-west, out of the town limits, along Bismarkerstrasse.

As she drove, she took one hand off the wheel to check her camera was where she normally kept it in the glove compartment. Then she felt under her jacket to make sure the Makarov was in its shoulder holster, even though she knew it was. If Jäger and Tilsner were planning to do Verbier harm – to kill him even, to stop him exposing them – then she would have two choices: to use force to try to stop them and protect her suspected murderer, or use the camera to record what was going on as evidence. She couldn't do both at once.

They turned right, down a narrow lane, before hanging back slightly. If she turned now, it would be obvious she was following. If she didn't, she might lose them. Jäger and Tilsner seemed to have no such fears. Perhaps they didn't care if Verbier realised they were tailing him.

She overshot the turning, then did a U-turn across the road, first checking no other traffic was in her way. Then she turned into the lane. If Jäger and Tilsner saw her turn into the lane in the distance now, then at least they might think that she had come from the other direction – and that therefore she was an innocent member of the public.

The lane swung round to the right, and was fringed by apple trees, laden with fruit. An old woman was collecting some of the apples, using her long skirt as a makeshift basket. Up ahead, Müller could see both Jäger's and Verbier's cars parked by what looked like a huge wall made of brick and render, with an arch at its centre. Jäger and Tilsner were exiting the Volvo.

She couldn't risk going any further. She parked near the apple-picker, making sure the Lada was shielded from view by the tree and a hedge. Then she retrieved the camera from the glove compartment, and started walking towards the walled structure, nodding at the woman on the way.

As she approached, she saw what looked to be Verbier in the centre of the arch. Tilsner seemed to have his neck in an arm-lock, Jäger seemed to be jabbing him with something. Was it a gun?

She had a split second to make a choice. Camera or Makarov?

She levelled the camera, and fired off as many shots as she could.

48

When I come round, it is night-time. At first, I believe I have died. There is a mass of bodies around and above me, and I've collapsed at the bottom against the barn wall. There is a very small gap under the wall. I put my nose up to it and breathe in the fresh air as silently as possible.

I want to go and find Marcellin. I hope against hope that he has survived like me, even though I know in my heart that when he let go of my hand, that was it. He was giving up. Still, I want to find his body, cradle it, mourn for the brother who has been stolen from me by these animals that think of themselves as the master race: a master race that behaves worse than pigs. The stain on their name will never be erased.

I will never rest until I avenge the death of my two brothers. Never.

That thought fires me with new purpose. I try to wriggle free from under the bodies. All of them, I realise, are lifeless. Perhaps the Germans have gone. Perhaps I can escape. Perhaps I can rescue Marcellin's body, even if it's too late to save his life.

I still hear the occasional groan and cry. Not everyone is dead. There are other survivors.

Then I freeze. Play dead.

The Nazis are back.

The doors are opened.

In the dim light, I can see smoke escaping from the doors. There's some fresh air in the choking atmosphere at last.

One of the SS guards is calling out. 'We have medicines and bandages here to help those who are injured. Please make yourselves known.'

Other guards are shouting the same message. I hear different voices calling out, asking for help. I almost shout out myself, only the confusion of not knowing whether I am injured prevents me. I do not know if the pain in my legs and body is just the weight of dead men on top of me, or if I have actually been wounded in one of the grenade explosions.

That moment of doubt saves my life, at least for now.

Because it's a trap. Automatic fire breaks out again. I hear the cries of the wounded and dying. I realise they're aiming at anyone who's identified themselves as alive. I sense a hail of bullets in my direction, cracking into the masonry above my head, thudding into the bodies above me. They are protecting me.

A wall of human death is preserving my fragile life.

I keep still. Terribly still. Counting the seconds, the minutes, the hours. I know that at some stage, if I can cling on long enough, the Americans will come.

They will see this horror for themselves. They will let history be the judge.

With my limited knowledge of the German language, picked up mostly at Dora, I get the feeling that arguments are breaking out amongst our captors. But still they do their evil work. Now the doors are open, some of them are using pitchforks to skewer the dead and drag their bodies out, treating them as worse than useless carcasses of bad, rotting meat. At one point, I think one of the bodies belongs to Marcellin. I want to cry out, I want to run to him, but I'm not sure. I have a view with just one eye, along the line of the rear wall of the barn to the door.

I couldn't be sure.

And if it was him, he was dead.

The most pitiful sounds are the cries and appeals of the badly wounded. Some of them speak in languages I don't understand. Some of the fractured German I don't understand. But then I hear a voice I understand all too well.

A fellow Frenchman, crying in French.

'Shoot me, please shoot me,' he cries. 'I cannot bear it.' He screams in agony. I can only assume he is badly burnt. I cannot see him through the pile of bodies.

Then I hear the shot, and his screams are no more.

I find myself drifting in and out of consciousness.

When I wake, I hear more shooting and more cries, and something in me snaps.

I summon up all my remaining energy and finally work myself free.

I crawl towards the door.

I'm just about to try to make a run for it, when a Russian prisoner, naked and covered in soot and burns, walks straight out. I see him grabbed by one of the few remaining German soldiers, forced to kneel by a trench, and shot in the back of the neck.

I'm almost frozen in shock. A Hitler Youth member sees me. He raises his machine pistol. We lock eyes and I realises he is only a young boy. Barely past puberty. Fourteen-years-old, fifteen at most.

I am about to be slaughtered by a young boy.

A young boy whose mind has been perverted by his sadistic rulers of the so-called master race.

Transformed from a boy, into a killing machine.

49

August 1977
Gardelegen

Müller didn't know what she was expecting to see from her hiding place behind the hedge. There had been some sort of altercation, but no shooting or arrest.

Verbier now appeared to be kneeling down in front of the structure, but Jäger and Tilsner were moving off, back towards Jäger's Volvo. Müller had to make sure she wasn't spotted. Crouching down below the level of the hedge, she ran back towards the Lada. She lowered herself down beside the car, indicating with a raised finger to her lips that the apple-picking woman should remain quiet and not give her away. The woman gave a small nod of complicity, before turning back to her task of collecting more fruit.

The Volvo passed, seemingly without spotting Müller. She raised herself but then saw that Verbier, too, was returning to his car. Once again she crouched down, once again she made a silent plea to her fruit-picking accomplice. This time the woman laughed and said: 'Don't worry. I won't give you away.'

Once the Citroën, too, was past her and on its way back down the lane, she thanked the woman, and began to climb back into the Lada.

She quickly swung the car round, hoping at first to keep following the Frenchman. But by the time she turned the corner in the lane and could see straight down to the main road, the car was out of sight. And she didn't know which way he had gone.

In any case, she now had important evidence. The fingerprints and the photographs. She needed to get back to the Hauptstadt and set Schmidt to work.

Once she was back in Berlin, she sought Reiniger in his office. The man might be pompous and dull and always tried to play by the rules. But as far as Müller knew, he was also trustworthy, and the number of people she could trust was dwindling quickly.

'Is this room secure, Comrade *Oberst*?' she asked him.

'What do you mean, *is it secure*?'

'If I have a conversation with you here, can I be certain it's not being eavesdropped.'

Reiniger sighed. 'If we can't have a private conversation in my office, then the world has arrived at a pretty messy place.'

'I would rather be certain,' said Müller.

'All right,' said Reiniger, putting on his jacket. 'Let's go for a walk around Alexanderplatz. There's usually safety in numbers.'

After they'd bought a couple of coffees, and found a quiet corner, they sat down. Müller stared Reiniger hard in the eyes.

'You've always looked after me, Comrade *Oberst*, and I am very appreciative of that.'

'Think nothing of it, Karin. As you say, it's about trust. You are an honest detective. I want to try to promote your career, although things haven't been going so well recently. But I don't think that's entirely your fault.'

'What I'm about to tell you may make you angry.'

'Go on. I might as well hear it.'

Müller gave a long sigh. She didn't want to turn into a snitch. But she needed some sort of protection, some sort of help. Reiniger was best placed to provide it.

'You know the murder cases that I've been removed from.'

Reiniger glared at her. 'I hope you haven't been interfering again. There's only so much I can do to protect you if you defy orders.'

'Just hear me out, Comrade *Oberst*, please.'

Reiniger gave a small nod.

'What if I told you I had photographic evidence of two Stasi officers meeting the murder suspect in those cases, evidence of them threatening and assaulting him, but *not* arresting him?'

'Well, that would be very odd indeed – and very dangerous for them, and you. The last I knew, there wasn't an actual suspect – more a nebulous counter-revolutionary group that are considered to be responsible.'

'We know that's a lie. Unfortunately we don't know why.'

'Careful, Karin. And how – precisely – can you, an officer who isn't even on the case, know that that theory is even erroneous, let alone – as you call it – a *lie*? That's a very serious charge.'

'I have fingerprint evidence.'

Reiniger. 'Really? And how did you acquire that, given you are off the case? And why didn't you hand over this evidence to the Ministry of State Security, given they are now in charge of it?'

'You know very well why.'

Reiniger gave a long, drawn out sigh before pausing dramatically. Müller could hear the rapid drumming of her pulse in her ears, filling the silence. 'Bring me the fingerprint evidence. Show me the photographs. Then we will see. But I don't fully understand what you want me to do.'

'I need some help. I can't do this alone.'

'But you have a deputy. You have a chief forensic scientist at your disposal.'

'The forensic scientist, yes. A deputy that I trust? I'm afraid I don't have that at the moment, Comrade *Oberst*. I think you can probably guess why.'

Reiniger nodded slowly. 'As I say, bring me the evidence. Make sure that it is absolutely watertight and cannot be challenged. Then we will see.'

Müller sought out Schmidt. She found the *Kriminaltechniker* poring over some slides in the lab, evidently working on something for someone else. That would have to wait.

She took him to a quiet corner. 'Where can we talk with reasonable secrecy, Jonas?'

'I always think the dark room is a good place, Comrade *Major*.'

'Good idea. I have some film evidence I need developing too. In secret. In fact, I need to be there while you do it.'

They moved to the dark room. Schmidt turned on the red safelight – illuminating himself in such a way that it almost looked like he was glowing in the embers of a fire. It made Müller shiver; it was too close to what she imagined the poor souls in that awful barn near Gardelegen must have looked like. Then she had a sudden thought – was that strange wall, where Verbier had been kneeling down, the remains of the barn?

She voiced the thought to Schmidt. 'Just before we start, Jonas, tell me that the exact location of that barn where the massacre took place?'

'Just to the north-west of Gardelegen, a couple of kilometres away. The Isenschnibbe estate. Hang on a minute, I can show you what it looked like.' He turned the main lighting on, lifting the red glow that had so unnerved Müller, and then opened his briefcase. 'Here's a pamph—'

Before he finished his sentence, Müller grabbed it from his hand. There was a photograph of some sort of memorial on the cover. It was where she had been today – where she'd seen the strange truncated wall. Where Verbier had knelt, presumably to pay his respects to those who hadn't survived. Where Jäger and Tilsner had disturbed him, threatened him, assaulted him. Desecrating that hallowed space. In an instant, her vision of the whole case flipped. Was Verbier really the murderer here? Had all of those guilty of such a barbaric atrocity been punished? Or had he found out that some had secured amnesties in questionable circumstances? Müller would never believe in taking an eye for an eye, a life for a life – but if this was the case, was he merely, in his own warped way, trying to right a wrong? Which further begged the question, if this was the case, what were Jäger and

Tilsner doing? Simply trying to protect themselves? She tried
to swallow back the nausea. Jäger was capable of anything. But
Tilsner?

'Are you all right, Comrade *Major*?'

'Yes, yes, Jonas. Sorry. It's just such an awful period in
Germany's history. Anyway, thank you. While the lights are on,
before we get on to the photographs I've taken, I've got this.'
She handed the sealed evidence bag to Schmidt. 'That wrapper is from a bouquet of flowers. It should have four sets of
fingerprints on it. Firstly, the flower seller's. Secondly, my own.
Thirdly, a hotel receptionist's. But it's the fourth set of prints I'm
interested in. Even after that I handled the bouquet again – so
my prints may obscure that fourth set.'

'If what you say is the case, we should still be able to get a
clear print. As long as the flower vendor used a new wrapper
that hadn't been handled previously.'

'Ah, I hadn't thought of that.'

'It doesn't matter. Even in that scenario, we may get something. Good work. And clever too. I'd never have thought about
handing someone flowers to get their prints. But it's the sort of
gift that isn't easy to refuse.'

Müller decided to accept the praise rather than reveal it had
been a happy accident. Sometimes it was useful for your subor-
dinates to believe you were wiser than was actually the case.

'Did we get prints from the Ronnebach murder, and the
Höfler killing?'

'Yes we retrieved some. I collected copies in person from my
opposite number in Karl-Marx-Stadt, and got the forensic team

in Leinefelde to send me a set. Of course, we don't know if any of them relate to the suspected killer.'

'No. Perhaps it's a long shot. But I'm convinced the fourth set of prints on the bouquet wrapper do belong to the murd . . .' She stopped herself mid-sentence. Müller realised she was no longer prepared to label Verbier that way. She knew too much now. 'I'm convinced they are the prints of our suspect.'

'You actually met him?' asked Schmidt, a look of awe across his face.

Müller nodded. 'But I wasn't in a position to arrest him. I was under cover. I had no back up, and – until we do find matching prints – no real evidence.' She pointed at the bag containing the wrapper. 'That is our evidence. You need to make sure there are no mistakes, Jonas. And this must remain strictly between you and me. The same goes for the photographs when we develop them. I went out on a limb to support you. For now, I've over-looked things. For now.'

'I understand, Comrade *Major*,' said Schmidt, shame-faced. 'I assure you, you can rely on me. I won't let you down again.'

'I hope so, Jonas. I won't give you a third chance. Grab this one while you can. If anyone from the Stasi approaches you, if *anyone* approaches you, including Reiniger, you tell them noth-ing. The only person you talk to is me. The fingerprint analysis must be done in secret. The photos we're about to develop must be kept secret. In a moment, you'll see why.'

Müller handed him her camera, and Schmidt once again turned the lighting to filtered, red safe-mode.

Schmidt got his developing trays and solutions ready.

'Do you know if you used Orthochromatic or Panchro-matic film?'

'I've absolutely no idea what you're talking about, Jonas.'

'In which case, I'd better use a developing bag to be on the safe side. That will keep the light out.'

After several minutes of adding various chemicals into the developing drum, and Müller starting to get a headache from all the smells, Schmidt washed off the film and hung it up to dry. From these small negatives, Müller didn't expect him to be able to see who the subjects were – she'd been at too great a distance.

The forensic scientist confirmed as much. 'If you're hoping to get a clear view of the faces of the people in these, you might be disappointed. I think you were too far away. We can try enlarging them when we print them off, of course, but unless you've got a very steady hand or it was very strong light, there's no guarantee. You needed a camera with a longer lens. But I can see where it is taken. I can see the relevance.'

That might be the case, but if the enlargement did work, then the subjects of Müller's camera work were likely to come as a big shock to him.

Once Schmidt had done the enlarged prints, he started rocking the developing bath from side to side. The faces were not totally clear, but clear enough.

'Good grief!'

'Keep your voice down, Jonas. You can see why I'm insisting on absolute confidentiality.' In the black and white photograph, Tilsner's face was reasonably clear, and straight on to the camera.

The armlock he had Verbier in was obvious too. Jäger's face was in profile, but still instantly recognisable. There would be no way they could deny it.

'What's going on here, Comrade *Major*? I thought *Hauptmann* Tilsner worked for us? And – if you don't mind me asking – if Comrades Jäger and Tilsner *were* on official business, why were you spying on them. Isn't that putting yourself at risk?'

Suddenly, Müller was less sure of herself. That was something she hadn't considered. The Stasi had taken over the case. Perhaps they *were* on official business. After all, it was no secret that Tilsner helped the Stasi. He'd virtually admitted as much. Jäger *had* admitted as much, at the end of the graveyard girl case. But then she remembered about Harald Scholz – Jäger's real name, his childhood name. She remembered that Scholz – so Lehmann said, and she had no reason to doubt him – had been one of the Hitler Youth guards that had gone to the barn. And now, there was a photograph of him back there, if Müller was correct in her assumption of where Verbier had been on the night of 13 April 1945, jabbing his finger in the chest of one of the very few survivors. There was no way this was official business. No way at all.

50

Continuation of transcribed and translated interview
with Hitler Youth member Günther Palitzsch, conducted
by Captain Arthur T. Wagner of the Ninth Army War
Crimes Branch on 25 April 1945, at 1515 hours

Wagner: Do you feel able to carry on, Günther, now you've
had a break?

Palitzsch: Yes. Sorry.

Wagner: There's no need to apologise. It's important that
we get this correct and that your account is as full, as
truthful and as accurate as possible. Now, you began to tell
me about the initial events at the barn. But how long did
you stay there? And what else did you witness?

Palitzsch: There were more shootings. The north-west
door was blasted open by a hand-grenade exploding inside.
Grenades were being thrown in all the time. I don't know
how anyone survived, really.

(PALITZCH PAUSES AND HOLDS HIS HEAD IN HIS HANDS)

Wagner: Take your time. There's no rush.

Palitzsch: I did see one prisoner escape, though. I think he was Polish. He burst out of the barn, and was grabbed by a dog in the dark. Guards were shooting towards him, but he must have known some German. He told people to stop shooting. In the confusion, it sounded like an order from a superior. He managed to escape across the fields. I heard he managed to hide in another barn until the Americans came. But some of the others who escaped weren't so lucky, and the paratroopers went after them with grenades.

Wagner: How long did you stay at the barn?

Palitzsch: Until about 10 p.m. I think. But then we were ordered back in the early hours to clear up everything.

Wagner: What did that involve?

Palitzsch: Various groups had been mobilised to take part. The Hitler Youth, in other words us, about 150 or so from the *Volkssturm* – the home guard – then another thirty or so from the fire brigade and emergency service. They were digging trenches to bury the dead, that sort of thing. But some of them refused. They couldn't stand all the shooting, the moans of the wounded. Some of them just left – defying their orders.

Wagner: When did you see the French prisoner?

Palitzsch: There was an incident involving a Russian. He came walking, naked, out of the barn. An *Unteroffizier* made him kneel by one of the trenches and shot him in the neck.

While that was happening, I saw this other prisoner come towards the door. I was worried the *Unteroffizier* would get him too. We just sort of locked eyes with each other.

(PALITZSCH BECOMES UPSET AND ASKS FOR ANOTHER BREAK – INTERVIEW SUSPENDED FOR THE DAY)

51

August 1977
Keibelstrasse People's Police HQ, East Berlin

Heavy rapping on the locked dark room door interrupted Müller and Schmidt just as they were finishing up.

'Quick. Give me the first set of prints, Jonas.' Müller jammed them in her briefcase. 'Is there anywhere completely safe for you to put the evidence bag and the negatives?'

Schmidt nodded, and had already pre-empted her. 'I use this wall safe for anything sensitive. Only I know the code.'

More banging on the door. Then muffled shouts. 'Karin, Jonas. This is urgent. Can you let me in, please?' It was Reiniger.

Müller waited until Schmidt had closed the safe, and set the combination lock, before she let Reiniger in.

He immediately handed her a piece of paper. 'Karin, you need to ring this number urgently. It's not good news, I'm afraid.'

'What is it?' shouted Müller as she rushed to a phone.

'I don't want to discuss it in an open office. But once you've spoken to them, if you need any help, be sure to let me know. And I wouldn't do it here. Go to the privacy of your own office.'

Müller found herself hyperventilating as she sat down in her office, about to make the call. The piece of paper with the number on quivered in her hand. She tried to control her breathing. It had to be something serious and important for Reiniger to interrupt them.

She dialled the number, her hand still trembling.

'*Major* Karin Müller of the People's Police here. I was told you wanted to speak to me.'

'Ah yes, Comrade *Major* Müller. I'm the head of children's services for the Friedrichshain district. It's concerning your children.'

Müller's heart hammered in her chest. 'There's nothing wrong, is there? They're all right?'

'They are well but they are now in our care.'

Müller felt her world crash down around her in an instant. Her whole body – her very insides – felt frozen to the core. She found herself struggling for breath. In her selfishness, by letting herself get too absorbed in her work, she had lost the most precious gifts she'd ever been given. The children she'd longed for, and that she'd been told, time and time again, she would never be able to have. Their birth had been a miracle – and she was in danger of tossing it away. She wasn't going to let that happen.

'What do you mean "*in your care*"? They're well looked after – they have a full-time carer.'

'Your grandmother, yes. You have a full-time job.'

What was happening here? It seemed like a deliberate attack on her and her family. 'Yes, but I look after them too.'

'Well, I am afraid your grandmother has been arrested.'

Müller stifled a gasp. She had to try to regain control of the situation – she had to fight back. 'Arrested? That's ridiculous. She's a pensioner.'

'It's out of our hands, I'm afraid, Comrade Müller. Your grandmother failed to pick the children up from the summer club in Volkspark Friedrichshain, and so she has been arrested and charged with child abandonment.'

Surely Helga wouldn't have forgotten? There must be something more to it than that. 'That's absurd. There must have been some sort of mistake.'

'There is no mistake.' The woman's voice had an icy coldness, as though she would brook no argument. She sounded almost if she were reading from a script. 'The situation will come up for review in a month's time. If there has been no improvement in your domestic situation, the children will formally enter the Republic's children's home system where they will receive a proper socialist education. You can be sure that they will come out as fully formed socialists as adults.'

This was like some sort of horror film. It couldn't be happening.

'Can I see the children?'

'Not at present, no.'

Müller bit her lip. She was trying to stay in control, but could feel her throat tightening, the tears starting to fall even as she attempted to choke them back. 'Please. I'm asking you as a fellow woman.'

'We can review the situation in a month's time.'

Müller felt desperate. She had brought all this on herself. She'd been playing the heroine, posing as a prostitute, following cars all over the country while here – in Berlin – her life had been torn apart.

She knew there was no point trying to argue with the woman. 'Do you know where my grandmother is?'

'I'm not certain, but the information we have is that she's being taken to Hoheneck Women's Prison.'

Hoheneck. It had as bad a reputation for women as Hohenschönhausen and Bautzen did for men. It would also be impossible to visit there while she was carrying out her job – it was right in the south of the Republic, near Karl-Marx-Stadt. She ended the call. There was nothing more to say to the official. It wouldn't have been that woman's decision. A darker hand was at play here, she was sure. She had dared to stand up to the Stasi. This was their way of paying her back, by ripping her children – barely seventeen months old each – from the bosom of their home. If she wanted them back, the Stasi would want her to tell them everything she knew. To hand over the fingerprints. To hand over the photographs of Jäger and Tilsner's meeting with Verbier. Was Jäger behind this?

She held her head in her hands, her elbows resting on her desk. Part of her wanted to give in, to give the Stasi what they wanted, even if that involved conspiring to continue in the cover-up of what some of their officers had done at Gardelegen at the end of the war. Surely she had to put Jannika and Johannes first? Somehow she had to win them back. She couldn't have them ending up like Irma Behrendt. Or worse like her friend Beate. That was what the Republic's children's home system could do to you at its very worst.

But a little nagging voice was saying the complete opposite. That what she should do is stand up for herself. Fight fire with fire. The question was, did she have enough ammunition to win the fight?

52

Tierpark, East Berlin

Perhaps it was Jäger's dark sense of humour – wanting to meet in the Hauptstadt's zoo, the Tierpark, somewhere Jannika and Johannes already loved visiting, despite being too young to fully appreciate it. He was toying with her. Showing her what she would be missing if she didn't cooperate.

She saw him standing with his back to her, by the polar bear enclosure – the designated meeting place. He turned as she approached, almost as though he knew she was there. Perhaps he had an earpiece hidden under his fashionably long hair, and a radio link to a nearby agent who been tailing her.

He looked to have aged since she last saw him up close. There was a hint of crow's feet at the side of his eyes, which were surrounded by dark circles. He looked like a tortured soul. She immediately felt she had the upper hand.

'Thank you for agreeing to meet, Comrade *Oberst*.'

'It's always a pleasure, Karin. Shall we go and sit on the bench?'

They moved over to the seat near the family cemetery of the Treskows, an enclave built into the zoo, and a less-popular spot for visitors. You were less likely to be overheard there.

'You've heard about my family situation, no doubt?'

'I have. It's most unfortunate.'

'The timing wasn't good either. It came as I was doing a little historical research, and somehow I think it might help me.'

Müller could see from Jäger's eyes that he was beginning to sense that this time, the balance of power might have shifted. Normally it was Müller asking for something from him. She wouldn't be asking this time. She would be demanding.

'You see, I know that you were *Harald*.'

'Don't use that name,' he spat.

'I know what you were. And I know where you were that night. You know the night I mean, don't you?'

'I wouldn't threaten me like that, Karin. There are those at Normannenstrasse who want a much more serious outcome for you than what has just happened.'

Müller gave a thin smile. 'I know I can't fight the Ministry for State Security. We're all on the same side after all, aren't we? But I can fight corrupt officers within the Ministry. And I can bring pressure to bear on you, just like you have brought pressure to bear on me.' She reached down, and pulled some papers from her briefcase. 'As part of my historical research, during my recent leave, I happened to visit Gardelegen. Guess who I saw having a friendly chat at the memorial?'

She showed him the photograph; Tilsner with Verbier in an armlock and Jäger jabbing his finger into the Frenchman's chest.

Jäger tossed the photograph aside. 'This means nothing. As a full colonel of the Ministry for State Security I can interview who I want, when I want, and how I want.'

'I'm sure that's the case in the Republic. But what would happen if newspapers in the West got hold of this? What would happen if they found out that Nazis – and that's what you are, Harald, make no mistake – currently hold down senior positions in the Ministry for State Security? Do you think you'd still be a full colonel then? They wouldn't be able to get rid of you fast enough. All that education about the Fascists doing this, the Fascists doing that, the overwhelming need for an *Anti-Fascist* protection barrier. And then there is a Nazi – more than one no doubt – sitting right in their midst.'

'You know you are treading on dangerous ground, Karin, making threats like this. I said at the beginning of this conversation, there are those who would like you dealt with more permanently.'

'Like you did to my ex-husband?'

'That wasn't my doing. I tried to protect him.'

'So you say, Harald. But you see, your whole life is a lie. So why should I believe anything you say? Anyway, I wouldn't make what you say are threats without taking out some sort of insurance policy. I've made sure that should I die unexpectedly – even if it's framed in terms of an accident – which I know is your favourite modus operandi – if I die unexpectedly, then I've taken steps to make sure the material will be released to the Western press at that point too. Automatically. It's all written down. It's all photocopied. And I've talked to Verbier.'

Müller was winging it now. She hadn't made any such deposition. There were no arrangements for if she died. But it would do no harm for Jäger to think there were. But she had talked to Verbier – briefly. If only to offer her services as a prostitute. *Ha!* It was almost laughable. But there was a deadly serious motive behind her threats. 'I'm sure you have plenty of surveillance cameras at the Interhotel International in Magdeburg. It's well known for being one of the Ministry's favourite operating grounds – all Interhotels are. Go through the photos you have from the camera trained on the outside of Verbier's room. You'll see a woman in a black curly wig with dark glasses talking to him. It's me.'

'I know. I've already seen the photos.'

Jäger's revelation held little surprise for her. She'd half-expected as much.

'And I have to let you know that I can arrest Verbier, at any time, just like that.' She clicked her fingers. 'I have his fingerprints. I have matches with the murders in Leinefelde, in Karl-Marx-Stadt, in Eisenach.' She was stretching the truth now, but she didn't care. 'He's proved he's worked out where all the high-ups are who dirtied their hands with their evil work at the Isenschnibbe estate. If I arrest him, he will no doubt sing like a canary. The story for the Western press will get better and better.'

Jäger sighed, bent his head, and covered his face with his hands. 'You don't understand what it was like at the end of the war. I envy your generation. We carry the guilt every day. There were terrible things done, I admit. But we were just boys who were following orders. We were as sickened as everyone else. We only shot over people's heads or deliberately missed.'

'Who did?'

'Me and Günther. My best friend from childhood. He worked on the Isenschnibbe estate. He was forced to take part too, and you know who he is. I thought he was your friend too. I thought you were close. He told me Frau Rost recognised him and you saw it.'

'I don't understand,' said Müller, but slowly she was starting to.

'When you went to interview Frau Schneider the first time, and she wasn't in.'

The *estate*. The old woman who recognised him from the estate.

'Yes, Karin. The penny's dropped. Some years after it all, Werner Tilsner was given a new identity too. The condition was that we work as spies, enforcers, for the Stasi. Werner Tilsner was Günther Palitzsch. He had been fifteen and in the Nazi Youth like me. Participating in it was compulsory. And Günther – Werner – was also at the barn.'

53

14 April 1945
Gardelegen, Nazi Germany

I wait for the shot, frozen. Instead, he beckons me forward urgently. I don't know if it's a trap, but I am almost past caring.

While the rest of the guards are distracted by the prisoner who's just been killed with a shot to the neck, I run.

Straight towards the boy.

Expecting at any moment to be downed in a hail of gunfire.

I am nearly on him, and still he doesn't shoot. Then he fires off his gun, but deliberately over my head. I can see him virtually aiming for the sky.

'Go into the woods. Hide,' he says. He uses simple, easy German. I can understand him. 'There's another barn further on. Hide there.'

'We can't do this,' says his colleague. 'We'll be shot. Look out. Here comes Pfeiffer.'

I glance round. It's another Hitler Youth member bearing down on me, his gun raised.

'You, halt there!'

My legs go weak, knowing this is it. But I stumble on. Then I trip on the uneven ground.

'No, Willi, don't,' cries the first boy. He's leapt in between me and the one named Pfeiffer.

'Get out of the way, Günther. You're a coward. You should have shot him. Now I must do it.'

'No,' says the one called Günther, the one protecting me. 'The Americans are coming. Let him go. He's like a walking skeleton anyway.'

'I'm warning you, Günther. Otherwise I will kill you.'

Then the other boy – the one who'd been facing the barn next to Günther – puts his body in the way too.

'Will you shoot us both, Willi?'

'There's another coming out,' says the one called Günther. '*Scheisse*. He *is* half-dead.'

I start to get to my feet to run as the one called Willi is distracted. But I turn to see this other prisoner.

What I see leaves my legs weak.

No, no. It can't be!

A half-naked figure, barely recognisable as a man, is dragging himself towards us. An awful, putrescent wound on his upper arm, burns on his chest and face, skin taut against his bones as there is no flesh left on him.

He is like a ghost.

It's Marcellin, back from the dead and screaming in agony.

'Shoot me. Shoot me, please, shoot me.'

'Marcellin, no!' I scream.

But the one called Willi has already raised his gun, and fires it into my brother's chest. Again, and again, and again.

Günther and his friend try to hold me back. But I must reach my brother. I must cradle him in my arms.

But when I do, his eyes have rolled to the back of his head.

He has gone.

I look up at Willi with pure hatred in eyes and heart.

He laughs. 'You're next.'

He raises his gun again for me.

To deliver the bullet which will finally take me from this hell.

54

Continuation of transcribed and translated interview with Hitler Youth member Günther Palitzsch, conducted by Captain Arthur T. Wagner of the Ninth Army War Crimes Branch on 26 April 1945, at 1000 hours

Wagner: You were telling us about the prisoner who appeared at the barn door, Günther.

Palitzsch: Yes. I think he thought I was going to shoot him, but I wasn't going to shoot anyone. I got the impression that he was desperate and didn't care any more. He was just running straight at me.

Wagner: But you didn't shoot? What about those next to you?

Palitzsch: Most people, I think, were watching what went on with the Russian, the one who was shot in the back of the neck by the SS officer and pushed into the trench. It was awful.

Wagner: What was the name of the SS officer who murdered the Russian?

Palitzsch: I don't know. I didn't recognise him.

Wagner: Are you sure about that, Günther? If you try to protect people now, after all that happened, with all the evidence we have, and then it turns out you are lying . . . well, that could increase the chances of you being prosecuted for war crimes.

Palitzsch: I understand that. But I swear to you I don't know who he was.

Wagner: Let's return to the prisoner running towards you.

Palitzsch: I whispered to Harald – Harald Scholz who was next to me – I said to him to shoot over his head, not at him. He was so thin, I expected him to die of starvation anyway. I did shoot, but I made sure the shot went well over his head.

Wagner: Are you sure it isn't that you simply missed? That you were trying to kill him, but you weren't a very good shot?

Palitzsch: Ask the prisoner, ask Harald. They know the truth. I showed him the woods where he could run to and hide. Told him about the second barn. Why would I do that if I intended to kill him? But then Pfeiffer saw what was happening.

Wagner: Pfeiffer?

Palitzsch: Willi Pfeiffer. He was the head of our troop – the *Kameradschaftsführer*. The prisoner was running towards the woods, but it was more a slow, painful shuffle, dragging his legs, stumbling. And then he fell, and Pfeiffer raised his pistol and was about to shoot him. I leapt up and made sure my body was between Pfeiffer and the prisoner. If he wanted to shoot him, he would have to shoot me first. Then Harald joins me, so we're a sort of human shield. Then another prisoner starts running towards us from the barn. He's in an awful state. Naked from the waist up, burns over his body and face, and a terrible gaping wound on his arm. He looks half-dead. He was half-dead. At first I think he's trying to escape, but then he falls at Pfeiffer's feet and in this croaky voice pleads with him to shoot him. The first zebra appears to recognise him, cries out his name.

Wagner: Which was?

Palitzsch: Something French. Marcellin, I think. But I'm not sure. The first zebra rushes back towards this Marcellin, but before he reaches him Pfeiffer fires into this Marcellin's body, again and again and again. The first zebra falls to the floor, cradles this Marcellin in his arms, and then Pfeiffer raises his gun again and is about to shoot him too.

Wagner: What stopped him?

Palitzsch: People all around us were shouting that the Americans were here, that we had to get out and retreat quickly. Get away from that terrible place. We just ran off then, as quickly as we could. Before Pfeiffer had a chance to kill the other one too. I looked round once. The barn was still smouldering. I could still see the silhouette of that first zebra crouched over the one called Marcellin, cradling him in his arms. They were silhouetted on the brow of the hill.

I felt deeply ashamed then, that the lies of the Führer, the man we had all once believed in, had led us into committing such a terrible act.

Wagner: But you say that you personally did not kill or injure anyone?

Palitzsch: I know. But I was still a guard of that convoy, that last march. I was on guard outside that killing place. I witnessed things, atrocities, that I . . . I never believed man was capable of committing against his fellow man.

Wagner: That all sounds very noble, Günther. But are you sure you're not just making a fine speech to try to save your own skin?

Palitzsch: (GÜNTHER PALITZSCH BECOMES TEARFUL AGAIN BUT THEN COMPOSES HIMSELF AFTER TWO OR THREE MINUTES)

Sorry. I'm ready to carry on.

Wagner: We've pretty much finished, Günther, unless you had anything more you wanted to say.

Palitzsch: Well . . . only that I wanted to know what happened to him. That prisoner. The one I tried to save.

Wagner: He survived, Günther, although it was touch and go at one point. He's been in hospital recovering from severe malnutrition, dehydration, and smoke inhalation. I have no idea whether he'll ever be able to live a normal life again. If he does recover fully, think about the mental scars he will have, never mind the physical ones. He was one of three brothers used as slave labourers by the Nazis. His younger brother died in Mittelbau Dora camp, where they were forced in sub-human conditions to help build V1 and V2 rockets. The two older brothers survived a gruelling train transport from near Nordhausen to just outside Gardelegen. They were then forced to endure what was little more than a death march around villages surrounding the town. You and your townspeople then herded them like animals into that barn. The majority of prisoners died. More than a thousand. Marcellin Verbier was shot dead as you describe, though by all accounts it is unlikely he would have survived in any case. We hope that the sole surviving brother will soon be well enough to tell us his account. For your sake, you had better hope it tallies with your own.

(CAPTAIN WAGNER ENDS THE SESSION AT 1021 HOURS)

55

Müller didn't know if her game of brinkmanship with Jäger would pay off. She wasn't certain what connections the Stasi colonel had inside police headquarters at Keibelstrasse: it was possible he could make inquiries of any unofficial informers within the People's Police ranks and find out that Müller's claim to have a fingerprint match had been premature. But what she was banking on was his fear of Müller exposing the fact that he'd been a member of the Hitler Youth movement *and* involved in the Gardelegen massacre. That, despite holding a senior position in an organisation dedicated to flushing out fascists and counter-revolutionaries, he'd been part of a disgusting fascist atrocity – albeit as a teenager.

But as the hours ticked away in her curiously empty flat, the phone failed to ring. Müller felt like there was a huge weight pressing ever more firmly on her chest until she was almost struggling to breathe. She twisted her blonde hair in her fingers as she waited. She knew there were things she had to do, like expose the cover-up that happened after the massacre, prevent further murders and catch the culprit – whether that really was Verbier, or not. If it was Verbier, was his motive revenge? If so, why wait until now? Yet she felt paralysed and impotent in the face of her twin children's potential entry into the Republic's severe children's home system, and her grandmother's incarceration in one of its most feared jails.

She heard a key turning in the apartment's front door, which suddenly sent hope soaring. She clasped her hands to her chest.

Helga!

The two women rushed into each other's arms.

'I'm so, so sorry, Karin,' cried the older woman, burying her head into her granddaughter's shoulder. Then she pulled back, alarmed. 'But where are Jannika and Johannes?' The desperate look in Müller's face must have been all too clear. 'Oh no! What's happened?'

'I'm sure it's nothing,' lied Müller. 'Come and sit down first. I'll make you a coffee.'

But Helga stayed rooted to the spot. 'Where are they, Karin?'

'Come and sit down at least, then I'll explain. I'm sure it's all a misunderstanding that will be sorted out soon.'

Helga allowed herself to be led through to the living room, and gently eased down onto the sofa.

'It's not my fault, is it? It was like a nightmare. I was stopped by *MfS* agents on the way to the holiday club. They were insisting on going through my papers. They wanted to know why I was still registered as living in Leipzig, yet I gave my address as Strausberger Platz. It meant I was late to pick up the twins.'

Müller held her grandmother in a tight hug. 'No, it's absolutely not your fault, Helga. If anything, the fault is mine. I ought to be able to separate work from home life. But I'm afraid—'

Once again, Helga pulled out of the hug, and stared hard at Müller. 'Tell me they're all right, Karin. Where are they?'

'Temporarily, they're being cared for by Friedrichshain's children's services department.'

'Why?' cried Helga. 'You're here. I've been freed now. They have no reason not to be at home with us, where they belong.'

'I know. I agree,' said Müller, fighting back tears. 'It will be sorted out, I'm sure. Very soon, I hope. What about you? It must have been a horrible shock.'

'I don't think they were ever serious. I think it was all designed to put pressure on you. I wasn't even assigned a proper cell. Yes, I was frightened. I didn't know what was going on at first. But I never really believed they were going to be able to keep me in prison. I hadn't done anything wrong.'

Müller was tempted to say that an obstacle such as being innocent wouldn't necessarily stand in the way of the Stasi. For example, her own apartment was bugged – something she had kept from Helga, and the children themselves, who in any case were far too young to understand. And, of course, there were the visits of the Barkas campervan with the twitching curtains outside the apartment block. It was there less often these days, and the occupants inside didn't always bother to properly conceal their surveillance cameras behind the curtains. But she bit her tongue. It was nothing Helga needed to know.

Within a couple of hours of Helga's return, Müller received a phone call. A glowing warmth suffused her body as the disembodied voice at the other end of the line explained that Jannika and Johannes were being returned to her custody. She could collect the twins immediately. Müller's tears began to fall at last – tears that she couldn't stop, no matter how hard she tried.

'Oh God, Karin! What is it?' asked an alarmed Helga.

Müller beamed at her grandmother, though she knew her mascara would be running down her face by now: that she would look like the bereaved spouse of the victim from one of those West German crime dramas Helga was addicted to.

'It's nothing to worry about, Helga. These are tears of happiness. We can go and collect the twins right away. They're coming back home.' She didn't mention that the only reason it had all been sorted out so swiftly was because of her threat to expose Jäger. For him to have acted so fast, he must be a very scared man.

Müller pushed thoughts of Gardelegen, Verbier, and the series of murders he may have been responsible for out of her mind for the rest of the day. She was officially off the cases, and therefore felt no guilt in devoting the rest of the afternoon and evening to her family. They deserved it.

They travelled out to the Müggelsee in the Lada, and Müller treated the whole family to ice creams in a lakeside café. Then Müller and Helga sat on deckchairs at the Strandbad, the twins playing happily together – for once – with their buckets and spades in the sand in front of them. In a few hours, Müller's life had been transformed. But as she felt the glow of happiness in having her family back together, a passing cloud that shielded the sun temporarily reminded her of the darker forces that had brought her to her knees. She wouldn't forget. She wouldn't forgive. She would solve this case, and if this meant the downfall of Jäger and Tilsner, well, so be it. She knew things about them now – she had a powerful hand. The fact that her children had been returned and Helga had been freed, merely served to demonstrate its power.

'So what are you saying?' asked Reiniger, studying the photographs from the memorial of Verbier, Jäger and Tilsner.

'I'm saying, Comrade *Oberst*, that a senior member of the Ministry for State Security may be caught up in all this – *is* caught up in all this. Therefore I don't think justice is best served by leaving this in the Stasi's hands. They're potentially compromised.'

'But when we had this conversation before, I asked you to bring me not just the actual photographs, but also the fingerprint evidence you said you have.'

Müller could see the colonel was considering her request. She didn't want this to be the stumbling block. 'Comrade *Kriminaltechniker* Schmidt is confident of finding a match with the prints I provided from the wrapper the flowers were contained in. But he wants to be certain, and there is a lot of fingerprint evidence from the various crime scenes to sift through. Some of those prints are partial ones. So he's not quite there yet. But if we delay now, the Stasi could just close ranks. I believe I've identified the murderer.' Again, Müller felt uncomfortable about using the 'M' word, given what she now knew about Verbier. 'But he may not have been working alone. We need to do house-to-house inquiries in Gardelegen to try to piece this together. To try to find out who from that time was involved, and whether they may have been working together with our suspect to commit these crimes – or whether they may be next in line to be targeted. If you delay, Comrade *Oberst*, and then there is another murder, how would you feel? I believe I have demonstrated that this is clearly nothing to do with the Committee for the Dispossessed as the Ministry for State Security allege.'

Reiniger rubbed his hands across his face. He looked tired and conflicted by a choice between doing what good police work demanded, and what his political masters would require. 'You realise you're asking me to go to my superiors, to get them to go to the very top, and then countermand the Stasi? If you're wrong, that'll be you finished. You'll lose the flat in Strausberger Platz. The Lada. Everything. You might be putting your children's future in jeopardy, too, because Stasi officers have long memories.' Müller knew what Reiniger was saying was correct. 'And I won't be able to defend you this time, because I'll be finished too.' He looked rather forlornly at the three gold stars on his silver-braided epaulettes – first the left, then the right, as though if he went ahead with Müller's plan, he might be saying goodbye to them sooner than he'd like to.

'I understand what I'm asking of you, Comrade *Oberst*. But what we're talking about here are former Nazis who now serve the Stasi.'

'They were members of the Hitler Youth, Karin. There was no choice for them.'

'There's always a choice, Comrade *Oberst*. Perhaps not in joining the Hitler Youth. But they could have defied their orders if they'd had the courage to do so. You know that as well as I do.'

56

Reiniger's solution, if it was one, was something of a compromise in Müller's view. He managed to get permission for Müller's house-to-house inquiries, but only if they were conducted by local People's Police officers in Gardelegen, overseen by Müller. The local officers would be sensitive to what had happened there more than thirty-two years earlier – just before Müller herself had been born. For Müller, it was a lifetime ago. But the shame was still there. Everything was still raw. The name of the town itself would always be tainted by what had gone on in that barn on the night of 13 April 1945 and the following day. Where Müller and Reiniger disagreed was that she wanted to ringfence the inquiry from Tilsner. With what she now knew about the inquiry, she believed her deputy would be compromised. Reiniger demurred. Whether she liked it or not, Tilsner would be going back to Gardelegen with her.

The blond-haired, blue-eyed *Hauptmann* Janson couldn't hide his delight at seeing Müller again, or the fact that she'd managed to prise open the inquiry once more. In facing the same frustrations when the Stasi had taken over the inquiry into Schneider, Müller had forged an important ally.

'My men and I are thrilled to be asked to assist you, Comrade *Major*.'

'Good. And call me Karin, please. My deputy here is Werner.'

Tilsner nodded sullenly. He'd said little to her all journey, and she hadn't revealed to him that she now knew of his involvement at the Isenschnibbe barn massacre. But all throughout the drive from the Hauptstadt, little memories kept on jumping into her brain. Memories that only now made sense; Tilsner slamming the shot glass down when drinking Schnapps, which she'd been told was the Fascist way, and his over-the-top reaction to the West German politician's Nazi comments at the Eisenhüttenstadt steelworks.

Janson clapped his hands together, bringing her thoughts back to the present. 'Good. And you must both call me Berti. So, where would you like to start?'

'I think friends and relations of Lothar Schneider, and those of his contact inside the Potsdam Stasi jail, Ernst Lehmann. Schneider wanted to give me information – I got some of that via Lehmann. What do you think, Werner? Do you have any local knowledge? Didn't you say that you had relatives living in the area?'

Tilsner held her gaze and his face failed to give much away. If he knew that Jäger had told her about his previous life – as Günther Palitzsch, the teenage Hitler Youth member – then he wasn't revealing it. Perhaps she should have taken him aside and questioned him in private. But something told her she would find out more if she didn't reveal her full hand. 'I'm happy to go along with what you and Hauptmann J . . . , sorry, what you and *Berti* feel is best,' said her deputy. 'I told you. They were only distant relatives.'

Müller and Tilsner's first house call was once again to Lothar Schneider's widow in Stendaler Strasse. Müller was particularly interested in finding out what Verbier had been to see her about, that night she'd tracked him from his hotel in Magdeburg.

Tilsner and Müller sat next to each other on the sofa, while Frau Schneider turned her armchair round to face them.

'Did you get anything useful from the man my husband referred you to?' asked the woman.

'We did, yes,' nodded Müller. 'Everything seems to lead back to something that happened in Gardelegen at the end of the war.'

The woman shrugged, with a resigned expression on her face. 'It's something that we all have to carry the shame for. Everyone round here, though some more than others.'

'Was your husband one of those, Frau Schneider?'

'No. He was in the Hitler Youth brigade. But he refused to go up to Isenschnibbe that day. He risked his own life to do that. In effect, he was disobeying orders. He could have been shot himself. He and his friend. Perhaps that was the one who he left the note about. But he still felt the guilt, we all did. And he volunteered to carry one of the crosses.'

'So he did feel some involvement?' asked Tilsner. His voice seemed nervous again to Müller, as though he would rather be anywhere else than he was right now. Talking about any other subject than he was right now. As though he was simply asking a question to go through the motions and to make Müller think he was playing an active part in the inquiry.

'Yes, but from what he said, he helped save someone, rather than kill anyone.'

Müller's ears pricked up at this. 'How so?'

'He and his friend found an exhausted, starving prisoner in a barn – another barn, not far from Isenschnibbe. He was a Frenchman. They gave him food, water. Guarded him almost, to make sure none of the other townsfolk could get to him. And then they told the Americans where he was. That man – that Frenchman – has always been eternally grateful for their help, but Lothar said it was the least they could do. Lothar was a good man, *Major* Müller. A kind man. He always insisted he had no choice but to join the Hitler Youth. But his family were no Nazis. They had a small farm between Gardelegen and Estedt. His mother tried to feed some of the prisoners when they marched past. She was prevented from doing so by the guards.' Her voice quietened almost to a whisper. Müller glanced at Tilsner to watch his reaction. He had his head lowered looking at his notebook, but not taking notes. *Is that a tear in his eye? Is he crying for himself, or in shame at what happened?* 'They are a good family, and he was a good man. He didn't deserve what happened to him.'

'Was their farm nationalised when others were?' asked Tilsner, still barely looking at the woman. Müller rolled her eyes. He was still desperately clinging to that theory. It wouldn't wash any more.

'No,' said Frau Schneider. 'Some of the smaller ones weren't, but of course they had to give a portion of their income and their production to the state, like everyone else.'

But Müller knew that line of questioning was a red herring. A red herring planted by the Stasi. And Müller now knew Tilsner was closer to that organisation than she'd ever been led to believe.

She wanted to move the questioning to something more productive. 'The prisoner you talked about, the one your husband helped in the barn, has he visited you recently?'

'He was French. Why would he be here in the Republic now?' Müller noticed the woman's eyes dart to the right. Normally that would indicate she was telling the truth, yet Müller knew she wasn't. Unless . . . unless she hadn't been in that night. Or Verbier had actually been visiting her neighbour, Frau Rost, the servant from Isenschnibbe estate. The one who'd thought she recognised Tilsner.

Müller pressed the point. 'We know who this Frenchman was.' She turned to Tilsner and gave him a meaningful glare. 'Don't we, Comrade *Hauptmann*?' She saw him cover his eyes with his hand. *What's going on in his brain? Can he see them? The prisoners? The prisoners he herded to their deaths, along with all the others?* Then she turned back to Frau Schneider. The woman was doodling on a piece of paper, possibly to calm her nerves. She was doodling *with her left hand*. That was why – when she'd constructed the lie about Verbier – she'd looked to the right. Straight out of the police manual. The lies of right-handed people tended to lead to leftward glances. Those of left-handers, to the right. She was definitely lying.

'I know you want to protect him. But I know he visited you. I was following him.' The woman gasped. Müller felt Tilsner give an involuntary shudder alongside her on the sofa. Both had something they were hiding. 'What did he say to you, Frau Schneider? Can I also remind you that obstructing a police inquiry is a very serious offence.'

The woman dropped her doodling pen onto the pad and was instead wringing her hands together, her eyes downcast. 'I'm sorry. I didn't want to do that.' She gazed with pleading eyes at Müller. 'I was just trying to protect him, just as my husband tried to protect him all those years ago.'

'Why does he need protecting, Frau Schneider?'

'He was devastated when he heard about Lothar. He was comforting me, too. But I could tell he was nervous. That he didn't want to stay too long. I got the feeling that he almost felt he was being hunted again. He asked about the same names as you.'

Müller felt a flutter in her belly, like a trapped bird or flying insect trying to escape. 'What do you mean, he asked about the same names?'

'Ronnebach ... Höfler ... Unterbrink ... the same list of names you had. I knew something must have happened to them. Yet he was asking if Lothar had left him a message – about those very same names. I thought he must be in some sort of trouble when I heard that.'

'Were those the only names?' asked Tilsner. His voice was light, gentle. Almost artificially so.

The woman frowned. 'I think so ... No! Wait! There was another. He asked if Lothar had ever mentioned anyone who used to be called something or other.' The woman started rubbing her forehead, as though that would help her remember. 'It'll come back to me in a moment. But I thought it was a strange phrase anyway. "*Used to be called*", he said, but perhaps – although his German was good – it might simply be that he was translating a French turn of phrase, or something similar.'

Frau Schneider looked up at Müller, as though she'd finished speaking.

'And the name? You can't recall it?'

The woman screwed her eyes up. 'Yes! Sorry. It was Willi. Willi Pfeiffer.'

There was little more the woman could tell them, but Müller had felt Tilsner's discomfort alongside her on the sofa throughout the conversation. He was holding himself terribly still, almost as though he'd been turned to stone. But if he was uncomfortable hearing Frau Schneider's account, Müller had every intention within the next few moments of ratcheting up his fear even more.

As they exited the Schneiders' apartment, Tilsner rushed ahead of her, about to descend the stairs.

She drew her Makarov from its holster, and slipped its safety catch. Tilsner heard the echo of the tell-tale click, and turned, a look of disbelief and terror on his face.

'Don't attempt to leave, Werner. Otherwise I'll have to arrest you.' She beckoned him with the gun. Then pointed to the neighbouring apartment door to the Schneiders'. The one where the old woman lived. The woman who thought she'd recognised him.

'Stand there,' she ordered, pointing to the doormat.

As she jabbed the pistol into Tilsner's back, she rang on the doorbell.

The old woman opened the door, then frowned when she saw who it was.

'You two again. What do you want this time?'

Müller gave Tilsner another prod with the gun, just to remind him it was there. 'I brought my deputy back to see you. He suddenly remembered where you and he knew each other from, didn't you, *Hauptmann*?'

Tilsner inched forward, hunched over like a naughty schoolboy anticipating his punishment at the headmaster's study door. 'Hello, Frau Rost.' His voice was barely audible. A whisper – from a fifteen-year-old boy trapped in the hell that was 1945.

'Günther?' She reached up, pulling his face down towards hers so she could study it more closely. 'It is! Günther Palitzsch. Wherever did you get to? You never came back to see me.'

Tilsner didn't answer. He was sobbing uncontrollably in the woman's embrace.

57

Magdeburg, East Germany

The man noticed the note as soon as he opened his hotel room door. The business card that he'd wedged between the door and door frame had been a crude way of telling if anyone had ignored the 'Do Not Disturb' sign. It fell to the floor as he entered, right next to a folded piece of paper that had been slipped under the door.

He bent down to pick it up, then unfolded it.

> I KNOW WHO YOU ARE.
> I KNOW WHAT YOU DID AT THE BARN.
> AND NOW I'M COMING AFTER YOU.

The man smiled wryly to himself as he crunched the piece of paper into a ball and then lobbed it towards the waste-paper bin, with a *petanque*-style underarm flip of the hand. Years of practice with the empty oyster shells on the Ile de Ré meant the paper ball hit its goal.

There was one person left that he wanted to find. To each of the previous targets, he'd typed exactly the same message he'd just received. In fact, there was a good chance it was one of his own notes that had been saved, and now it had been sent back to him. The paper looked similar.

Now he was the target.

It was ironic, but in some ways he wasn't surprised. There was only one man who knew enough about what had gone on, but who was now powerful enough to turn the tables on him.

Perhaps everything had been leading up to this point.

The man he wanted to find had now found him.

The others had just been warnings. This was the one he really wanted.

Would he come for him here?

Probably not. Interhotels were notorious as centres of Stasi spying. And if – as the businessman suspected – this particular Stasi senior officer had been pulling strings for his own ends, using the spy ministry's resources to settle his own personal score, he wouldn't want to do it somewhere where he could be seen or overheard.

He had no doubt that the woman he'd given the flowers to – the one posing as a prostitute – was one of them. He'd almost been tempted, but since that fateful day in 1945 he'd never strayed, and wasn't about to now. She had been a beautiful woman – her features reminding him a little of Marie-Ange in her younger days. Of how she looked when he'd finally arrived back, and found that – no – she hadn't slept with the Boche soldiers. She hadn't had their babies. She'd been waiting for him. Finally, he'd been able to say those words he'd been dreaming about saying almost every minute, every hour of that nightmare ordeal.

So he'd given the woman the flowers. Not because she reminded him of Marie-Ange. His wife – older now, but still beautiful – was waiting for him back home in Loix. No, he'd given her the flowers because he knew she was one of them.

So that they would have his fingerprints.

So that they would have the proof about him – even if they chose to ignore it. That he sent the notes but wasn't at the crime scenes.

The likelihood was that the one who was hunting him wouldn't come to the Interhotel.

But there was one place that was particularly appropriate for this to be settled, once and for all.

The place where it had all happened more than thirty-two years ago.

The place he would never forget.

The killing barn.

58

February 1950
Head office for the Protection of the National Economy, East Berlin

'So Harald and Günther, why do you think I've asked you to meet me here?'

Günther Palitzsch was confused. When Harald had contacted him, he hadn't initially wanted to meet – in fact he didn't want anything to do with him, or anyone from back then. He just wanted to forget. But try as he might, he couldn't. Now they were standing in front of someone who was calling himself Hauptmann Winkler, although they knew him by a very different name. He worked for some sort of police service that wasn't really a police service. It sounded a bit more like an internal spying ministry. The Gestapo revisited.

'We weren't sure,' Harald said. 'Why did you, Pfei—?'

The man now called Winkler held his hand up. 'Don't use that name any more, please. Comrade Hauptmann, or Comrade Winkler will suffice. I asked you here to make you an offer. To help erase something from your past that, otherwise, might hold you back here in the Republic.'

Günther still hadn't got used to calling this newly formed country by its correct name, the Deutsche Demokratische Republik. To him it was still Germany, the same Germany where terrible things had happened in the recent past, only now it was split into two: communist this side, to the East, capitalist on the other, to the West. He couldn't help thinking it would have been better if the Gardelegen area had fallen on the other side of the border. But perhaps – after all that had gone on – the town and its inhabitants didn't deserve it.

'You know that as former members of the Hitler Youth who were involved at Isenschnibbe, you will never be able to progress here. But I can offer you a way forward. You're both young, good-looking, about to turn twenty. We're recruiting agents and I know you two are able, and you will be loyal to me, because I will be the one giving you new identities, should you agree to work with us.'

He took some documents from a desk drawer, and handed one set to Harald, and one to Günther himself.

Günther looked down. At the top of the pile was an East German identity card. He flipped it open to the photo page, and there was a portrait of himself staring back at him. Where did they get that from? The name wasn't his. Instead, this person was apparently called 'Werner Tilsner'. He leant towards Harald, looking over his shoulder. Again, it was a photo of Harald, but a different name, this time 'Klaus Jäger'.

Next in the pile was another ID card, from something called the Ministerium für Staatssicherheit. *It had the same photo, but this time there was no name. It was anonymous.*

'We will be bound together. We each have our secrets,' said Winkler. 'But I will be senior to you, and you will do my bidding. In return, you get a new life here in the Hauptstadt, and a chance to forget, a chance to forge a new career, to be a valuable member of the Republic.'

As the years passed, Günther Palitzsch was never entirely sure why he agreed to the arrangement – especially when he'd seen that Harald's designation would be 'Leutnant', and his would be a mere 'Unterleutnant'. That was probably the payback for when he'd refused to let the prisoner be killed – for showing that he was willing to disobey orders. But he had said yes. He wanted to be protected from what had gone on in the barn. He knew there were survivors, though only a handful. He'd seen the utter hatred in their eyes when they'd tried to confront the townsfolk who'd been forced by the Americans to go up to the barn and dig up and rebury the dead. How the American soldiers had had to hold them back, to prevent them tearing the townspeople of Gardelegen apart. He knew – one day – one of them would seek their revenge. It was only a matter of time.

His best defence was to accept Winkler's arrangement. It wouldn't give him absolute protection. But with a new name, a new job, and a new place to live, he could begin to forget what had happened at that barn on the 13th and 14th of April 1945.

59

August 1977
Gardelegen, East Germany

Müller eventually bundled Tilsner down the stairs and back into the Lada without the need for any more prompting with the Makarov. He couldn't meet her eyes, let alone speak to her. She wasn't sure she wanted to meet his. Frau Rost may have thought the sun shone out of the bottom of the boy she once knew as Günther Palitzsch. But the man Müller knew as Werner Tilsner – the man whose bed she'd once shared a couple of times – had revealed himself to her as a liar, a coward, and something much, much worse. A former Nazi. She would never, could never, forgive him.

Forensic scientist Jonas Schmidt came through on the radio as they were heading back to Gardelegen People's Police offices to catch up with Janson.

'Hang on a minute, Jonas.' She covered the radio handset with her hand, and turned to Tilsner. 'Step outside of the car and go and stand over there where I can see you.' She pointed to a spot far enough away that he wouldn't be able to hear her conversation with Schmidt, but near enough that she would have him covered by the Makarov if he did try to escape.

'Am I under arrest?' he asked.

'Not at present. But I can't trust you any more, if I ever could. Until I know precisely what part you have played in all this, there are things in this investigation that I will be keeping back from you.'

'It's not what you think, Karin. I didn't kill anyone at that barn.'

Still with her hand over the radio handset to prevent Schmidt overhearing, Müller held Tilsner's gaze till he dropped his eyes, like an animal signalling its subservience. 'Were you at the barn as a Nazi? Yes, you were. I don't care how old or young you were. I don't care what you did or did not directly do. If you were there, if you helped and were complicit in any way, then you are as guilty as any of them. Get out, now.'

She watched until Tilsner was a sufficient distance away from the Lada, and then spoke into the handset.

'Go ahead, Jonas.'

'It's the fingerprints, Comrade *Major*. I've got the results.'

Müller found herself fighting for breath momentarily. This was a critical moment.

'Go on.'

'You won't like it, I'm afraid, Comrade *Major*. I've cross referenced exhaustively against what you gave me on the bouquet wrapper and what was found at the scenes of the various murders. There isn't a match. Either your suspect was wearing gloves . . . or he's innocent, and wasn't there at all.'

Müller held her head in her hands. What did this mean? It wasn't necessarily an indication that Verbier was innocent. As Schmidt himself had pointed out, he could have been wearing gloves – or he could have wiped all his prints. But it meant she didn't really have the evidence she needed to arrest him.

A sharp tap on the front passenger window pulled her out of her thoughts. It was Tilsner.

She leant across and opened the door. 'Didn't I tell you to stay over there?'

Tilsner sighed. 'Can I get in, Karin? I've something to show you.'

She shrugged and beckoned him inside. Following Schmidt's revelations, she wasn't exactly sure how to proceed next. For all that he was utterly compromised, Tilsner was still a detective – for the moment, at least. He might have useful information or ideas.

'I wanted to show you something,' he said, reaching over to get his jacket from the rear seat. He pulled a piece of folded paper from the inside breast pocket.

As Müller unfolded it and read the contents, she pulled her head back in shock.

I KNOW WHO YOU ARE.
I KNOW WHAT YOU DID AT THE BARN.
AND NOW I'M COMING AFTER YOU.

She folded the paper up again, covering the message.

'When did you receive this?'

'Just before we were sent down to Karl-Marx-Stadt. Right at the start. That's why I've been so out of sorts.'

Müller gave the message back to him, then stared hard at her deputy again. 'Out of sorts? You've been lying, trying to undermine the investigation, keeping things from me all the way through. That's not my definition of being *out of sorts*. You recognised each of the victims, but you said nothing.'

Tilsner held his hands over his ears, and closed his eyes. 'I was scared, Karin. I am scared. That I will be next. Surely you understand?'

'No, I don't understand. Your best defence would have been to help me solve this case. You'd better change your attitude and start doing that from now on, to the extent that I'm prepared to allow you to. But I will never understand, Werner. Never. And once this is over, I will never work with you again.'

Rather than meet up with *Hauptmann* Janson to catch up on his team's progress with Ernst Lehmann's friends and relatives as she'd intended, they instead made for Gardelegen town centre and the library. Müller insisted that Tilsner tell her who Ronnebach, Höfler and Unterbrink really were. Instead, he wanted to show her.

First the librarian brought out Gardelegen town's copies of the interviews carried out by a Captain Wagner of the US Ninth Army's War Crimes investigation unit, undertaken and transcribed in the days after the massacre.

Tilsner seemed overly keen to show her his own interviews, even though that wasn't Müller's principal interest. He traced his finger along the passages where it described his claims of helping the Frenchman, of actually standing in the line of fire to prevent him being shot. Müller started to doubt herself. Perhaps Tilsner wasn't the monster she thought. If the evidence from Tilsner's teenage alter ego Günther Palitzsch was to be believed, then Jäger too appeared to have tried to intervene to save Verbier. The villain of the piece was the one called Pfeiffer, at least as far as the involvement of Tilsner's Hitler Youth unit was concerned – limited though that was in terms of the over-all massacre. Perhaps Tilsner had simply been following orders, but was that a sufficient excuse? No, it wasn't, not for what had happened at the barn. Tilsner had known full well what was going to happen to the prisoners – he'd overheard the one called Thiele, the one who appeared to be in charge, talking about it at the party thrown by the lady of the manor. Gerhard Thiele had been the highest-ranking Nazi in Gardelegen – the *Kreisleiter* or district leader and the man who seemed to have dreamed up this vile plan. Had he been held to account for his crimes? And what about this Frau Bloch von Blochwitz – the one who had offered up the barn as the venue for the mass executions? Whoever were the real architects of the massacre, Günther – or Werner – had known all about it, yet he'd still been part of the escort taking the prisoners to their deaths when they thought they were being freed and handed to the Americans.

'What about Ronnebach, Höfler and Unterbrink?' asked Müller.

'I'm not sure of their names then. Gardelegen's not a huge town, but it's big enough. There's no way I knew everyone who lived here and was involved. And some of them would be from neighbouring villages and so on. But I recognised each one of them.'

'Where from?' asked Müller.

'From the drinks party. And then at the barn itself. Two of them were leaders of some kind, high-ups, issuing orders at the barn. I think one was with the *Fallschirmjäger*. I think that was the one who was later called Ronnebach. One was with the *Volkssturm* – that was Höfler. Yes, I remember him. He had a bad limp in his leg. And Unterbrink – I seem to remember he was with the fire service.'

'But none of them was this *Kreisleiter* Thiele?'

'No. I might be able to identify them from some of the photos.'

She watched Tilsner talk to the librarian, then saw her help him with various folders which they brought to the table. Throughout, Müller couldn't help but think that seconds, minutes and hours were disappearing. Was this the best use of her time? Would she be better off tailing the Frenchman again, watching for his next move? She also knew she needed to phone Helga, to explain that she would be away longer than she thought, and to make sure everything was OK at home. She couldn't face a repeat of the children being taken into care. She knew they had to be her priority. So she had to make that call now. But if she did, would Tilsner just disappear? He was finally aware that she knew everything about him. Although he seemed to be more cooperative, there was still a desperate, frightened edge to his voice.

They started to leaf through the photographs together. Müller recognised the town hall, without its ivy cladding, behind a column of townspeople carrying white crosses on their shoulders.

'That was around the time I was interviewed by the war crimes investigators. All the able-bodied men of the town were forced to carry a cross each and were marched up to the Isenschnibbe barn, carrying spades and shovels with their other hand to dig the victims out of the trenches the SS and paratroopers had buried them in, and give them a proper burial.'

Tilsner suddenly pointed in excitement at one of the photos of the digging.

'There – that man in civilian clothes. That's Höfler. He must have been from the *Volkssturm*. They were among those who had to rebury the dead.'

'What about the other two?'

'If Ronnebach was a paratroop officer, as I seem to remember, he would have either fled ahead of the American advance, to defend Berlin, or he would have been captured. Unterbrink, I don't know.'

Müller felt reassured by Tilsner's renewed cooperation. She could have insisted he came with her to the public call box outside the library, but at the end of the day, whatever had gone on in the past, he was still her deputy. Perhaps she ought to be prepared to trust him.

60

As soon as Müller returned to the main reading room of the library from the phone box, she knew something was wrong. Tilsner was nowhere to be seen. Her renewed trust in him had been misplaced.

She rushed towards the librarian. 'Did you see which way my deputy went?'

'He went off with another man, towards the front exit.'

Müller raced to the entrance and looked right and left. There was no sign of Tilsner and his mystery 'friend'.

She rushed back to quiz the librarian again.

'Did he look as though he went willingly?'

The librarian frowned. 'I think so. They were laughing and joking. The man had his arm round your friend.'

'They were both laughing and joking?'

The librarian's frown deepened. 'Wait a moment, no. Only the other man was, come to think of it.'

'How were they holding each other?'

'You've got to understand I only saw this from the corner of my eye. They seemed to stumble a little. I thought the other man might have had a little too much to drink.'

Or he was walking awkwardly because whoever it was had Tilsner in an armlock, concealing a gun held against his ribs? For Müller, her own imagined, unspoken scenario was the most likely. But was it Verbier, or someone else?

Müller immediately ran to the Lada, which was parked up outside, then radioed through to *Hauptmann* Janson.

'Berti, can you put out an all-bulletins alert for my deputy, *Hauptmann* Werner Tilsner? It's urgent. I think he's been abducted at Gardelegen library, and I think his life may be in danger. I will meet up with you soon. And get one of your officers to interview the librarian and get a description of the man he was with. I should have done it, but I have one idea where he might have been taken.'

She cut off the link before Janson could ask where that was. Perhaps he would guess anyway. The one place that bound together Verbier, Jäger and Tilsner – although only the former had carried that name when they first met there in terrible circumstances.

The last remaining portion of the wall of the Isenschnibbe barn.

At the memorial to the dead.

As Müller accelerated out of Gardelegen towards the north-west, playing in her head were the imagined scenes from 13 April 1945, overlaid on the real vista before her through the car windscreen, and the photos of the aftermath and burial she'd viewed with Tilsner in the library minutes earlier.

She imagined the pitiful march from the cavalry school, with the convoy of wagons carrying those prisoners unable to walk. The prisoners in their zebra-like striped clothing, who'd already endured the death marches around Gardelegen, and before that the cruelty of the labour camps, and the inhuman conditions on the rail transport to the north and east.

As the silhouette of the last remaining wall of the barn started to take shape on the horizon, her mind took her back to a day a few weeks before she herself had been conceived. When crazed, fanatical followers of one of the most vicious tyrants to ever walk the earth set fire to the straw in that barn, and roasted the occupants alive. However it played out, she knew that this investigation would stay with her for ever.

Müller parked the car at the end of the lane that led to the memorial, out of sight of anyone who might already be there. Then she climbed a farm gate, and followed the fence line in a crouch, trying to make herself as invisible as possible.

At the entrance to the memorial grounds, she could see the silhouettes of at least three cars. One of them was sleeker, more pointed than the other two, with an aerofoil interrupting the gentle slope of its hatchback rear door. In profile, it looked a little like a space rocket.

She immediately recognised it as something different from any of the Republic's models, or even any of the usual imports from the West, rare though they were.

It was a French-manufactured Citroën CX, belonging to former labour camp inmate Philippe Verbier.

The man she'd assumed was her murder suspect.

But she was no longer sure.

Four figures were gathered by the memorial, but it wasn't until she drew closer that their faces became clear enough to identify.

One was Verbier himself. One was Jäger. And one was Tilsner. The fourth man was in profile so she couldn't recognise him from this distance although he seemed vaguely familiar. With horror, she realised what he was doing: holding a gun to the side of Tilsner's head.

To get any closer, to hear what they were saying and to identify this fourth man, she risked giving herself away.

But it had to be done.

She reached into her shoulder holster and drew out the Makarov. Then as quietly and slowly as possible, she released the safety catch, trying to hold it back with her finger to avoid it snapping and revealing her position.

This field had been left fallow as meadow, rather than ploughed. She dropped to her stomach and edged forwards along the ground, a little like she'd seen East German and Soviet troops doing on news reports of their big exercises near the state border – imagining an invasion from the West.

She reached the edge of the field.

On the other side of the wall in front of her were the four men.

To her left-hand side was a bush. She used it to shield herself as she stretched to full height, straining to hear the conversation, and to see the identity of the man holding the gun.

She risked one peek from behind the foliage.

Immediately, the blood chilled in her veins, despite the oppressive summer heat which was causing beads of sweat to form on her forehead.

She knew the man.

She'd seen his photograph when investigating his son's activities in the Guben medical experiments case. His son was Jan Winkler.

He was Comrade *Generalmajor* Winkler, one of the most powerful men in the Ministry for State Security.

The Stasi.

As she strained to hear, slowly the words he was saying began to take shape.

'It's up to you now, Verbier. I had to choose who to shoot all those years ago. Now you can choose. Who's going to be first? But to be clear, there is no point getting your hopes up. None of you are getting out of here alive – except, perhaps, you, if I decide to spare you. But then you will be going to jail for the murders of Ronnebach, Höfler, Unterbrink and Schneider. And for the killing of these two gentlemen here. So that would almost certainly be the death sentence.'

Then Müller heard Jäger's voice. It was higher pitched than normal. Faster. Panicked. 'Don't be an idiot, Winkler. You'll never get away with this.'

'Don't call him Winkler,' spluttered Tilsner. 'Let's give him his real name. Willi Pfeiffer. Sadistic little Willi Pfeiffer. You know he's the one who killed Marcellin, don't you, Philippe?'

'Shut up, Tilsner. Otherwise I'll shoot now.'

'I know,' said Verbier. 'But you will find no evidence for me killing the four you mention. I only found out about poor Lothar the other day. Was that you, Pfeiffer?'

'All of it was him,' said Jäger. 'He was worried that you really were about to pick us off one by one because of your notes. Only a few people knew who he really was so he decided to eliminate those who knew. That's why you asked us to meet you here, Winkler, isn't it? To eliminate the remaining three who knew all about your role at Isenschnibbe.'

'Shut up, Klaus.'

There was a moment's silence. Müller considered her options. Was she a good enough shot to take out Winkler without hitting Tilsner? She'd had the training. She risked one more look over the wall from behind the bush, before crouching down again. She couldn't be sure. Winkler still had her deputy held tightly against him. It was too risky.

'In any case we have the evidence against you, Verbier,' Winkler continued. 'The notes you wrote to Ronnebach, Höfler, Unterbrink, myself, and Jäger and Tilsner here were all typed on French manufactured paper, with ink from a French typewriter ribbon. That's pretty damning, don't you think?' Although she was concentrating on getting a clear line of sight – without taking out Tilsner as collateral – Müller couldn't help thinking back to the blue French envelope in Martin Ronnebach's weekend cottage. It hadn't contained a lover's letter. It must have been one of these notes.

'I didn't send any notes to Günther or Harald. I owe them my life. Why would I try to scare them? You must have faked those two. I hold my hands up to the note to you and the other three – but my revenge was just psychological. I wanted to scare, not kill. I just wanted some of you who'd got off scot-free to get a feel for some of the terror and cruelty that you meted out on others. That didn't include these two. I would never stoop to the level of a Nazi like yourself. You probably still have a photo of the Führer in your bedroom, don't you?'

'Shut up, Verbier. Otherwise it's you first.'

There was a moment's silence. Then Müller heard the safety catch of a gun being released.

Winkler's voice spoke again: 'Kneel down there!'

Müller risked raising her head above the wall again, partially shielding herself behind the bush. She brought the Makarov up, aiming at Winkler. He was standing behind Tilsner, who was now kneeling on the ground. But she hesitated, her finger on the trigger. She still didn't feel confident enough to target Winkler, without hitting Tilsner.

'Don't do it, Winkler,' shouted Jäger. As he did, Verbier calmly walked between the kneeling Tilsner, and Winkler's raised pistol. He was protecting Tilsner – just as Tilsner, or rather Günther Palitzsch, had protected him thirty-two years ago. Protecting Müller's deputy with his own body.

Now, if Müller fired, she would almost certainly hit the Frenchman as well. She crouched down again, and moved a few metres sideways along the wall separating her and the field she was in from the memorial. She had to find a better angle to fire from.

Verbier challenged Winkler. 'You'd better do what you wanted to do all those years ago, then. You'll have to kill me, if you want to kill him.'

Müller estimated she'd crawled enough metres now to have changed her angle of fire. She didn't have the bush as cover any more. She raised herself with the gun pointed at Winkler.

In that instant, Jäger saw her, and shouted out: 'No, Karin!'

Winkler turned to train the gun on her. He was too late, but by turning became the target Müller had trained for at the police university.

She had eight bullets in her Makarov. She needed just one.

A single bullet. Aimed at the lower portion of the so-called T-zone – the line between Winkler's eyes and the tip of his nose.

It happened instantaneously, but appeared almost in slow motion.

Like a feature film slowed down.

But this was real, and in real time, the bullet slammed into the soft tissue and cartilage. There was an explosion of blood, and then – Müller knew from her training – the bullet penetrated the lower brain stem, the medulla oblongata.

The sounds of the shot echoed around the monument grounds, and off the remaining wall of the death barn.

Winkler's cries were strangled in his throat as he slumped to the ground. It was then that Müller noticed two other guns on the floor by his side, presumably from disarming Tilsner and Jäger.

Jäger moved to check Winkler's body for life.

Tilsner locked eyes with Müller, as Verbier helped him up from his kneeling position. She could see her deputy's whole body shaking from the fear and shock. 'Thank you,' he mouthed. Müller didn't respond.

Then – from the corner of her eye – Müller saw Jäger make a move for his own gun.

'Freeze!' shouted Müller. 'All three of you. Put your hands above your heads.'

She knew she still had seven of the Makarov's eight bullets left. She was prepared to use them if necessary.

Someone must have heard the gunshot. The sound of police sirens was growing closer – probably from *Hauptmann* Janson's team, alerted to the shooting by a member of the public. Either that, or Janson had worked things out for himself.

'We need to sort this mess out, Karin,' said Jäger. 'The police will be here in a moment. There's not much time.'

She still had her gun trained on the three of them.

'I don't trust you. Or him.' She waved her gun towards Tilsner. 'And I saw you threatening Verbier. Both of you. I have those photographs. Tilsner had him in an armlock.'

The Frenchman intervened now in a calm voice. 'You're mistaken, officer, I'm afraid. Yes, we all met here the other night. But it was partly an explanation on my behalf – partly a reunion. What you interpreted as aggression from Günther and Harald . . . well, I should say Werner and Klaus, wasn't that at all. We were hugging each other, after I'd told them what had been going on. It was the first time we'd seen each other since that day. The day they saved my life. But we were scared, yes. I'd heard about Lothar by then. They told me about the other murders – and I realised for the first time that I would be the prime suspect, because I had sent those three threatening notes, other than the note to Lothar. If you thought you saw us arguing, it was probably heated discussions because we all feared we might be the next one to be killed.'

If Jäger or Tilsner had tried to make a fine speech, Müller knew she would have ignored it and arrested them. But with Verbier, this was something different. She knew there was no fingerprint match. Perhaps she had misinterpreted the photographs, and seen what she wanted to see.

She lowered the Makarov, slid the safety catch back into place, and started to return it to her shoulder holster.

'No,' said Jäger. 'Give me your gun. I can sort this out. You know I can.'

The sound of the police sirens were getting even nearer. They had only seconds left.

If Müller was going to do this, she wanted things to be as safe as possible. She emptied the remaining bullets, and then handed the weapon to the Stasi colonel.

'You go and stand on the lane and head off the police. Make sure they don't come too near. Tell them there has been one casualty and ask them to call for an ambulance. But tell them the Ministry for State Security is dealing with the incident.'

Before she turned towards the lane, Müller watched Jäger wipe her prints from the Makarov, and then saw him curling Winkler's lifeless fingers around the grip and trigger, pressing the flesh firmly against the metal to create a new set of finger-prints. Then he arranged Winkler's dead arm so to appear as if he had fired Müller's gun at himself.

Somehow, he had disarmed a police officer, and then used her gun to commit suicide. It ensured Müller and the *Kriminalpolizei* were kept completely out of the equation. If you thought about it, it didn't make any sense.

Of course, no one would have the chance to think about it, to question it, to find out what had really happened.

Because this was the Stasi at work, constructing a lie.

Müller knew it was what they did best.

After Jäger's work was done, and he'd handed over to the local Stasi, he invited Müller and Tilsner for a drink. Jäger said that Verbier had been allowed to return to his hotel, to his fire prevention work, and eventually back to France. There would be no action taken against him in relation to the threatening notes, confirmed the Stasi colonel.

She didn't want to go drinking with former Nazis. Especially in the town where they lived. But that apparently wasn't what the Stasi colonel meant – the drink would be once they had arrived back in the Hauptstadt. Müller agreed – but only because she wanted to spell out a few home truths to them.

She waited in the bar for the chance to speak to each of them alone. When Jäger went off to make a phone call, that presented the first opportunity.

She stared hard at her deputy. 'You realise I can't just sweep this all under the carpet and carry on.'

'I'd warn you against trying to expose us. Jäger could turn very nasty.'

'I'm not worried about him.' And Müller realised that this was true, probably for the first time since meeting him at the start of the graveyard girl case. She no longer felt that frisson of fear in his presence. 'And I'm not worried about you. I won't be working with you ever again.' Then she lowered her voice. 'I refuse to have a Nazi for my deputy, but that won't be an issue anyway.'

Tilsner began to protest. To retell the story about how he had saved Verbier, how he was only obeying orders. How he hadn't been a Nazi – that teenagers had no choice but to be members of the Nazi Youth.

Müller raised her hand. 'I'm not interested, Comrade *Hauptmann*. It's over. We're finished.'

The chance to talk to Jäger alone wasn't immediately forthcoming, so Müller took matters into her own hands. 'Could you leave us for a few minutes please, Comrade *Hauptmann*?' She wasn't going to call him Werner, she wasn't going to bend and be friendly to the two men. She was resolute in what she planned to do.

'I hope you two haven't fallen out, Karin,' said Jäger, trying to lighten the mood.

'It's no concern of yours whether we have or haven't. What I want to know from you is how much you knew of what Winkler – or Pfeiffer, if you prefer – was up to.'

Jäger protested his innocence. Of course he would, thought Müller. He claimed Winkler had been acting on his own, a rogue Stasi officer trying desperately to cover his own back. Killing the others in a way meant to mimic the barn massacre, creating fires that produced smoke so that death – from asphyxiation and smoke inhalation, rather than burns – would be long and lingering, lashing their hands so they couldn't get away. Ronnebach had only freed himself thanks to burning off his wrist bindings, burning himself in the process. But he had then found that his escape was blocked, just as escape routes from the barn at Isenschnibbe had been blocked by the SS guards, and – in his small way – by Pfeiffer, a.k.a Winkler. Everything had been carefully constructed so that the finger of suspicion would point at Verbier, as it did. And more importantly, to get rid of witnesses to his own involvement. If she took this fine tale at face value, then Jäger himself was exonerated. Only she knew that Jäger . . . Harald Scholz, like Tilsner, could have chosen to play no part in the massacre at all, could have refused to guard the convoy, refused to have lain in wait, guns aimed, in case prisoners tried to break free from the death trap. Others had refused. Jäger and Tilsner hadn't.

It sickened her, but at the same time she knew it was something she could use to her advantage. In the realms of the Stasi, Jäger was still a powerful man. Perhaps even more so now that Winkler was out of they way. The Stasi colonel might even get promoted to take the place of the man whose suicide he'd faked.

She felt no guilt as she reached into her pocket for her natural mother's metal box that she always kept close to her.

'Remember this?' she asked.

'Yes.'

'And what's inside it?' The box had contained a photo of her teenage mother cradling Müller as a baby, before she was taken away for adoption by the Russian authorities who controlled this part of occupied Germany in the immediate years after the end of the Second World War. She'd already removed that photograph to a safe place. The box also contained the metal dog tag belonging to a Red Army soldier – the man Müller believed was her natural father. Several months ago, she'd asked Jäger to help her trace him when they met at the Soviet war memorial during the Guben medical experiments case. He'd failed to provide her with any information – though Müller remained convinced that Jäger could discover it if he wanted.

'Yes,' said Jäger. 'But I haven't had the chance to do anything about it yet.'

Müller gave an ironic laugh. 'I asked you last year. You've had plenty of time; you just haven't had the inclination. This time I'm not asking.' She opened the box, and removed a piece of paper on which the details from the dog tag were written. 'Here are the details again. Make sure this time you get the information I want, and if my father is still alive, make sure you arrange all the necessary visas, tickets, and travel documents to allow me to visit him, wherever he is. Get one of your messengers to deliver them to me at my apartment in Strausberger Platz.'

'That's a big ask.'

'As I say, it's not a request. If you don't do it, then a dossier about your wartime activities, and the fact that you were a Nazi and yet you're now a senior officer in the Stasi, will be made known to the West German press.'

Jäger took the piece of paper with the details, folded it, and put it in his wallet.

He didn't give Müller a reply.

He wouldn't even meet her eyes.

Müller left the bar soon afterwards, and didn't bother to say goodbye to either of the men. If she could help it, she had no intention of seeing them ever again. Neither would be missed. She wanted to move on with her life.

She had one more person she wanted to meet before returning to Helga and the twins. But first she stopped at her office at Keibelstrasse.

It was late now, and the typists had long gone home. Müller loaded a sheet of *Volkspolizei* headed notepaper into the Optima electric typewriter and began to compose the letter she needed to write. The words came easily, and she typed slowly and carefully – not wanting to have to use correction fluid and go over anything again. It seemed a natural process. It seemed the right thing to do.

Reiniger was still in his office.

'You always seem to catch me at the end of the day, Karin. Perhaps we both need to go home to our families sooner. Family life is just as important as work life, I'm sure you agree. And I'm glad all this Gardelegen stuff has finally been sorted out.'

Müller shrugged. 'Was it really *sorted out*, Comrade *Oberst*? Our case is over. But I'm sure that the stain on that town, and what happened there at the end of the war will always be there.'

'You may be right, Karin. But it's important we remember, and make sure a cold-blooded massacre like that never happens again.'

She sighed. 'Unfortunately, once again no one is facing justice. No one is on trial.'

'That isn't your fault. You did all you could. The culprit committed suicide. Obviously, given who it was, nothing about the case, or about the murders, can now be made public. But several people can rest easier in their beds at night.'

She stared hard at Reiniger. Perhaps he hadn't thought about his choice of words. Perhaps he genuinely believed them. They were, of course, true. Several people *would* indeed rest easier in their beds. There was one problem.

They were all Nazis.

They had all been involved in the horrific massacre at Gardelegen.

Müller could only hope that what they'd done came back to haunt them in their dreams, night after night.

That was her wish for *all* of those involved, no matter how small their part. And that included Tilsner and Jäger.

She'd been holding the envelope in her hand behind her back. But now she leant forward and pushed it towards Reiniger across his desk.

He frowned. 'What's this?'

Müller smiled. She felt a huge weight being lifted from her shoulders. She couldn't wait to get back to the apartment in Strausberger Platz to smother Jannika and Johannes in kisses, and open a celebratory bottle of *Sekt* with Helga. Her grandmother had money saved from not paying her rent in Leipzig for well over a year – they could manage on that for a few months. After that, who knew what the future held? But it wasn't something she worried about. It was something she looked forward to.

Reiniger had started to open the envelope.

Müller turned towards the door without answering.

She glanced back once before she left the room, and watched as Reiniger read her words – the words of her resignation letter – with pursed lips, and ever deepening furrows on his brow.

Her own thoughts had already raced ahead, anticipating the reunion with her little family.

Her own face was creased, too, in a broad smile.

EPILOGUE

Snow lay on the ground in this part of the far north-east, though it was only October. One of the two weekly flights from Moscow had even been cancelled due to a fierce blizzard. These were the first blasts of winter after a few short weeks of summer.

It meant this second flight was fully booked, and the German woman on board had to use all her powers of persuasion at Domodedovo International Airport to ensure that as a non-priority passenger, she was not re-booked for the following week when the weather might have closed in even more. After all the permits she'd had to apply for, all the favours she'd had to call in, she didn't want to be denied now.

Viewed from the air as they descended over the Chukotka peninsula – almost within touching distance of the United States – the patches of wind-blown snow looked like splatters of white emulsion paint; an abstract explosion over the fast-freezing tundra. Then the bumpy landing on the Ugolny airstrip, and finally – after nearly ten hours – she could stretch her legs. Her marathon journey hadn't started in Moscow either, but in Berlin – at Schönefeld – on an Interflug Ilyushin Il-18 before the change of plane in the Soviet Union, to another Ily-ushin, the much larger Il-62.

The woman felt elated and nervous at the same time. When she'd discovered the address she'd been given corresponded to a Soviet military base in the far north-east, she'd almost given up hope. A citizen of the Republic would never normally be permitted to come here. But now here she was.

The taxi driver didn't understand her instruction in school-girl Russian at first.

'Anadyr-1,' she said. 'I need to you to take me to Anadyr-1.'

'Anadyr town?'

'No. *Anadyr-1*. The military base.'

'*Gudym?* The base? I can't take you there. It's not permitted.'

The woman got the Russian translation of her authority document from the folder. The driver read it, then shrugged.

'It's up to you. But they will stop us at a checkpoint before we get there. And if I get arrested, you will have to pay to cover my wages. I can't afford to lose a day's work.'

The taxi driver wasn't arrested, but the woman thought *she* might be. Instead, after paying the man what seemed a ludi-crous amount of her fast-diminishing supply of roubles, the woman was taken to a holding area at the checkpoint and ordered to wait.

Telephone conversations in too-rapid Russian followed, which the woman couldn't understand. She knew her trump card was the rank of the man she wanted to see. As far as she knew, he was the man in charge. His rank: *Podpolkovnik*. The equivalent of the German *Oberstleutnant*. Lieutenant Colonel. She couldn't imagine there were many more senior in this far-flung place.

After a few minutes, more Red Army soldiers arrived at the checkpoint and she was ordered (at least she felt she was being ordered) into the front of a Soviet Gaz four-wheel-drive. Then they were through the gates, heading towards one of several three-storey concrete buildings lined up in terraces up the low hill which overlooked the base. The soldiers had Kalashnikovs over their shoulders and marched her into a bare office, with just one table and two chairs. Again, she was ordered to wait.

Only a matter of seconds later, a fit, balding, wiry man in perhaps his early fifties, entered the room. The woman got to her feet. She felt her throat constricting, and tried to say all the words she'd rehearsed.

In the end, she didn't have to. The man approached her, a broad smile on his face, and pulled her into a tight hug. She could feel him trembling just as much as she was, could feel the moisture from his tears as well as the stubble on his cheek rubbing against her skin.

Still holding her, he pulled back slightly, and began to speak in broken German.

'Karin, Karin. This is the most wonderful day of my life. To meet the daughter – my *only* daughter, my only *child* – that I never knew I had.'

Dedicated to all those forced labourers who lost their lives on the 'death marches' to and around Gardelegen and at the Isenschnibbe barn in April 1945.

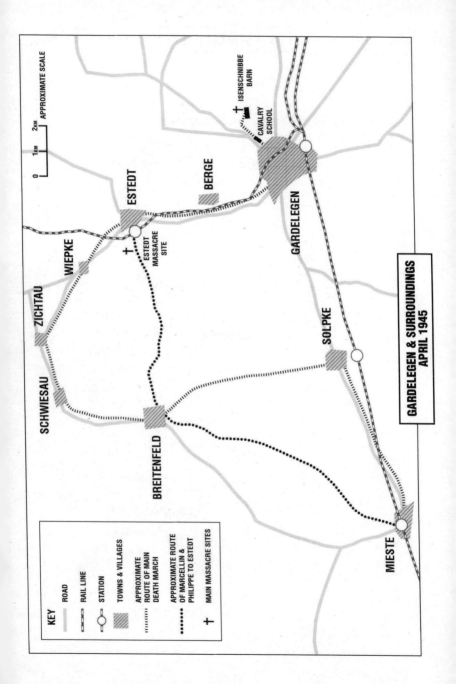

GARDELEGEN & SURROUNDINGS
APRIL 1945

KEY

ROAD

RAIL LINE

STATION

TOWNS & VILLAGES

APPROXIMATE
ROUTE OF MAIN
DEATH MARCH

APPROXIMATE ROUTE
OF MARCELLIN &
PHILIPPE TO ESTEDT

MAIN MASSACRE SITES

APPROXIMATE SCALE

0   1KM   2KM

ESTEDT

BERGE

ISENSCHNIBBE
BARN

CAVALRY SCHOOL

GARDELEGEN

WIEPKE

ESTEDT
MASSACRE
SITE

ZICHTAU

SCHWIESAU

SOLPKE

BREITENFELD

MIESTE

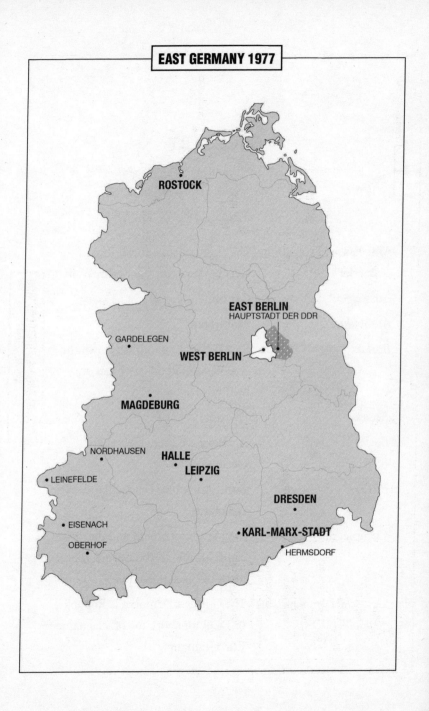

EAST GERMANY 1977

ROSTOCK

EAST BERLIN
HAUPTSTADT DER DDR

GARDELEGEN

WEST BERLIN

MAGDEBURG

NORDHAUSEN   HALLE
                LEIPZIG
• LEINEFELDE

                      DRESDEN

• EISENACH
         • KARL-MARX-STADT
OBERHOF
         HERMSDORF

GLOSSARY

Anti-Fascist Protection Barrier	The euphemistic official East German term for the Berlin Wall
Aussteigen!	Get out!
Autobahn	Motorway
Barkas	East German manufacturer of the B1000, a small delivery van or minibus
Bezirk	District
Boche	A pejorative French term for Germans
BRD	Bundesrepublik Deutschland. West Germany
Compiègne	A WW2 internment and detention camp located in the northern French town of the same name
Deutsche Demokratische Republik (DDR)	The German Democratic Republic, or DDR for short, the official name for East Germany

Fallschirmjäger	Paratroops
FDGB-Heim	Free German Trade Union holiday residence
Grenzübergang	Border checkpoint
Hauptmann	Captain
Hauptstadt	Capital city (in this book, East Berlin)
Interhotel	East German chain of luxury hotels
K	See *Kripo* below
Kaffee Mix	'Coffee' with 50% made up of ersatz ingredients in response to the 1977 East German coffee crisis
Kameradschaftpolizei	Comrade police force – prisoners who served as guards in labour camps
Kapo	Short form of the above
Keibelstrasse	The People's Police headquarters near Alexanderplatz – the East German equivalent of Scotland Yard
Kommando	A detachment or detail of slave labourers
Kreisleiter	Nazi Party county leaders – the fourth rank of the Party, below *Gauleiter*
Kriminalpolizei	Criminal Police or CID
Kriminaltechniker	Forensic officer
Major	The same rank as in English, but pronounced more like My-Yor

Milice	Paramilitary organisation formed by the Vichy regime to combat the French resistance
Ministry for State Security (*MfS*)	The East German secret police, abbreviated to *MfS* from the German initials, and colloquially known as the Stasi – a contraction of the German name
Mutti	Mum, or Mummy
Oberleutnant	First Lieutenant
Oberst	Colonel
Oma	Grandma, granny
People's Police	The regular East German state police (*Volkspolizei* in German)
SA	*Sturmabteilung* – literally Storm Detachment – a paramilitary wing in Nazi Germany
Scheisse	Shit
See	Lake
SS	*Schutzstaffel* – literally Protection Squadron – the Nazis' foremost agency of security, surveillance and terror
Stasi	Colloquial term for the Ministry for State Security (see above)
Tierpark	East Berlin's Zoo

Unterleutnant	Sub-lieutenant
Vati	Dad, or Daddy
Volkspolizei	See People's Police above
Vopo	Short form of *Volkspolizei*, usually referring to uniformed police officers, as opposed to detectives
Wehrmacht	The German armed forces from 1935 to 1946

AUTHOR'S NOTE

Although this novel is a work of fiction, the events up to and including April 1945 are based on historical facts and accounts of the survivors of Mittelbau-Dora, and the Gardelegen and Estedt massacres.

Philippe Verbier and his brothers are fictional characters, but all of the things that happened to them – up until Philippe's escape – did actually happen according to the handful who survived the massacre. Verbier's story up to and including 1945 is an amalgamation of some of those experiences.

One of the fullest accounts of the massacre that I used as source material is Dr Karel Margry's excellent twenty-five-page article in the *After the Battle* magazine, issue number 111. For life in Mittelbau-Dora and some details about Isenschnibbe, I consulted André Sellier's superb *A History of the Dora Camp* – notable not just because it was the first book-length English-language account of conditions there, but also remarkable because Sellier was himself an inmate. Another valuable source for me was *The Death Marches – The Final Phase of Nazi Genocide* by Daniel Blatman.

What of the perpetrators of this atrocity? The SS officer responsible for the transport of the prisoners from Mittelbau-Dora who ended up at Gardelegen, Erhard Brauny, was tried and sentenced to life in prison. He died in 1950. But the man considered to be the main architect of the massacre, Gerhard Thiele, reportedly escaped on 14 April by disguising himself as a German soldier. He found sanctuary in West Germany using false papers until his death in 1994, aged eighty-five. But his wife continued to live in the GDR – and never gave away the whereabouts of her husband.

Accounts differ, but it's thought some dozen or so prisoners survived the massacre, hidden under bodies, clinging to rafters or by tunnelling out. They included Poles, Russians and one severely injured Frenchman.

Although the site of the Gardelegen massacre was on territory which became part of the Soviet zone, and then East Germany, I would stress that the 1977 East German police case and investigation is entirely fictional. I thought long and hard about the ethics of bolting a fictional story onto a horrific real-life event. In the end, I concluded that anything that serves to raise the profile of the Gardelegen massacre must be a good thing. If I'm wrong, I apologise.

Despite the fictional nature of the 1970s end of the story, the idea of Nazis being recruited by the Stasi is rooted in reality. For example, *Der Spiegel* in 2014 published research about Auschwitz SS guard Josef Settnik and how the Stasi made him an offer he couldn't refuse: his past in the SS would be forgotten if he cooperated with the Ministry for State Security and spied on members of his own Catholic community. There are several other examples. The article quotes Henry Leide of the Rostock branch of the Federal Commissioner for the documents of the State Security Service of the GDR as saying: 'Nazi perpetrators had a great opportunity in the GDR to get away scot-free if they behaved inconspicuously or cooperated.'

The inspiration for this novel came after I visited the site of the Gardelegen massacre in 2016. It was a very moving experience, and I was struck by the fact that a) I was the only visitor b) there were no obvious signposts to the memorial from the main road and c) instead of genuine floral tributes, there were plastic ones (perhaps this is understandable as wilted, old flowers would look even worse). The memorial stands towards the end of a country lane on the edge of Gardelegen, and one young woman seemed to be intent on destroying the sense of remembrance by sitting in her car at the entrance presumably in ignorance of where she was, playing deafeningly loud rock music. I glared at her, she got the message, and turned it down or off.

But it felt like a forgotten piece of history. Something that should be respected better, and visited more. When my children were at school, 'educational visits' were often to exotic places like China – which seemed somewhat inappropriate and expensive for state schoolchildren. Surely sites like the remains of the Isenschnibbe barn would be cheaper and more relevant, to learn what the politics of hate can bring about at their worst excess?

Thankfully, by the time you read this, things will have changed. The foundation stone for a new visitor centre at the memorial was laid on 4 June 2018 and building work is already well underway. So if nothing else, if you've enjoyed this novel – despite its sometimes grim contents – I'd encourage you to make a detour there and pay your respects to the more than a thousand slave labourers who lost their lives at the hands of the Nazis at Isenschnibbe on 13 April 1945.

ACKNOWLEDGEMENTS

First off, huge thanks to my beta-readers from what was the GDR. Once again, former BBC News colleague Oliver Berlau did an invaluable job by reading an early draft of this manuscript and picking up on several things I'd got wrong. This time Oliver was joined by pianist Andreas Boyde, who also grew up in East Germany – and who showed me extracts from his Stasi file. Thanks so much to both of you, and it goes without saying that any remaining mistakes are solely down to me.

I'd also like to thank my wife, Stephanie, for providing invaluable help and for finding the time to read and comment on my manuscript while writing a novel of her own.

Thanks to everyone who turned up to my book events at libraries, festivals and bookshops over the last year and who said nice things about the books on Twitter and Facebook. Particular thanks to fellow author Jane Thynne who did a double act with me at several venues, despite me mucking up the technology on more than one occasion.

Former BBC colleague Jat Dhillon is owed special thanks for helping spread the word via my promotional postcards.

Above all, writing this novel wouldn't have been possible without the excellent support and editorial skills of my editor Sophie Orme and the team at Bonnier Zaffre, and as always I'm hugely indebted to my agent, Adam Gauntlett, and his colleagues at Peters, Fraser & Dunlop literary agents.

Want to read
NEW BOOKS
before anyone else?

Like getting
FREE BOOKS?

Enjoy sharing your
OPINIONS?

Discover

READERS FIRST
Read. Love. Share.

Sign up today to win your first free book:
readersfirst.co.uk